The Coming

The Coming

Joe Haldeman

ACE BOOKS, NEW YORK

SF

THE COMING

An Ace Book
Published by The Berkley Publishing Group,
a division of Penguin Putnam Inc.,
375 Hudson Street, New York, New York 10014.
The Penguin Putnam Inc. World Wide Web site address is
http://www.penguinputnam.com

First edition: December 2000

Library of Congress Cataloging-in-Publication Data

Haldeman, Joe W.
    The coming / Joe Haldeman.
        p.   cm.
    ISBN 0-441-00769-4
    1. Human-alien encounters—Fiction.   2. Life on other planets—Fiction.
3. Astronomy teachers—Fiction.   4. Mass media—Fiction.   I. Title.
PS3558.A353   C66   2000
813'.54—dc21
                                                                    00-029306

Printed in the United States of America

10   9   8   7   6   5   4   3   2   1

This book is for two guys who live a thousand miles apart and have never met: Ricky and Rusty. Both, by coincidence, were marines in the Pacific in World War II.

Ricky is Ottone Riccio, poet and prophet and rascal. Every teacher needs a teacher like him.

Rusty is James Hevelin, who is never called James except by the government. He is the friend every man needs and not many find.

In some world everyone has a Ricky on his left and a Rusty on his right, and it's a good world.

The author gratefully acknowledges the influence of James Gunn's beautiful novel, The Listeners, *on this book.*

October first

 Professor Bell

Reporters.

Normally her desk was no neater than it had to be, a comfortable random pile of notes, journals, and books. So long as she knew where everything was, who cared? But she had just spent fifteen minutes nervously straightening things up, desk and worktable. It was not quite six in the morning.

There would be reporters.

She looked at the coffee machine in the anteroom. The smell was a magnet. No, not now. Her heart was already racing. Doctor said two cups a day.

She pushed a button on the desk. "Previous," she said, and the diagram on the wallscreen was replaced by a double page of equations and numbers. "Previous," she said again, and got a double page of numbers and words. "Left." The screen reconfigured and gave her a single magnified page of words. She stared at it and shook her head.

It was an old and old-fashioned office, dating from before the turn of the century. It had an antique blackboard that she enjoyed using, the only one left in the physics building, and one whole wall, floor to ceiling, had built-in shelves for books printed on paper. Some of that space had been converted into a large display screen, but she did have rows of paper volumes bound in leather, cloth, and cardboard. The head of the department can be eccentric.

"Music," she said; "random Vivaldi, then random Baroque." An oboe began a familiar figure. "Louder, ten percent."

She sat down for a minute, listening, and then got up and slid a large book from the shelf, one she'd bought on impulse Monday. She leafed through the yellowing pages carefully. It was a book of news photographs from the old *Life* magazine, documenting a war that her great-great-grandfather had fought in. Grainy patriotic pictures and ads with meaningless prices. *Lucky Strike Green Has Gone to War.* What on Earth did that mean? Lucky Strike was evidently a tobacco cigarette; maybe green tobacco had some weapons application back then.

At the sound of the elevator, she closed the book and returned it. Her husband came into the outer office. "Coffee any good?"

"Just made it, half-real." He poured a cup. White stubble on his chin, rumpled workclothes. He got up almost as early as she did, but didn't bother to shave and dress till noon.

"I didn't quite understand your message." He sat down on the chair normally reserved for nervous graduate students. "Or quite believe what I heard." She always expected to get the house when she called home. Norman was a cellist and composer, and spent the first hour of his workday warming up, meditating over scales and intervals, and ignored the phone. But the house had told him it sounded important, and so he picked up the message. He'd called back immediately and said he was coming over.

He looked around the neat office. "You have someone in?"

She laughed. "I've been tidying. Waiting for a longer parallax verification."

"Parallax, yeah. *Relax.* Sit down, you make me nervous." He gestured at the wallscreen. "This is it?"

She nodded. It was a neat column of words: *WE'RE COMING,* repeated sixty times.

"Well . . . by itself, it doesn't exactly make one—"

"Norman. The signal came from a tenth of a light-year away. In English."

"Oh." He sipped his coffee. "We don't have anyone that far out?"

"Of course not."

"Creatures from outer space."

"Something from outer space." The phone rang and she picked up the wand. "Bell." She leaned forward, elbow on desk, staring blankly at the column of words. "Anytime is okay. Is he the science reporter?" She rolled her eyes. "Please. Can't we wait for a science reporter?" She exhaled slowly. "I understand. You have the address? Right. Bye."

Norman smiled. "Science reporters aren't up at six?"

"They're sending their 'night man.' He's probably used to murders and things."

"They couldn't wait?"

"No, it's out on the nets. I called the Marsden Bureau in Washington as soon as I was sure what it was."

"Oh, you're sure what it is?"

"No, no." She stood up and sat back down. "Just how far away, how fast. You know what the blue shift is?"

"An article of clothing?" She gave him an exasperated look. "I guess it's like the red shift, but blue."

"Right. It tells how fast something is coming toward us, rather than away." She pointed at the column of words, stabbing. "This thing came in a burst of gamma rays. Its source is coming at us with almost the speed of light."

"Sounds dangerous."

"It's slowing down. If it weren't, I couldn't say anything about the blue shift—I mean, they could just be broadcasting in high-energy gamma rays."

He frowned. "I don't understand."

"It's complicated." She waved the complications away. "Anyhow, I can tell how fast it's slowing down. From that . . . what it boils down to is that this thing popped into existence going the speed of light, exactly one-tenth of a light-year away, and it's decelerating at such a rate that it will reach Earth in exactly three months. New Year's Day."

"No coincidence."

"Of course not. They're giving us a creepy message. Those two words, combined with the blue shift and position, say, 'We know a lot about you, and we are vastly superior technologically. Ready or not, here we come.' "

He rubbed the stubble on his throat. "Jesus." They both looked up when the elevator door chimed. "The night man cometh."

Daniel Jordan

Dan didn't like the way the old elevator squeaked and shuddered. They were supposed to be fail-safe, but he'd covered a story over in Jax a few years before, where one newer than this had dropped twenty floors. Broken necks and fractured skulls and only one survivor, her muffled screaming terrible as the Rescue Squad rappelled down to cut open the roof. He pushed on the squealing door to speed it up, then held the door for the cameras to roll out behind him.

He checked his watch: 6:17. The Kampus Kops wouldn't start ticketing until seven. Maybe the press card on his windshield would protect him. The station only paid for two tickets a week, and he'd already had them.

Dr. Bell, 436. He turned to the right and the cameras followed. The small one stopped every couple of meters to take atmosphere: bulletin boards, an empty classroom, the sign that said DEPARTMENT OF ASTRONOMY AND ASTROPHYSICS. Dr. Bell was waiting for him in a doorway, a small stocky woman with short black hair streaked with white; a kindly face with an expression difficult to read. Dan introduced himself and they went into the office.

The guy sitting by the desk looked like the janitor, but Dan had a good memory for faces and made the name connection. He held out his hand. "Norman Bell, of course. I went to your concert in the park last spring."

The man shook his hand and looked amused. "You cover music as well as astronomical anomalies?"

"No, sir." Something about the man compelled honesty. "Actually, I'm tone-deaf. It was a date."

He laughed. "She must have been worth pursuing." He stood up. "Well. I'll get out of your way."

"Please stay, Norman." She looked at Dan. "Is that all right?"

He shrugged. "As long as you don't stand or sit together. Confuses the cameras' tiny brains." They would scurry around getting two-shots, long shots, intercuts, reaction shots. Half the footage would be of a scruffy-looking man in gray workclothes, temporarily irrelevant. "I think it would shoot best with you at your desk, Professor. I'll sit over here." He indicated the chair that Norman had just vacated.

"I'll go lurk by the coffee machine. Want some?"

"No thanks. Just came from Burgerman."

"That's how you got here so fast," Dr. Bell said. "I hope it didn't interrupt your breakfast."

"Oh, no," he lied, "just hanging out with the city cops. Trade gossip." He looked at the big camera and whistled, then spoke slowly: "Establishing shot. Bee Gee two-seventy from behind subject to my left." The camera drifted behind Bell and then wheeled out in an arc. "That's for editing back in the studio. I just repeat the questions there and they can paste my face in from any angle. So the cameras don't have to worry about me now."

The camera completed its circuit and said "okay" in a monotone. "Begin at the beginning," Dan said.

"How much do you know?"

"Almost nothing. You got some weird signal from outer space and the night desk thought it was important."

"It is." She leaned back. "I got to the office a little after four. The screen was blinking for attention."

"Can you recreate that?"

"Sure." She pushed a button on her desk. "Find today, 0405."

The screen began to blink red, saying ANOMALY RECORDED GRB-1 0355 EST.

Dan whistled and pointed at the screen. The large camera rolled up to it and seemed to concentrate. "Daniel," it said in a soft woman's voice, "please come adjust my raster synchronization."

Dan shook his head. "That's automatic in the new models." He got up and peered through the camera and fiddled with a pair of knobs until the picture of the wallscreen settled down.

He returned to his seat and the small camera climbed up onto Bell's desk and stared at her. She looked at it warily. "Am I supposed to talk to it?"

"No, just talk to me. What does the message mean?"

"GRB-1 is a gamma-ray burst detector. The "one" is optimism; we never got money to launch the second, which would've been a backup.

"Anyhow, some sources send out bursts of gamma rays, sometimes for hours, sometimes minutes, usually just seconds. This satellite detects and analyzes the radiation. It has a small telescope, essentially a fast wide-angle lens, that covers the whole sky every two seconds. If it detects a gamma-ray burst, the bigger telescope can be on it in about a second."

"Does it have any practical applications?"

"One never knows, but I doubt it. Except that if the Sun ever did that, it would fry everyone on the daytime side of the planet. It would be nice to have a few hours' warning."

"Do you have a picture of the satellite?"

"Sure." She pushed the button. "Find GRB hyphen one comma artist's conception." A dramatic holo of the satellite appeared, silhouetted against the sun peeking crimson from behind the curve of the Earth. Dan pointed at it and the big camera, which had been tight on Bell, turned around and got a shot of the wallscreen.

"That's pretty but falsado," she said. "GRB-1's up in geosynchronous orbit; the Earth's just a big ball that gets in the way."

"So what's this anomaly? I mean, what does the word mean?"

"It means something unexpected, a mystery. In this case, we recorded the gamma ray burst, but when the computer tried to find out what source it was, there was no object there, in previous records. I mean down to twenty-fifth magnitude, which is about as faint as they get.

"That was the first anomaly, which was interesting. The second was startling. Whenever we get a burst that's more than a few seconds long, we send out a request to the Japanese gamma-ray observatory on the Moon, for backup data. Their detector's more powerful. It found the burst but said that our position was a tiny hair off. We checked and no, our position was accurate. What it was, was parallax."

She anticipated the question. "You hold your finger up at arm's length, and look at it first with your right eye; then with your left." She demonstrated, blinking. "The finger appears to change position with respect to things farther away. That's parallax.

"Stars, let alone galaxies, are too far away for there to be a measurable parallax between the Moon and GRB-1, the right eye and the left. This thing was only about a tenth of a light-year away. It's not a star."

"So what is it?"

"That's the third anomaly, the fantastic one. I went to analyze the spectrum of . . . I went to analyze the signal. It was a long steady beep for sixty seconds, and then a jumble for sixty seconds, and then another steady beep, and then an identical jumble." She paused. "Do you know what that means?"

"You tell me," he said quietly.

"It means the signal isn't natural. The sixty-second minute is not an interval that occurs in nature."

"Yet it was coming from somewhere farther than humans have ever been?"

"That's right. And it's obviously a signal. I put it through a decryptation, what we call a Drake program. It's simple frequency modulation, like FM radio. This is the message." She pushed the button and said, "Previous previous."

Dan pointed at the screen and the camera obeyed. "They're coming?"

"Yes, initially at almost the speed of light. At the rate they're slowing down—fifty gees' deceleration!—they'll be here in exactly three months. That's New Year's Day."

He was silent for a moment. "Suppose it's a hoax. Could it be a fake, a joke?"

"Well, somebody could get to my computer, verdad, and set me up for a practical joke. But they couldn't get to the Moon. I mean, I just told them where to look, and there it was."

"So something's out there." Dan laughed nervously. "An invasion from outer space."

"We'd better hope it's not an invasion. You extrapolate back from the first signal, and when that thing first appeared it was going point-nine-nine-nine . . . fifteen or sixteen nines . . . of the speed of light." She leaned toward the little camera and spoke carefully. "If you took all of the energy that all of the world produces in one year, and put it all into a space drive . . . we couldn't make a golf ball go that fast. If it's an invasion, we've had it. Perdido."

"Dios," Dan said under his breath. "Use your phone?" He reached past her and picked up the wand; checked his watch while he was punching. "Charlene, listen up. Dan. You have to cut me a fifteen-second teaser on the seven o'clock. Then a three-minute lead at eight, and a five-minute lead at nine. And get . . . listen, it's my ass, not yours. And get Harry and Rebecca down here *right now* for depth and color, for nine."

He listened. "Just tell Julie to be down in Room Six in fifteen minutes. I'm gonna show him two crystals that'll blow him into the next county. The next *century*. We're gonna scoop the whole fucking world."

He nodded at the phone. "The Second Coming, bambina. The Second Coming." He hung up the wand and pulled a data crystal out of the small camera, and then stood and extracted a similar crystal from the large one.

"Thanks, Professor, you were great. Gotta run. Couple science types be here in a half hour." He started for the door.

"Your cameras?"

"They'll use 'em." He sprinted down the hall, crashed through an emergency exit, and ran down the stairs.

‖‖‖‖ Norman Bell

Norman winced at the ugly clanging the emergency door precipitated. A pure tone would do the job. His wife called maintenance and the noise stopped.

He stood up and stretched. "Guess you're stuck here. Bring you back something to eat?"

"Where you going?"

"Greek place, Nick's."

"Hmm. One of those spinach things. Spinach and cheese. No hurry."

"Spanakopita." He bent over slowly to pick up his bicycle helmet. "Don't forget to watch yourself on the news."

She was looking at a screen full of numbers and letters. "I wonder what channel."

Norman tapped the number on the side of the large camera. "Seven would be a good bet."

Downstairs, he unlocked the ancient bike and pedaled *squeak-click-squeak* though campus, taking the long way downtown to avoid traffic. There weren't too many cars at this hour, but drivers were erratic. The ATC didn't kick in until seven.

He checked his watch and pedaled a little faster. He would have to cross University Avenue, and it was best to be off the main roads well before "the bitching hour." Some drivers would go a little crazy, their last few minutes of manual control, trying to make an extra block or two before the ATC system engaged and turned them into law-abiding citizens—or at least turned their cars into law-abiding machinery. Until then, an orange light meant "grit your teeth and step on it."

He got across University without incident, and kept up the rapid pace for the few blocks remaining, just to get some exercise. He was a little winded by the time he locked up outside the Athens,

Nick's, and was glad Nick had the airco on inside. It was going to be a bad one today, close to eighty already, with the sun barely over the trees. He could remember when it was never this hot in October in Gainesville.

He selected a honey-soaked pastry and asked for strong Greek coffee and ice water, then put three bucks in the newspaper machine and selected World, Local, and Comics.

He read the comics first, as always, to fortify himself. The world news was predictably bleak. England and Germany and France snapping at each other, the Eastern Republics choosing up sides. Catalonia declaring itself neutral today—the day after its sister Spain aligned with Germany, squeezing France. Europe has to do this every century or so, he supposed.

The coffee and roll came and he asked for a glass of ouzo. Not his normal breakfast drink, but this was no normal morning.

"Nick," he said when the man brought the liquor, "Would you mind turning on the seven o'clock news? Channel Seven; Rory's going to be on."

"You' wife? Sure." He shouted something in Greek and the cube behind the bar turned itself on.

Still five minutes to go. The local station was filling time with its trademark "Girls of Gatorland" nude montage. He watched a pretty young thing display her skills on the parallel bars, and then went back to the paper.

Water riots in Phoenix again. Inner-city Detroit under martial law, the national guard called in after a police station was leveled by a predawn kamikaze truckload of explosives. A man in Los Angeles legally married his dog. In Milwaukee, twins reunited after sixty years immediately start fighting.

The local section had an unlovely, but possibly useful, photo-essay that showed the types of facial mutilations that various local gangs used to tell one another apart. They were more like social clubs nowadays, however fearsome the members looked. Ten years ago there was a lot of blood spilled. Now they just have those strange tournaments, killing each other in virtual-reality hookups, with dozens playing on each side. Why couldn't Europe do that?

Too American, he supposed, though the Koreans had actually started it.

He folded up the paper as the news program started. The lead story was Detroit, of course. There was dramatic footage of a water-dumping helicopter that was fired upon and had to drop its load a block away from the fire and retreat. The crowd shots around the ruins of the police station showed little grief; one group of boys was cheering, until they saw that the camera was on them, and scattered.

Rory's discovery hadn't made the lead, but it got more time than Detroit. It wasn't often they had a story that was both inter-planetary and local.

There was an interesting déjà vu feeling to watching it, seeing which parts of the interview were chosen, and how they were mod-ified. They didn't actually monkey with Rory's responses, but some of the questions were changed. Predictably, there was nothing about parallax or the noncoincidence of the human minute being part of the signal; nothing about what the distance and speed im-plied. That would come in a later broadcast. This seven o'clock one just established their scoop.

Nick had brought the ouzo and stood by Norman, watching the broadcast. "Your wife gonna be famous?" he said. "She gonna still talk to you?"

"Oh, she'll talk to me." Norman sipped the ouzo and looked away from the screen, which was featuring a graphic feminine hy-giene commercial.

"Guys from outer space," Nick mused. " 'Bout time they admit-ted they was out there."

"Really."

"Sure—been in the papers since I was a kid. Damn air force shot one down a hundred years ago. They got the dead aliens in a freezer."

"Nick. You don't believe that."

"It was in the paper," he said. "Hell, it was on the *cube*." He raised both eyebrows high and bent to polish a table that was al-ready spotless.

"This could be pretty big," Norman said. "Rory didn't think

there was any way it could be a hoax. Otherwise, she wouldn't have called the news."

"Well, you don't never know, do you?"

"I guess in about a week we'll find out. You wouldn't care to make a gentleman's bet?"

Nick stared at his reflection in the plastic tabletop and scowled comically. "Where you from, Mr. Bell?"

"Boston."

"Well, I never make bets with people from Boston."

"I was actually born in Washington, D.C."

"You kiddin'? That's even worse."

The news picked up with outer space again. They'd had time to contact the Moon. A confused Japanese astronomer, the one who had verified Rory's signal, was on live, providing more questions than answers: What do you mean, message? Speed of light? Who is this Aurora Bell? Rory hadn't identified herself personally, of course, she was just some code name like UF/GRB-1.

When the announcer explained to the scientist that Professor Bell had decoded the signal as "We're coming," repeated sixty times, his eyes narrowed. "Is this some sort of a college prank?" Then someone off-camera handed him a piece of paper. He stared at it for several seconds and then looked up. "We . . . um . . . we apparently have verifed the Florida analysis. 'We're coming'?"

"So what does it mean, Dr. Namura?"

The delay was longer than the usual Earth-Moon time lag. He shook his head. "I suppose it means they're coming. Whoever 'they' might be." He spread his hands in a gesture more Gallic than Oriental. "I really don't have the faintest idea. Of course we can't rule out the possibility of a hoax. Not to accuse your Mr. Bell." He glanced off-camera and back. "Mrs. Bell, Dr. Bell. Excuse us. We really do have to discuss this." He walked away, the camera starting to track the back of his head, and then cutting to the moonscape in the holo window behind where he'd been standing.

"Tell you what, Mr. Bell. I say it's a hoax. If I'm right, you owe me a hundred bucks. If I'm wrong . . . you and me gotta trade jobs for a day."

"What, you can play the cello?"

"Maybe. Never tried."

Norman laughed. "It's tempting, but I'll pass. Never was much of a pastry chef." He pointed. "Oh, yeah. Rory wanted a slice of spanakopita."

"Sure thing. Fresh this morning."

A small dark man came in and let the door slam behind him. He was in formal evening wear and looked as if he'd been up all night. "¿Qué pasa, Professor?"

"Not much," Norman said. The man had called him Professor ever since he found out his wife outranked him. "Invasion from outer space."

"Yeah, right. Lay ya odds."

"Better talk to Nick about that. Thanks." Norman took the spinach pie, paid, and left.

||||| **Willy Joe**

||| | "What the hell he's talkin' about?" Him and Nick probably been in the back room, coupla fuckin' mariposas, everybody knows about Greeks, and the musicians, hell, do anything. Take turns down the ol' dirt track. Otherwise why's he always here in the morning? Half the time, anyhow.

"They got some weird radio thing at the observatory. Had his old lady on the news."

"It's always somethin', ain't it?"

"Siempre." Nick brought out a small cup of strong coffee, a sausage pastry, and a glass of retsina wine. He set them down in front of Willy Joe with a neatly folded five-hundred-dollar bill under the saucer. "So how's business?"

Willy Joe palmed the bill and took a sip of coffee. "Always good, first of the month. Runnin' me ragged, though."

"Pobrecito," Nick muttered as he walked back to the pastry counter.

"So what's that mean?" he snapped. "What the fuck you mean by that?"

"Just an expression."

"Yeah, I know what it means. You watch your fuckin' mouth." Willy Joe shifted, slumping back in the chair. The new belt holster was uncomfortable in the small of his back. He didn't have to carry a gun on these collection rounds, anyhow. Who'd fuck with him? Not to mention Bobby the Bad and Solo out in the car.

Got this fuckin' town by the nose, now the new mayor's in. Bought an' paid for before the Commission election back in '40. The bitch last year was hard to handle. She found out what it was to push on Willy Joe, though. Might as well piss in the sea, bitch. Nothin's gonna change.

He unfolded his list and checked off the Athens. It was the last twenty-four-hour joint; the others wouldn't be open for a while. He took the phone wand out of his pocket and said, "Car."

"Solo here."

"Look, we're ahead. You guys go do what you want till quarter to nine. Make it nine, outside Marlo's." He put his thumb on the hang-up button while he drained the retsina. "Sanchez."

"Buenos."

"Willy Joe. Where you at?"

"Second and North Main, like you said."

"Okay; you try and keep up with Solo. Black and red Westinghouse limo pullin' out from the Athens."

"No problema if he stays in town." Sanchez was on a bicycle. With the ATC going in the morning, you could keep up with traffic on foot without overexerting yourself.

The limo moved smoothly in a diagonal from the curb, between two cars and into the left lane. Headed for the ghetto, interesting. Bobby the Bad was okay but a little dumb. Solo was new; friend of a friend in Tampa. He acted a little too tough. Willy Joe would love to get something on him. Someday he might need a little lesson in who's boss.

"Nick." He held up the empty wineglass. "Another retsina. You got the sports page?"

"Get you one." He brought the bottle over and then put a buck in the paper machine.

Willy Joe snatched the sports section. "See if I got any money left." He took a leatherbound notebook from an inside pocket and checked his bets against the columns of results: Thoroughbreds at Hialeah, dogs at Tampa, jai alai in town. He knew from last night's news that he'd lost his biggest wager: convicted murderer Sally Anne Busby chose the wrong door and was electrocuted. The bitch. He'd played a hunch and put a thousand on lethal injection.

Won a dog trifecta, though. All told, he was down $378. So he'd bet double that today. He spent twenty minutes drawing up a list distributing the $756 among safe bets and long shots, and then called his bookie.

The cube had some black broad talking to the professor's wife. "Did you ever expect this sort of thing to happen?" she asked. "Is there any precedent?"

"Nick, you wanna put somethin' else on the cube? Enough about the fuckin' president."

‖‖‖ Marya Washington

"Nothing I'd call a precedent," Professor Bell said. "As you certainly know, there have been ambiguous SETI results—"

"Search for Extraterrestrial Intelligence," Marya supplied for her audience.

"Yes . . . that may come from other intelligent species, or they may be radio signals generated by some natural process we don't completely understand."

"Like intelligence," Marya said.

"Quite so." She smiled broadly at the younger woman. "But in more than twenty years of analysis, we haven't gotten any clear semantic content from the three suspect sources. This one is as plain as a slap in the face."

"And as aggressive?" She held up two fingers in front of her chest, out of sight of the camera.

"That's not clear. If they were attacking us, why announce that they were on their way? Why not just sneak up?"

"On the other hand," Marya said, "if their intent is benevolent, why don't they say more than 'ready or not, here we come'?" One finger.

"Well, they have three months to go. This first signal might just have been to get our attention."

"They certainly have done that. Thank you so much, Dr. Bell, for taking time here at the University of Florida to explain this interesting new development to our audience at home; this is Marya Washington reporting live from Gainesville, Florida; we now return you to your local stations." She smiled into the large camera until it clicked twice. Then she leaned back in the chair and yawned hugely.

"Caramba. I guess astronomers always discover things at ungodly hours."

"Used to be. It's around the clock now."

"I suppose. Well . . . thanks, Aurora—can I call you Aurora?"

"Rory."

"Thanks for your patience. I wish we'd had more time, but we're competing with some big hard news." She laughed. "As if a police station being blown up was anything compared to this."

"Oh, my. Was anyone hurt?"

"Eleven dead they know of. It was leveled."

"Funny I didn't hear the explosion."

"Oh, no, no. It was up in Detroit. It may not have been directed at the police, either. They were holding some Mafia guy who was going to sing to the grand jury on Monday. . . . You didn't know about any of this, did you?"

"No, I—I'm afraid I don't pay much attention to the news."

"Me neither, for a reporter. Since I specialize in science stories. My big newsmagazine is *Nature.*"

Rory picked up a beige crystal. "*Astrophysical Review Letters.* All the latest gossip." She tapped it on the table, thinking. "So what about this special? What will you want me to do?"

Marya interpreted the gesture as impatience. "Oh, don't worry. No rehearsal or lines or anything. I'll just be interviewing you the way I did today, but in more depth. Bother you as little as possible."

"But I really do want to be involved. SETI is pretty far from my specialty, but I seem to be thrust into it. Besides, it was a passion with me thirty years ago, when I was an undergraduate."

"Was that about the time they found the first source?"

"Five or six years before that, actually. By the time they heard from Signal Alpha, I was pretty much committed to the physics of nonthermal sources, academically—not much time for little green men."

"Who didn't materialize anyhow." Marya took a leatherbound bookfile from her purse, flipped through the pages, and pulled out a blue crystal with SETI-L printed in small block letters across the top. "You have the Leon survey book?"

"No. Heard of it." She took the crystal and slipped it into the reader on the desk. It hummed a query note, copyright, and Rory told it "general fund." It copied the crystal and ejected it. Rory looked at it. "This has the raw data?"

"All three stars. The reductions, too."

"Well, we might want to redo them. It's been a few years, early forties?"

Marya squinted at the back of the crystal. "Twenty forty-three."

"Don't know how much has happened in eleven years." She asked the desk for the department roster, and it appeared on two screens. "You'll be talking to Leon, I guess—he's where, Cal Tech?"

"Berkeley. I called his office and left a message asking for an appointment. But who do you have doing SETI here in Gaines-ville?"

"No one specializing . . . but Parker's pretty sharp. He does our radio astronomy courses, intro and advanced, and he's kept up on SETI. Keeps the undergrads excited." She wrote his name and number down on a slip of paper. "Excited as I was . . . and will be again, looks like. Mysteries."

"It should be a good show. Network gave me two days to come up with forty-five minutes, though, so I have to move." She put the crystal back, and hesitated. "Um . . . can you sort of assign me someone? Someone less senior than Parker, some grad assistant I could call at any ungodly hour for information?"

"No, I can't get you a grad assistant," she said, and studied Marya's reaction. "You're stuck with me, I'm afraid. I wouldn't let anybody else share in the fun. Parker can give us both an update, but I'm your pet astronomer for the project. Finders keepers."

The elevator bonged. "Well, hablar del diablo. Here comes Parker." A tall man, unshaven and bleary-eyed but wearing a coat and tie with his kilt, shambled down the hall toward them. He had small rimless glasses and a goatee.

Pepe Parker

He leaned against the doorjamb, a little out of breath. "Rory . . . what the hell?"

"A reasonable question. Pepe Parker, this is Marya Washington."

He peered at the attractive black woman. "I know you. You're on television."

"Not at the moment," she said. "Newsnet asked me to put together a special on this message."

"And I took the liberty of volunteering you."

"Oh, muchas gracias. I had so much time on my hands."

"If you'd rather not—" Washington said.

He raised one hand. "Kidding. Look, I don't have half the story: Lisa Marie had the news on and recognized your voice; she punched 'record' and woke me up. Or tried to. I was up at the dome till past three."

"What on earth for?"

"Don't ask. Don't get me started. Be nice if somebody besides me could make the goddamned bolometer work. So you got some LGMs?"

Washington looked at Bell. " 'Little Green Men.' I don't know what else it could be. Open to suggestions."

"Could it be a long-delayed hack? That occurred to me on the way over. Some eighty-year-old probe with a practical joke encoded."

"Nice try. You haven't seen the spectrum, though. Eighty years ago there wasn't that much energy on the whole planet."

"And it's actually English?" She nodded slowly. "Holy Chihuahua. What's it doing now?"

"Carrier wave. It's a 21-cm. signal blue-shifted to 12.3 cm."

"Yeah, okay. How fast is that?"

"Call it $0.99c$. Decelerating."

"Oh, yeah—Lisa Marie said you said it would just take three months? To slow down and get here? Fifty goddamned gees?" Rory nodded.

"What if it didn't slow down?" Washington asked. "What if it hit us going that fast?"

"Terminado," Pepe said. "If it's any size."

"Let me see." Rory turned to address the wall. "How much kinetic energy is there in an object massing one metric tonne, going $0.99c$?"

"Four-point-four-three $\times 10^{21}$ joules," it answered immediately. "Over a million megatons."

"Crack this planet like an egg," Pepe said. He was amused by Washington's avid expression. "I think she's got a lead for her story," he said to Rory.

"I'm not the one you have to worry about," Washington said. "By noon you're going to have stringers from every tabloid in the country down here. If I were you I'd have some secretary send them all to the Public Information Office."

"Do we have one?" Pepe asked.

"Yeah, some kid runs it," Washington said. "I talked to him, Pierce, Price, something." She took a Rolodex card out of her breast pocket and asked it, "Name and office number, Chief, University of Florida Public Information Office." It gave her "Donato Pricci, 14-308."

Rory wrote it down. "Good idea," she said. "God knows when we'll get any science done around here. You straight newspeople are going to be bad enough."

"We try," Washington said. "But wait until you meet the science editor from *Dayshot*. He's also the astrology columnist."

"Maybe we better put the secretary down by the elevator," Pepe said. "The front door. Maybe with a couple of fullbacks."

Washington checked her watch. "I better get down to the station. See what local talent can cover; how many people I'll have to bring in. *Try* to bring in."

She squeezed past Norman, coming through the door. He put the white box with the spinach pie in the cooler under the coffee machine. "Buenos, Pepe. Program looked good, hon."

Rory looked momentarily confused. "Oh, the early one. We just did another."

"I don't know about that million megatons," Pepe said. "That'll be on every front page in the world tomorrow morning."

"What million megatons?" Norman said.

Rory gestured at the wall. "I asked it how much kinetic energy the thing had."

"If it were to hit us without slowing down," Pepe said.

"Save Germany and France some trouble." He tossed the folded-up newspaper sections onto the table by the coffee machine. "Comics and world."

"From the sublime to the ridiculous," Pepe said.

The phone chimed and Rory picked it up. "Buenos . . . why, Mr. Mayor. Such an honor."

⦀ Mayor Southeby

"Mr. Mayor, right." Cameron Southeby lived across the street from Rory and Norman; they'd been neighbors for nine years. "So what can I do to help you? What can you do to help me?"

Rory told him that the situation wasn't clear yet; there might be a lot of reporters—if she could figure out some way to send them over, she would.

"Do that. We eat 'em alive." He swiveled around and looked out the glass wall over the city, two hundred feet below. "City of Trees" was becoming an embarrassment. "City of High-Rise Parking Lots" wouldn't help real-estate values, though. "Seriously . . . keep me in mind, Rory. You know our university liaison, June Clearwater?" She didn't, but read him off the Public Information name that Washington had given her.

Pricci the Prick, Southeby thought, remembering his grandstanding over a little assembly permit. "I'll get them in touch with each other," he said. It was his day for Italians. He fingered the card that said *WJC 9:30*—Willy Joe Capra, one of his favorite people. He touched the envelope in his side pocket.

Rory told him not to get his hopes up about this having any far-reaching effect on the city. It might turn out to be a seven-day wonder; it still could be some subtly arranged hoax.

"But you said on cube that you were sure it *wasn't* a hoax." Southeby's vision of his town becoming the focus of the world's attention evaporated, replaced by a nightmare of worldwide derision.

Rory told him to pick up his shorts; all she meant was that just because *she* was sure there was no hoax didn't mean there couldn't be someone smarter than her behind it, second-guessing her suspicions. The straightforward explanation was still the most probable, but . . .

"Oh . . . okay. Well, you must have a million things to do. I'll let you go. Mañana."

Norman Bell

Norman watched his wife's expressions with amusement as she finally extricated herself from their blowhard neighbor. "He's trying to find a money angle?"

"Good old Cam."

"I'm going through the market on the way home. What you want for dinner?"

"Whatever. Something I can reheat. No telling how late I'll be."

"Keep it in mind." He picked up his helmet.

"Don't forget your sunblock."

"You kidding?" Actually, he had forgotten, but he kept a tube in his bike bag. "Give me a call when you start home. I'll hot it up."

"You do that." Her husband spoke in accents of cool New England, but he used southern expressions he'd picked up from her cornball uncle, whom she loathed.

It was a ten-minute pedal down shady back roads to the Farmers' Market in the middle of town. Halfway there, he started sweating in spite of the shade, and stopped to put on the sunblock.

They'd been doing this for about ten years, using the space between the federal building and City Hall as an open-air market two days a week. It was a "free" space, as Norman knew, with a catch: you had to put down a five-hundred-dollar deposit, which would be refunded at closing time, or more likely a week later. That kept marginal farmers at home.

He locked his bike and walked past the seafood display, expensive fish, shrimp, squid, and eels attractive on beds of shaved ice. Save it for last. The place was pretty crowded, as he knew it would be at this hour, city workers killing time before going to the office at nine. The crowd was bright and young and chatty—lots of new students, this time of year. He liked to drift through, eavesdropping.

He had two cloth bags, and as he wandered from one end of the market to the other—from fish to coffees—he checked out prices and planned what he was going to buy where, on his way back. Rory thought the market business was a silly affectation, the city manufacturing nostalgia for a simpler time that had never existed in the first place, and although Norman couldn't disagree, it was still a high point of his week. Prices were cheaper in the supermarket, but the produce was suspiciously uniform there, and the crowds were just crowds.

"Dr. Bell!" Lots of warm brown skin and a little tight white cloth: Luanne somebody, a student from three or four years ago.

"I saw the news this morning—isn't that just . . . *total?*"

"It's something," Norman admitted. "So where have you been? Haven't seen you around."

"Oh, I went to Texas for a master course, keyboard. No work there, surprise. So what do you make of it?"

"I don't know any more than you do; just what was on cube. Aurora does think it's real." He studied her. She was radiating sexual signals, but they communicated display rather than availability, just as he remembered from before. He wondered how much of it was deliberate, like the carefully bedraggled hair and the makeup so subtle it was almost invisible, and how much was just in her nature. She liked being looked at; glowed in his attention. Any man's attention.

"When I left a few minutes ago, she was talking to the mayor. Fishing for an angle to bring fame and fortune to Gainesville. Or to Cameron Southeby."

"*That* zero is mayor? I should've stayed in Texas."

"You know him?"

"Knew him." She touched his arm and whispered, "When he was police commissioner," raised one eyebrow, and walked on.

He watched her go. Interesting walk: "She moves in circles / and those circles move." What illegal thing might she have been involved in? He had no doubt that Cam was on the take, but Luanne had seemed so prim and shy as a student. Oh, well. Probably a leather-underwear-and-handcuffs prostitute on the side. Some of the quietest people had bizarre private lives. He had met one or two, pursuing his own private life.

Suppose this thing does turn out to be creatures from another planet, landing on the White House lawn on New Year's Day. How would that change things? Would the Europeans lay down their arms in celebration of the universality of life? Sure.

It would all boil down to what they brought along with them. The threat of absolute destruction might indeed unify humanity against the common enemy, but what good would unity do against an enemy who could crack the planet like an egg?

Maybe they would bring the truth, and the truth would make us free. As it had so effectively in the past.

He wished he were older. At sixty it was hard to have a sense of humor about dying. Maybe in another thirty years.

He studied the various coffees and invested in a moderately expensive blend: an ounce of Blue Mountain with three ounces of French roast. It made more difference to Rory than to him. She had perhaps one cup a day at home, and liked to savor it. He drank it constantly, fuel for music, but not the real stuff. Coffee-est or MH Black Gold. One good cup of real in the morning and then twenty cups of anything black and strong.

He turned around and paused, looking at the thirty or so stands, remembering which ones had what. He checked his list; crossed out coffee, added green peas and smoked ham. Make a nice soup and let it cook all day. Bread and salad, already on the list.

His day for young women. "Good morning, Sara."

"Buenos, Maestro." She was the bartender and co-owner of Hermanos Mendoza—the Brothers Mendoza, who had gone north in a hurry twenty years before, leaving behind a stack of unpaid bills and their name.

Sara always touched her neck when she said hello to you. She had been in a terrible fire a few years back, and even after they rebuilt her face she'd had to talk through a machine in her throat for a while. She still wore long sleeves and high necklines. Her face looked sculpted, less mobile than you would expect.

She shifted a large bag of onions so some of the weight was on her hip. "So how's the music business?"

"Lento, as we say. Slow. You want to buy a song?" Actually, he realized, one was forming in his mind. The first few notes of a mock-bombastic overture. A greeting for the aliens.

"If I could afford a song from you, I wouldn't be tending bar."

"There you go." He sang to the tune of the last century's "The Teddy Bears' Picnic": "If I could afford a tune from you / I wouldn't be tending bar."

"Wow. You just make that up?"

He smiled. "Trade secret."

"You take care." She shifted the big bag of onions onto her shoulder and walked away. Completely different from Luanne, her walk was stiff and mannish. It was probably from the fire; months of immobility and then walking in braces. Brave girl, Norman thought.

Sara

She could feel his eyes on her butt, every man's eyes. One more operation. Cut through the scar tissue, give her two buttocks again. Then learn how to walk again like a woman.

Not covered by Medicare. Rebuilding a womanly butt was not covered; it was "cosmetic." If you wanted cosmetic surgery you had to save up for it. They had paid for this so-called face and the two hard sponges on her chest. They opened her labia up and gave her pubic hair again, which of course is not cosmetic because who sees it?

Nobody had, not socially. Not until she could afford the last operation. She kicked open the door to the bar with unnecessary force.

"*Nuestra Señora de las Cebollas,*" said José, the morning man. Our Lady of the Onions.

"Hey, next time you carry 'em and I'll cut 'em."

"Sure you will." The bar's big specialty was the onion flower: a machine slices the onion carefully in a crossed dice, three quarters of the way through. Then when somebody orders one, you just dip it in light spicy batter and deep-fry it for a few minutes. It opens like a flower in the cooking and turns sweet.

All very delicious, but someone had to peel a few dozen onions before eleven, and it wouldn't be Sara. "I'll take over the coffee. You get on the onions."

"Let me take a leak first."

"Oh God, yes. Don't pee on the onions."

"Flavor of the week." No customers, which wasn't unusual at nine sharp. José had crowds on the half hour, five-thirty, six-thirty, seven-thirty, eight-thirty. Things were calm by the time Sara came in.

She put on an apron and took a cloth to the machines. They had a hundred-and-fifty-year-old cappuccino monster that still worked, and José liked to mess with it. Sara didn't. She made cappuccino with the milk jets on the espresso machine, and nobody complained. When everything was shiny, she made herself a cup and sat down.

"Chee-wawa," José said, coming out of the men's room. "I work like a dog since dawn and my boss comes in and drinks coffee."

"Some bosses drink blood, José. Be grateful."

He popped an orange drink and sat next to her at the small table. "Qué día."

"Already? What's happening?"

"Oh, the usual. Drunks, bums. Invaders from outer space."

"We get 'em all."

"No, I mean verdad. People from outer space."

"Really. What did they want? Beetle juice?"

"No, I mean *verdad*! You don't watch the news."

"How could I watch the news when I don't have a cube at home?"

"Okay. A good point."

"So what about these invaders?"

José poured the orange drink over ice and squeezed a half lime into it. "Government bullshit, you ask me."

"It was on television?"

"Yeah, some woman at the university. She got some message from outer space. We got aliens on the way."

"Hold it. This is really true?"

"Like I say, government bullshit. Next week they come up with some alien tax we got to pay."

"Did you record it?"

"What I record it with? You leave a crystal here?"

"It was on CNN?"

"I guess, I don't know. Whatever was on."

"You're a big help." Sara got up and started doing the tables. Wipe each one down with a cloth, reposition the silverware. "I mean really, it's real?"

"Your friend the musician's wife, the professor? She was on the cube."

"Oh, yeah. Dr. what's-her-name Bell. The astrologer." She sat back down. "So really. It's really real."

"Would I bullshit you?"

"All the time. But I mean, this is real."

"Verdad. Really real."

"Holy shit. Do you know how *big* this is?"

"Yeah, yeah. That's all they talk about, all morning."

She sipped her coffee. Then she drank half of it in two gulps. "Holy shit."

"I wouldn't get all worked up over it. It's just the government."

"José, look. The government doesn't always lie. What could they gain from this?"

"Alien tax."

"Oh yeah, sure. But I mean, don't you see? We're not alone! There are other people out there."

" 'Course there are. I knew that all the time."

"Oh God, of course. Your tabloids."

"So what's wrong with my newspapers? They're right? That's what's wrong with my newspapers?"

"Just . . . just let's go back, about three squares. You saw this on the cube."

"Bigger than shit. Like you say, CNN."

"CNN. And it wasn't a joke."

"No way. *Verdaderamente.*"

Sara was strongly tempted to go to the bar and pour herself something. Not so soon after dawn, though. She sat back in the chair and closed her eyes.

"You're thinking."

"Happens." After a moment: "So have they called out the army yet? NASA going to blow them back to where they came from?"

"Not yet. They're not due for another three months."

"Nice of them to tell us." The door banged open and Willy Joe flowed across the floor and onto a bar stool, the one nearest the men's room.

"Cup of espresso, Señor Smith?" José said. He nodded.

Sara checked her watch. "You're two minutes early."

"It's the goddamn aliens. Screwin' everything up." While the espresso machine was building up pressure, José punched "No Sale" on the antique register and took out a pink five-hundred-dollar bill.

"Hey. Be obvious," Willy Joe said.

"I'm an obvious kind of man." He put the bill under the saucer in front of Willy Joe.

"I could make you real obvious. You don't watch your fuckin' trap."

"Yeah, yeah." He poured the coffee, making a sound like a chicken, just audible over the machine hiss.

"José . . ." Sara warned.

He served the coffee. "It's okay. Señor Smith knows I know his boss."

"You know too many people, génie. Get you some trouble someday."

"Enjoy your coffee, sir," he said with a broad smile. "I hope it is done to your liking."

"You boys want to put your dicks back in? Customers coming."

"You watch your mouth too, lady."

Sara turned and made a sign only Willy Joe could see: right thumb rammed up through left fist. "Y tu madre," she mouthed, her face turning red.

"Yeah, well, fuck you, too." He turned back to his coffee. Two women and two men came in, suits from the federal building. Sara took their orders and passed them on to José.

At exactly nine-thirty, the mayor strode in. He said hello to Sara and José and one of the suits, Rosalita. He sat down two stools away from Willy Joe and ignored him.

"Café con leche, Mr. Southeby?" José said.

"Oh, let me be daring. The chocolate one."

"One chococcino, coming up."

Sara brought him a place mat and setting. "So what about these aliens, Cameron? You made it all up, confess."

"Ah, you see though me like a window, m'dear," he said theatrically. "Anything to keep from raising taxes. Tourists by the planeload."

She patted his shoulder. "Send some of them here," and went on to seat two new customers.

José brought the hot-chocolate-with-espresso, and ground a scatter of fresh chocolate on the top. "Merci gracias," the mayor said, and took a careful sip. He sipped and studied the menu for a few minutes, then went into the men's room.

Sara had seen the little dance every month since Cameron took office. Mayor goes into the men's room and comes back out. Willy Joe suddenly feels nature's call, and stays in the bathroom long enough for the mayor to finish his coffee and escape. Willy Joe comes back out, leaves a stunning five-dollar tip, and slithers on to his next stop.

She could blow the whistle on them. She could have her fingers broken, one by one, too. She could have them broken *off*, and fed to her. Willy Joe was just a hood with delusions of grandeur. But the people he collected for played for keeps.

She sat down again. Busy, slack; busy, slack. Were all businesses like this? Did whores spend two hours on their backs and then two hours doing crossword puzzles?

Here comes Suzy Q., the poor daft thing. Sara stood up and went to the bar, but José was a step ahead of her. He'd filled a large foam cup with sweet coffee and hot milk.

She took it outside with some pastry from yesterday. Suzy Q. accepted her morning gift with calm grace. Fix up the random hair, the pungent rags, and she could look like Queen Victoria or Eleanor Roosevelt. Stern ugliness, imposing.

"How goes it this morning, Suzy Q.?"

"Oh, it's hot. But hot is what you got. Am I rot or not?"

Sara laughed. "You're rot, all rot." She patted the old woman on the shoulder and went back inside.

Suzy Q.

Now she knows how to treat somebody. She has so much pain herself she sees other people's pain clear. I remember when she had the fire and that thing in her throat, she had to use a crutch to come out but she come out with my coffee. Wish I could kill someone for her, there must be someone she needs killed, I could do them like old Jock and put them in the swamp. But it's not a swamp no more, no, it's all apartments on top of old Jock, would he be pissed? Always carrying on about so many people come to Florida, and himself come down from Wisconsin. The Big Cheese, he used to work in some Kraft plant up there, but he got too cold and come down here to pick at me until I couldn't take no more and had to hit him, hit him four times with that frying pan, till the brains come out his ears. More brains than you'd think he had, the way he carried on.

My lordy lord, this coffee is good. I do miss old Jock sometimes, I should have wrote down the date the year, so I'd know how long he's been gone. I told people he just run away with some little girl from Café Risqué, and they say sure, Suzy Q., he always was that way, and by the time they get around to building on the swamp I guess there's not much left. I did go out there once to check and he was all white and wormy and popping out of his clothes. I found a big piece of old plywood to put on top of him. He did smell something fierce. But I guess nobody went out to the swamp back then.

I could use a tomato. I got six paper dollars and some change. The Lord provides for this believer but he don't provide tomatoes in this town, just coffee. I could chop up a tomato in that rice, and a little sugar.

Sometimes I feel like I'm going crazy. Seems like everyone talking about aliens from outer space today. I try not to listen but there it is.

Bet I can get a tomato for two dollars, I don't mind a few spots. And who's in my way but Normal Norman.

Norman

He had a small bouquet of flowers. "Suzy Q. How's by you?" He handed her a blossom.

She took it, sniffed it, and stuck it in her scraggly hair. "The usual. Except for the aliens. You know anything about the aliens?"

"Nope. Just that they're coming."

"Everybody wants to come to Florida." She waggled a hand at him. "You're in the way of my tomatoes."

"Sorry." He stepped aside and she pushed her grocery cart past him. It held about a dollar's worth of bottles and cans, and some random newspaper sections, neatly folded.

The old lady was really only one year older than Norman. In high school she had been the quintessential cheerleader, always there if you had a football or basketball letter. Norman was band and orchestra, no letters. Alien Boston accent.

They used to call her Snowflake. It had snowed in Gainesville the day she was born.

She'd started to go crazy with her first husband, didn't do too well with the second, and when the third ran away she just popped. Had she ever gone to a shrink? Norman didn't know; he'd stopped going to reunions and didn't have any other source of gossip about his generation.

He looked up at Hermanos and considered going in to have a cup with Sara. No, better get on home and record the theme that was building in his head.

He unlocked the bike and loaded the groceries and pedaled slowly back across campus, humming the new melody as he went. It was between classes, a lot of attractive undergraduate bodies hurrying, but he wasn't distracted. This might turn out to be something interesting.

He left the bicycle in the atrium and set the produce bag next to the refrigerator; sort it out later. He hurried into the music room and snapped on the antique Roland and slipped a blank crystal in the recorder, labeling it *Alien concerto/1st pass.*

He chorded out the twelve-bar opening with the screen off, and then turned it on to review what he'd done. He played a second version, looking at the screen, simplifying here, elaborating there. But he wasn't happy with his changes; they were moving the piece toward a conventional kind of drama, almost like a march.

Should not have had that ouzo. Booze in the morning wasn't conducive to work. He left the keyboard on but stretched out on the couch, asking the room for Hermancina's rendition of the second movement of Beethoven's *Pathétique.* He closed his eyes and let the slow, stately passage fill him.

The phone chimed, of course. He asked the music to hold and picked up the wand. "Buenos."

The voice at the other end identified itself as *People* magazoid and asked whether Professor Bell was in.

Norman didn't bother to point out that *he* was Professor Bell, too. "She's at work. She doesn't want to be disturbed."

They asked for her number at work. "It's unlisted," he said, and hung up. Of course it wasn't unlisted, but a reporter ought to be able to figure that out.

He pushed a button on the wand. "Rory's office," he said.

Aurora

Rory sighed and picked up the wand. "Yeah?" She smiled at her husband's voice. "Oh, hi." He told her about the *People* magazoid call. "Well, if they don't track me down in the next half hour, this number won't work. At eleven-thirty they're going to start routing everything through some publicity office."

He asked whether she was getting any work done. "No, we're just killing time before the big meeting. Barrett and Whittier live."

University chancellor and dean of sciences, respectively. "Some government people beaming in." She checked her watch. "Five minutes. Anything interesting at the market?" He described the dinner menu and told her about meeting Suzy Q. and giving her a flower.

"Poor damned thing. She's been on the street since I was a kid . . . yeah, I'll give you a call if I'm going to be late . . .'dios."

Pepe looked up from his work. "Who's on the street?"

"Poor old woman named Suzy Q. Pushes a grocery cart around?"

"I've seen a few of those."

"She went to high school here with Norman. You don't remember Bolivia."

"Rory. I was two years old then."

"Sorry . . . anyhow, her first husband was a marine, went down there and won the war. But he came back with a time-bomb virus. She woke up one morning and he was dead, melted in a puddle around his own skeleton. She just came undone."

"Jesus. I didn't know people brought it home with them."

"It was rare. He must have gotten it right at the end of the war." She paused. "Pepe, what happens if there's a war now?"

"To me?" She nodded. "Well, I'm still a Cuban citizen, even though I've been away for seven years. You know I've only got a blue card."

"I know. Could they call you up? Cuba's not going to be neutral."

"You know, I'm not sure?" He took off his glasses and polished them with a tissue. "When I left I was reservado, like inactive reserves here. You stay that way until age forty, or until you do active service. Or until they change the law, which they might have done without telling me."

"But as a reservado you'd be safe. Especially living over here."

"Truthfully, I don't know. But they'd have a hard time finding me. I'd be in Mexico mañana." He blinked through his glasses and imitated a broad Mexican accent: "*¿Cuba? ¿Dónde está esta isla Cuba? Soy campesino mexicano solamente.*"

"Sure. You sound like a campesino with a Ph.D."

"Seriously, I'd go home and fight if the island herself was in danger. But I don't care about Europe."

"Good. You know how Norman and I feel. I'd hate to lose you, but if you need help disappearing . . ."

He held up a hand. "Gracias. Best not to talk about such things."

"I suppose." Her wall chimed. "Meeting in two minutes, Room 301." Today it had the voice of Melissa Mercurio, a thirties movie personality. A seating diagram came up on the screen:

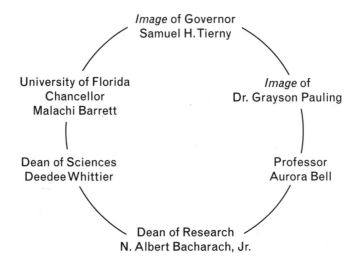

Image of Governor
Samuel H. Tierny

University of Florida
Chancellor
Malachi Barrett

Image of
Dr. Grayson Pauling

Dean of Sciences
Deedee Whittier

Professor
Aurora Bell

Dean of Research
N. Albert Bacharach, Jr.

"Oh, the governor," Rory said. "This will be a feast for the intellect."

"I should know who Pauling is," Pepe said. "Sounds familiar. NSA?"

"No, cabinet. He's the president's new science adviser. 'Science and technology.' " She pushed a button and got a paper printout. "I don't know anything about him. Life sciences, I think. More politician than scientist, I'd imagine."

"Buena suerte."

"Yeah." She opened a few drawers and found a notebook. "Maybe we can get away for lunch? Go down to Sara's and get a beer?" Dos Hermanos was the department's official bar.

"Love it."

Rory walked down a floor and went to 301, a room usually reserved for first-Friday get-togethers and holiday parties. They'd put in a round table that was too large for six people, holo flats in place for the governor and Grayson Pauling.

The holos were dark and the chancellor hadn't shown up yet. She said hello to the two deans and took her place to the right of Bacharach.

She suppressed a smile at his sour "buenos." They had been at odds for three years, ever since Bacharach had inherited the "Dean of Research" title. Some people would covet the job, but to Bacharach it was a necessary evil—five years of afternoons spent in argument and analysis and the annual excruciation of presenting the budget to the board and trying to explain science to them.

Rory suspected that he didn't like teaching any more than he liked committee work; he'd really prefer to be left alone with his particle physics. It was more than delicious that her astrophysics budget had slowly climbed under his tenure, while particle had to eat a major cut in spite of his arguments.

She did like him in spite of his dourness and departmental politics. He was an odd-looking man, very tall, huge hands. A ponytail and beard that reminded Rory of her father's generation.

Deedee Whittier was Bacharach's opposite. She loved academic infighting; she was a master of finely tuned sarcasm and the art of playing one person against another. Rory approved of her, though. She could have used her position—as Bacharach did—to limit her teaching to intellectually challenging seminars in her specialty. Instead, she took on two huge lecture courses, Life Sciences and Biology I, and the students had twice voted her Teacher of the Year. Rory had eavesdropped on her lectures and envied her charisma. She envied her trim athletic beauty, too; almost as old as Rory, she looked more than ten years younger.

Chancellor Barrett hurried in, checking his watch. "Damned reporters." He sat down heavily next to Whittier. "So. We're all in our places, with bright shiny faces."

"Good morning to you, Professor Mal," Rory said.

He tilted his head toward her. "And to you, Professor. Deedee, Al. Anything new, Aurora?"

"Not since this morning's broadcast. You saw it?"

"Yes, twice." He took out a large white handkerchief and rubbed his face with it. He was a big round man who didn't take well to the unseasonal heat. "That fellow on the Moon, that Japanese. Do you know anything about him?"

"I didn't. I looked him up about an hour ago. He's a radio astronomer doing a project for the University of Kyoto."

"He's legitimate? He couldn't be part of a hoax?"

"Mal . . . how the hell could I know? He might be in the pay of the Mafia."

The chancellor winced, just as a soft *ping* warned of an incoming transmission. "Don't say 'Mafia' when the governor's here."

"Heavens, no. Let's keep relations out of this." The two deans laughed.

The governor's image faded in and solidified. He smiled broadly. "Good morning, all. Buenos días." Murmur of returned greetings. "So what's the joke? Can I be in on it?"

"Reporters," Chancellor Barrett said quickly. "Though I suppose they are no joke to a man in your position."

"Ah, no. No. But we have to live with the little darlin's, don't we? Ha." He studied a prompt screen, which had the disconcerting effect of making it look like he was staring accusingly at Dean Bacharach. "Now. God knows I don't want to interfere with your science work. This is really serious stuff, I know. But it could be a real shot in the arm for the state of Florida, too. Surely you can appreciate my position." He looked around at the holographic ghosts who sat at his table in Tallahassee. Rory suddenly realized that that was why this table was so large; it had to be the same diameter as the governor's.

"I won't try to kid anybody. Florida has had a couple of bad years." A bad decade or two, actually. The barrier dikes around Miami and the other coastal cities had cut into tourism, even before last April's flood. The southern part of the state was permanently tropical and growing hotter; light industry was moving away because nobody wanted to live there. The long-running sitcom *Flying Cockroach*

Blues had not helped. If it weren't for Disney and the Three Dwarves, the whole state would go Chapter 11 and slide into the sea.

"This can help change our image. I mean, Florida has always been strong science-wise, but people don't know that. They think about hurricanes and floods and bugs and, uh . . . cancer. But Florida's a lot more than that, always has been." The chime sounded again and the governor looked at the appropriate blank space. The image of a gaunt, weary man appeared.

"Good morning, all." Grayson Pauling looked around. "Don't bother with introductions. I've been briefed."

He looked at Rory. "Dr. Bell. You are on record as being politically, shall we say, agnostic. Can we trust you to cooperate with the government?"

"Is that a threat?"

"No. Just reality. If you don't care to work with us, you may get up and leave now. There are 1,549 astronomers in this country. One or two of them must be Republicans."

"If you're asking whether I can work within the system—of course I can. I'm a department head. Academic politics is so convoluted and smarmy, it makes Washington look like summer camp."

"Point well taken. Speaking of Washington . . . please join me." The room shimmered and snapped and suddenly Rory found herself sitting at a round table in the White House, evidently. A large window behind Pauling showed a manicured lawn with a high wall, the Washington Monument beyond.

She didn't know you could do that, without setting it up beforehand. It was an impressive demonstration.

Even the governor was caught off guard. "Nice . . . uh . . ." He cleared his throat. "Nice place you have here."

"It's the people's place, of course," Pauling said, deadpan. "It belongs to you more than to me."

"What sort of cooperation are you talking about?" Bacharach asked, not hiding his hostility. "You want Profesor Bell to keep the facts from the public, the press?"

"Under some extreme circumstances, yes." He put his elbows on the table and looked at Bacharach over steepled fingers. "And under such circumstances, I think you would agree with me."

"Being?"

"Panic. When Dr. Bell mentioned a million megatons this morning, and the possible destruction of the planet . . . that was unfortunate."

"A calculation anyone could make," Rory said. "Any student computer would give you the answer immediately."

"Ah, but only if you asked the questions. And the student asking that question wouldn't have a hundred million people watching her on cube." He shook his head. "You're right, though. It's not a good example. A sufficiently bright college student could make the calculation."

"A sufficiently bright junior-high-school student, Dr. Pauling," Bacharach said, almost hissing. "Do you actually have a doctorate in science?"

"Al . . ." Chancellor Barrett said.

"*Political* science, Dr. Bacharach. And a bachelor's degree in life science."

"Dean Bacharach does not mean to imply—"

"Of course he did," Pauling said. To Bacharach: "I trust you are satisfied with my credentials . . . to be a politician?"

"Eminently satisfied."

"I think we'll get along together splendidly. For as long as you stay on the project." He sat back slowly. "Now. The Department of Defense is assembling a task force to deal with the military aspects of this problem. They'll be in touch with you, Governor."

"What military aspects?" Rory said. "Do they plan to attack this thing?"

"Not so long as its intentions are peaceful."

She laughed. "Do you have any idea of how much energy a million megatons represents?"

"Of course I do. Our largest Peace Reserve weapon is a hundred megatons. That would be ten thousand times as large."

"So isn't it rather like ants plotting to destroy an elephant?"

He smiled at her. "An interesting analogy, Dr. Bell. If the ants worked together, they could sting the elephant, and make it change course."

Deedee Whittier spoke for the first time. "Rory, would you be practical for once in your life? Do you think we'll get a nickel of federal money if we don't let the generals come in and play their games? This is going to be an expensive project, and the state is flat broke. Is it not, Governor?"

"Well, I wouldn't actually say we were, uh, *broke*."

"I like your directness," Pauling said to Whittier. "Let me return it: your state's worse than broke; it's in debt up to its panhandle. Largely because of a government so corrupt it makes my fragrant city seem honest by comparison."

"Corrupt?" the governor said. "Young man, that's simply not the case."

"Not your office, Governor." He made a placating gesture with one hand. "Lower down, though, surely you're aware . . ."

"Yes, well, yes. Government attracts both good and bad." Tierny's administration hadn't attracted a surplus of good people. He was the kind of governor only a newspaper cartoonist could love, and he would have long since been impeached if his machine hadn't owned the senate and judiciary before he came into office.

"I suspect you won't have much to do with the Defense people," Pauling said. "Most of the resources that come into Florida will come through Cape Kennedy."

"More good news," Rory said. "No surprise, though."

"The NASA can get things done when they're allowed to," Deedee said. "Your own gamma-ray satellite, didn't it go up ahead of schedule?"

"My *one* gamma-ray satellite. The backup is rusting away in some shed down at the Cape."

"Perhaps something can be done about that," Pauling said smoothly. "Gamma-ray astronomy seems a little more important than it was yesterday. I'll have my office look into it." Rory just nodded.

The governor cleared his throat loudly. "One reason I wanted to be in on this meeting was to ask you educated folks a simple question. I don't think it has a simple answer, though." He paused dramatically, looking around the table. "Have you given any thought to the possibility that the thing what's behind this thing . . . is God?"

"What?" Rory said. Whittier rolled her eyes. Bacharach studied the back of one large hand. Pauling openly stared at the governor.

"It might not be obvious to you scientist types, but that's just what your man in the street is going to think of first. All that thing said was 'We're coming.' What if it's the Second Coming?"

"Are you serious, Governor?" Pauling said.

He sat up straight and returned the man's stare. "Do you think I am the kind of man who would exploit religion for political gain?"

Rory decided not to laugh. "Why should God be so roundabout? Why not have the Second Coming in Jerusalem, or the White House lawn?"

"Actually, ma'am, I have given that some thought. It could be that God meant to give us three months to ready ourselves. Cleanse ourselves."

"He might be more specific," Deedee said. "The last time, he told everyone who would listen."

"God works in mysterious ways."

"So does the government." Deedee reached out of the holo field and brought back a plastic cup. "Let's leave that part to the holy joes, okay?" She sipped coffee and set the cup down. It hovered a disconcerting inch over the table.

"It is something we'll have to deal with," Chancellor Barrett said. "If that becomes a commonly accepted explanation, there may be some public resistance to our research. Even organized resistance."

"That's true, Mal," Deedee said, "but what can we do about it ahead of time?"

"There's the obvious end run," Pauling said. "Does your university have a religion department?"

The chancellor shook his head. "Philosophy. There are sub-heads in comparative religion and 'philosophies of social and religious morality.' "

"Well, find one of them who's ordained, if you can—a tame one—and make him a pro forma member of your committee."

"Hold it," the governor broke in. "You all act like this was some kind of a game. You'll look pretty sorry if it turns out that God really *is* behind it."

This time they all stared at him. He seemed dead serious. "Now,

I'm not saying that business and science aren't important. But this could be the biggest thing in history. Second biggest thing."

It actually was calculation, Rory decided. The idea had come to him while he was sitting there, and now he was going to hang on to it with all of his famous "bull 'gator" tenacity. He probably didn't have much support from organized religion, so he was going to milk this for votes.

"Now I understand the church and state thing," he continued, "and anyhow you scientists won't do much about the God end of it. Wouldn't expect you to. But Dr. Pauling's right. To be fair about it, you have to put some religious people on your committee."

"And you have a suggestion for one," Pauling said.

"As a matter of fact, I do. And he lives right near Gainesville, out in Archer, practically suburbs."

The chancellor forced an unconvincing smile. "That wouldn't be Reverend Charles Dubois."

"The same! By George, Dr. Barrett, you don't miss much, do you?" Reverend Dubois would be hard to miss. He was prominent in almost every conservative movement in the county. He had delivered Alachua County's votes to the governor in spite of the pesky liberal presence of the university.

"Um . . . I'm not certain he would be qualified. . . ."

The governor was staring at his prompter. "He has a doctorate. He went to your own university."

Barrett looked a little ill. "He didn't earn his doctorate here?"

"Well, no. That was in California."

"Through the mail," Bacharach said. "That charlatan doesn't have a real degree at all."

"You know him?" Rory asked.

"I live in Archer, too. He tried to push through a zoning variance for his new church last year."

"We can't spend our energy worrying about local politics," the governor said. "Dubois is an energetic, intelligent man—"

"Who flunked out of UF his first—"

"Who has the trust and support of many elements of the community that do not automatically trust you academics." He glared into an uncomfortable silence.

Bacharach stood up. "Malachi, thanks for asking for my input here. I'm obviously not helping the process, though." He turned around abruptly and disappeared.

Rory realized she was in the same room with him; if she stood up and stepped away, the illusion would vanish, the dean and the chancellor staring at ghosts. Maybe she should. This was getting pretty far from the astrophysics of nonthermal sources.

Well, there was no way to keep the politicians and religionists out of it, anyhow. Might as well start dealing with them now.

"Governor," she said, "with all due respect, I wonder whether we might want a representative of the religious community who's more widely known. This Dubois man may be notorious in some circles, but I've never heard of him, and I live just twenty miles away."

Deedee smiled at her. "Aurora, I'd bet that everything you know about local politics could be inscribed on the head of a pin."

"She has a good point," Pauling said. "We should find someone of national stature. Perhaps Johnny Kale could find the time."

"Or the pope. Everybody trusts the pope." Deedee looked into her coffee cup and put it back down. Johnny Kale had been the pet preacher of the last three administrations. He had as much clout as a cabinet member.

Even Rory had heard of him. "But he's kind of old-fashioned," she said, although she meant something less charitable.

"Well, perhaps that's what we want," Pauling said, "for balance. Most of the *country* is pretty old-fashioned, after all."

Rory wasn't very political, but she knew a turf battle when she saw one. The governor was thinking so hard you could hear the dry primitive mechanisms grinding away.

"There's no reason we can't have both men," he conceded. "Reverend Kale at the national level and Reverend Dubois down here."

"At any rate," Chancellor Barrett said, "we have to keep a sense of perspective. This is still primarily a scientific problem. Absent some startling revelation."

"I don't know how much revelation you need," the governor said.

"More," Barrett said.

"I guess you find it easier to believe in ETs than God?"

"Save it for the speeches, Governor." He turned to Pauling. "What sort of many-headed beast are we cooking up here? At the federal level we have you, Defense, NASA, and now that sanctimonious camp follower Kale. No doubt we'll have a boatload of senators before long."

Pauling nodded. "Half of Washington will find something in this that's relevant, as long as it's hot. I'll try to deflect them so they don't interfere with your science."

"What science?" Rory said. "Unless they begin broadcasting again, everything we do is idle speculation. Until they're close enough to observe directly."

"How long would that be?" Pauling asked.

"Depends on how big they are. Depends on what you mean by 'observe.' We have a probe orbiting Neptune that's the size of a school bus, and we can't see it optically. If that's the size of the thing, we won't see it until it's a day or so away."

"Three months' wait." The governor frowned. "That's a long time to keep people interested." Rory opened her mouth and shut it.

"We can work on that," Pauling said. "The preparations for various contingencies could be made pretty dramatic.

"When I was a kid I remember reading about plans to orbit nuclear weapons—not as bombs, but as insurance against a catastrophic meteor strike, like the one that got the dinosaurs."

"*May* have," Deedee said.

"Anyhow, it never got off the ground, combination of money and politics. I wonder if they could do it now."

"Not in eleven months," Deedee said. "No matter how much money and politics you throw at it."

"I wouldn't underestimate the Defense Department," Pauling said. "Remember the Manhattan Project."

"It was the War Department then," Rory said, remembering from her new book, "and the threat was more immediate and obvious."

"I don't know about this Manhattan thing," the governor said. "We don't need to drag New York into this, do we?"

Barrett broke the silence. "That was the code name for the team that developed the atom bomb, Governor."

"Oh, yes. Of course. World War II."

"I don't think it's conceptually difficult," Whittier said, "putting missiles with large warheads into orbit. I'm no engineer, but it seems to me you could cobble it together with existing stuff. Peace Reserve weapons mated piecemeal with the Super Shuttle. The problems would be logistics and politics rather than engineering."

"International politics more than national," Barrett said. "A lot of countries wouldn't care to see American H-bombs in orbit, no matter which way they were pointed."

"And there's a law against it," Pauling admitted. " 'Weapons of mass destruction' have been proscribed, in orbit, for almost a hundred years."

"Has anybody told the Pakistanis about this?" Rory said.

Pauling shrugged. "Outlaws don't obey laws. We have to step lightly, of course, especially given the European situation. There's no reason all the bombs should be American, and of course their launching wouldn't be under the control of any one nation."

"Dr. Pauling," Rory said, "don't let yourself be too impressed by a few hundred megatons in orbit. We're still the ants in this picture."

"We must remind ourselves of this constantly," the governor said, "and not fall prey to the sin of pride."

"How very true," said Pauling in a weary, neutral tone. "Hubris. Get you every time." He stood up. "I think we have a sense of how everyone feels. We need more data; we need time for the data we do have to sink in. Shall we meet again two days from now, same time?"

Rory was the only one who didn't nod or mumble yes. This was going to be nothing but an impediment.

Suddenly the three academics were sitting alone at their too-large table in Room 301. Barrett turned to Whittier. "So. Do you think we've lost Bacharach for good?"

"Pretty sure," Deedee said. "He doesn't have any real stake in staying."

"He could lose his position."

"Al wouldn't lift a finger to retain his deanship," Rory said. "You know that. He'd gladly trade the extra pay and perks if he could do science full-time again."

"I've always wondered how sincere he was about that. Perhaps we'll find out."

Rory got up. "I'll have some tentative scheduling for both of you tomorrow morning. Have to go confer with my second-in-command, over a beer."

"Thanks for your patience, Rory," Deedee said. "Difficult man to work with."

"Or against." Rory gave them a parting smile and closed the door quietly.

Deedee Whittier

"You've met the governor before, Mal?"

"Twice, at formal receptions. This is the first time I've had an extended colloquy with him."

"He's a piece of work. Not really that stupid, I assume."

"No. He has normal intelligence, or at least the equivalent in animal cunning." They both laughed. "And vast reserves of ignorance to work with. I think Pauling's going to be much more of a problem."

"He's going to take over."

"Already has. At least we don't have to deal directly with La-Salle."

Deedee nodded wearily. Carlie LaSalle, president of the United States, made Governor Tierny look like an intellectual. A completely artificial product of her party's analysts and social engineers, she gave the people exactly what they wanted: a cube personality who was *nice* to the core, with a gift for reading lines and a suitably inoffensive personal history. She was an anti-intellectual populist who had presided over four years of stagnation in the arts and sciences, and had just been reelected.

"We'll be walking on eggshells," Deedee said.

"I was thinking bulls and china shops, actually, with Garcia. I like him but think we're well rid of him. He won't disguise his contempt."

"No; he's no diplomat."

"What about Dr. Bell?"

"Aurora? She's pretty levelheaded."

"She was pushing Pauling harder than I liked."

"Mal, be realistic. Most of the professors in my department would gleefully take a blunt instrument to that son of a bitch. Besides, Aurora made the discovery, for Christ's sake. We're stuck with her."

He drummed his fingers on the table. "This is the problem. This is the problem all around. We're stuck with Tierny. We're stuck with Pauling and LaSalle. We already have to do a goddamned minuet around them. It would be real nice if we had more control over our own side. Our own half of the equation."

Deedee took a mirror and a blue needle and touched up the edges of her cheek tattoo, which was fading. Someday she would get a permanent one, to cover the cancer scar, but her dermie said to wait. It might grow.

She worked for half a minute, frowning. "So be plain, Mal. What do you want me to do about Aurora?"

"Well . . . as you say, we can't just dump her. I guess I just want to know more about her. Find some weakness we can exploit. Is that blunt enough?"

"Si, si. I'll put Ybor Lopez on it. He's trustworthy and a real computer magician. I'll have him put together a dossier on her. I . . . well, I have something to make him cooperative." She snapped her bag shut. "For you, Mal. Just this once."

"I appreciate it. I won't abuse the information."

"Oh, mierda. I know you won't. You owe me one, though."

"You have it." They got up together and left the room.

Deedee wished she had kept her mouth shut. Traitor to her class—she'd been a professor a lot longer than she'd been an administrator. And to pull this on Aurora, of all people. She'd never been anything but helpful and kind. Ybor would probably find out she was an ex-con or a dope addict. Like him.

They started to go down the stairs, but heard the crowd murmuring three floors down: reporters. They backtracked and used the fire stairs.

Deedee's office was two buildings away. She hurried through the noontime glare, the cancers on her face and shoulder saying, "You forgot your hat." The sunscreen was supposed to be good for eight hours, but she'd been sweating. In that air-conditioned room in Washington.

Lopez was locking up the office as she came out of the elevator. "Ybor," she said. "Hold it. We have to talk."

They went back into the outer office, a spare uncluttered place where Ybor ran interference for her. She sat him down in the visitors' chair and perched herself on the desk.

"I need your expertise, Ybor. And your silence."

"Something illegal, Dr. Whittier?"

"No. Shady, but not illegal."

"Okay. You can trust me."

She let out a long breath and chose her words. She used Spanish. "—I don't have to trust you, Ybor. Because I have you by the hair."

"No comprendo."

"—I've seen you shooting up, twice. Tell me it's diabetes."

He slumped. "How the hell did you ever see me?"

"—What is it?"

"Se llama 'José y María.' "

"Some kind of DD?"

"Sí." A designer drug. "—You give them some blood or sperm and they customize it."

"—As much as you know about science, you let them do that?"

"—It's hard to explain. You don't do anything?"

"—Nothing big. Nothing illegal."

"De acuerdo." Ybor switched to English. "Who do you want me to kill?"

"I just need your jaquismo. Get into and out of university personnel files and some municipal records without leaving any tracks. Try to find some dirt."

"So who's the villain?"

"She's a nice person, not a villain. I just need some leverage. Aurora Bell." She looked oddly expectant.

He shook his head slowly. "So what happens if I don't find anything? She's not exactly Mata Hari."

"I don't expect you to find something that's not there. Just do your best and be extra careful. How long?"

"Oh . . . this afternoon. Say four."

"Thanks." She slid off the desk. "Sorry about, you know. Anytime you want to go into rehab . . ."

"Yeah, well. You know. It's not like that."

"I *don't* know, actually. But so long as it doesn't interfere with your work, it's not a problem. Not for me." She walked out, leaving the door open.

Ybor Lopez

He shut the door and locked it and leaned against it for a few seconds, eyes squeezed shut, teeth clenched. Then he went to the supply closet and unlocked the backup files safe, a fireproof metal block to which only he had access. He took out the José y María hypo, dropped his pants, and put the applicator nozzle flat against the large vein in his penis. He fired it, wincing, and rubbed the sting away. By the time he had his pants pulled up and the hypo locked back in the safe, the drug was coming on.

He sat down and reveled in it, the clean pure power that roared through his veins, the light that glowed from inside. The absolute confidence. What could she know about this? He felt a moment of compassion, of sorrow, for people who went through life without having this. A gift from his own body, grown from his own seed. There was nothing wrong with it. It was the law that was wrong.

To work. Leave no tracks, all right. No voice commands. No backup crystal. Go under the machine's intelligence and use it like its twentieth-century predecessors: simple commands executed sequentially.

He did it all the time, for fun and the department's profit, as Whittier well knew. It was winked at; probably half the science and engineering departments had someone like Ybor, who could make an hour of computing time look like fifteen minutes. (The missing time would show up on accounts like Slavic Languages and Art History, who didn't have Ybors.) The same sort of skills could slip through the light encryption that protected the privacy of personnel records.

It took Ybor about half an hour to set up the program that would assemble a cybernetic image of the private life of Aurora Bell. It just took a few minutes more to have it do the same for Deedee Whittier, insurance. He pushed a button to start it running and went out to get some lunch.

Good timing. José y María did make you feel famished about an hour after you popped. It was a healthy hunger, though; felt good.

He walked down tree-lined Second Avenue to downtown, studying the undergraduate girls. His appreciation of their beauty had an exquisite purity, partly because he couldn't do anything about it until a day or so after the drug wore off. But that was not really a problem, he told himself. For every thing there is a season. He tried to ignore the persistant itching pain at the injection site, the slight numb erection.

It wasn't just the way they looked, moving in their soft summer clothes. He could smell them as they passed; smell the secret parts of their bodies as well as the public perfume, the astringent sunblock. He could feel the heat from their bodies on his face, on the back of his hand, as they passed. He could almost read their thoughts, at least when they were thinking of him.

What a wonderful day. He even loved the heat, the blast that glowed up from the asphalt as he floated across streets. It was as if he walked *on* the heat. Cars stopped for him respectfully, their horns music. Brakes squealing in beautiful unison as he triggered the street's emergency mode.

As he appoached Hermanos, the smell of meats frying was almost too much for him. He swallowed saliva and walked into the cool and dark.

What were all these people doing here? Usually Hermanos was uncrowded until after one, when the Cubans and Mexicans started drifting in. There were only two tables unoccupied. Ybor sat down at the bar.

The owner Sara waited on him. She made him uncomfortable. He had known her before the accident, when she was a lifeguard at the Eastside pool. He had studied her body for hours when he was eleven and twelve, and it disgusted him to think of what it must look like now. But he always went to the bar when she was serving.

"Hola, Ybor. What'll it be?"

He didn't have to look at the menu. "*Ropa vieja y vino tinto.*"

She wrote it down. "Old rags and new wine, coming up." She poured him a glass of red wine, cold, and went back to the kitchen.

Ybor took a sip of the wine and then held the glass between his palms, warming it. Like everything, the bar was transformed by the drug, made more real and more fantastic at the same time. The cheap paneling became a whorl of frozen life, tropical trees microtomed over and over. The liquor bottles with their rainbow of colors and flavors; from yards away he could smell them individually. The slow ceiling fans pushed gentle puffs of cool air over him, like slaves waving palm fronds. The mirror showed a young man capable of great things. Thirty-five was still young.

Sara brought the stew with a plate of warm tortillas and the green hot sauce Ybor liked. *Ropa vieja,* literally "old clothes," was beef slowly cooked in tomato sauce and peppers, until it fell apart into shreds. Ybor liked it but had chosen it mainly because he knew it would just be ladled out and brought to him. He could have starved to death while they were fixing a hamburger.

Sara watched him tear into it with a spoon in one hand and a rolled tortilla in the other. "I like a man who likes to eat," she said, smiling, and went off to fill a bar order.

This drug could make eating a cracker into a sensual experience. The spicy stew played an ecstatic symphony in his mouth, nose, palate; the act of swallowing was a complex and delightful counterpoint.

Sara came back. "So how about these aliens?"

"¿Cómo?" She going to carry on about immigrants again, interrupt this symphony?

"Right next door to you." She waved a hand at all her new customers. "All these reporters. All because of Aurora Bell."

That got his attention. "What'd Dr. Bell do?"

"What, you live in a goddamn cave?"

"Working all morning. What she do?"

"She got some signal from outer space. Some aliens coming to Earth, like in the movies."

"Aw, bullshit, Sara. You're bullshittin' me."

"Like you'd know bullshit if you stepped in it," she said cheerfully. She whistled at the set over the bar and told it CNN. "Just watch for a few minutes."

Now what the hell had he gotten himself into? The way Whittier had talked, of course she'd thought he knew.

The stew turned sour in his mouth and he swallowed with difficulty. Shit, what if they expected some newsie to hack the system and beefed up the watchdogs? They might catch the tap and it would point right back to him.

A live reporter standing in front of the building next to where he worked delivered a one-minute summation of the alien thing. There was Dr. Bell, sitting in her office with all the old paper books, talking about, Jesus, a million megatons? Okay, relativistic kinetic energy. Still. One hell of a bang.

There was some commotion behind him and he turned around to see Aurora Bell walk in with Pepe Parker. They were good-naturedly telling the reporters no interviews; this was lunch. The big guy who runs the coffee machine in the morning came out to stand behind her with a cast-iron frying pan. Subtle.

Pepe raised a hand in greeting and he returned it. They saw

each other every now and then at the dance clubs. Not a bad guy for a Cubano.

"Something wrong with the *ropa?*" Sara asked.

"Oh no, it's great. Let me have another wine, though."

"Tinto," she said, and refilled his glass.

‖‖‖ Sara

Wonder if he's a drunk. If he is, he's a cute one. Late for him, actually, he's usually in here for a wine or cerveza by eleven. Work all night, drink all day, but he doesn't seem to drink that much, just unsteady and bright-eyed from fatigue and coffee. He was a cute kid back in high school, junior high, always down at the pool looking at me, I wonder does he remember, does he know I remember? I looked at him, too.

José was taking the order of Dr. Bell and the guy who came in with her. Funny Ybor didn't know about Dr. Bell and the aliens, right in the building next door. Physics and astrology. Astrophysics, they just said, probably a combination.

Astrology had helped her a lot. Some of it was just made up, maybe all of it, but you had to make a decision one way or the other, might as well ask your chart. She carried hers in her purse usually, but this morning the battery light was on, so she left it plugged in at the house. She could get along without it for a day. Maybe when she got home she would ask it Is Ybor a drunk? Would he fuck a woman with a body like hers? She knew the answer to that and looked away from him as she pressed her knees together and felt a small helpless ripple of desire, not for Ybor in particular. Time to go to a feelie, or maybe back to Orlando to get serviced for real. There was a place in Gainesville but if she used it Willy Joe would find out. She would have to kill him. It would be a public-health measure, but they'd probably put her in jail anyhow. She thought about last time in Orlando and felt warm and wet and knew she was blushing, the big black man who called her his little doll. What was the name of that place, the Bluebird, the Blackbird? She knew where it was and knew the man's name, John Henry, claro.

José was in front of her. "Two Tecates on five?" he asked. "Preparadas. I've got my hands full."

"Tecates," she said slowly.

"You okay, amiga?" He stood there with order pad and frying pan.

Sara laughed. "Just thinking. Not used to it, I guess."

She opened the two cans of beer and sprinkled a pinch of rock salt on the top of each, and topped them off with lime. Disgusting combination, but the customer was always right, or at least was always the customer.

She carried the two beers over to table five and gave them to Rory and Pepe. "I saw Norman in the mercado this morning. He was acting funny."

"He usually acts funny," Rory said.

"I didn't know you were famous then. He was probably thinking about being second fiddle."

"Not his instrument," Rory said, and they both laughed. There was a loud crash in the kitchen and Sara went to check.

 Pepe

He watched her rush away, the peculiar walk. "It was a drive-by?"

Rory nodded and grimaced. "Just off University, student ghetto somewhere. A car door opened and some stranger splashed her with gasoline and lit a match. She heard some people laughing, at least two men and a woman. But she couldn't remember what kind of car it was or tell them anything about the man. I guess that was a year or so before you came."

"Pobrecita," he said, squeezing the lime into his beer.

"People wonder whether it had something to do with the brothers who owned the place originally. But they'd disappeared years before."

"That was back when the gangs were so bad."

Rory didn't use the lime. She brushed off most of the salt and sipped from the can. "A lot of random violence then. People think it's bad now. There were places you just didn't go after dark."

"Still are."

"Claro." She got a pad and stylus out of her bag and turned them on. She drew a row of neat boxes, frowning, and then erased them with her thumb. "I told Deedee and El Chancellor that I'd have some scheduling for them tomorrow morning. But until I hear from NASA and the Cape, everything's kind of moot. Defense, too, in a way. They'll oversee a lot of the funding."

"You mean you don't want to make up a table of organization just to have the government come in and kick it apart."

"Sí. No harm in doing a tentative one, I guess. Who's qualified for what, interested in what. If the feds change it, they change it."

"So where do I fit in?"

"Pretty face." She pretended to write it down. " 'Official . . . pretty face.' "

"How about 'nonadministrator'? I just do the science?"

"Muy buena suerte. You get to help me run this circus."

Pepe shrugged and suppressed a smile:

That's what I'm here for. Eight years of winning your trust, so I can make sure you divine half the truth, the right half.

And the decade before that, studying how to talk, how to think, how to act. Not in Cuba. Learning how to live with this alien food and drink.

In his way, he loved her. But that was of no importance. He knew what his job was going to be, over the next week, the next three months.

"Qué bueno," he said. "Do I get a pistol and chair?"

"I'll put in a requisition."

A man rushed up to the table. "Professor Bell."

"Yes?" After a moment she recognized him as the reporter from this morning. "Mr. Jordan."

"Dan. Don't want to take your lunch time, but look . . . they've put me on . . . God! . . . soft background, local color. It's not my . . . it's not . . ."

"It's not your story anymore."

"That's right. I'm just a local flunky now." He took a deep breath. "What I wanted, wanted to know, is could I get an interview with you and Mr. Bell sometime today, tonight?"

"Sure, sin problema. Just call first, what, eight?"

"Thanks. I've got your number." He looked at Pepe. "Perdón. I'll get out of your hair."

Daniel Jordan

He went back out into the heat and whistled for the camera to follow him. Lots of local color out here by the mercado, but nobody wants to stand in the sun and chat. He moved over to the shade of a pair of trees just past the coffee booth.

People walked by him. It must have been easier in the old days, when you had a big square camera and a human cameraman, a microphone in your hand and wires trailing everywhere. A pain in the ass, actually, but at least people would have to notice you.

"Excuse me, sir." He stepped in the path of a slow-moving, round middle-aged man. "I'm Daniel Jordan from News Seven. . . ."

"Good for you," he said, but stopped.

"I came down to the mercado to ask people's opinions about the Coming."

"That's what they're calling it?"

"Some people, yes . . ."

"Well, I don't like it. Sounds religious."

"Whatever the name. How do you feel about it?"

"Feel? I suppose it's a good thing. Make contact and all that. Been talking about it long enough."

"You don't feel there's any danger?"

"No, no. We were talking about that at the shop. Small's Jalousies and Windows? Government's gonna try to scare us, spend tax money protecting us from these goddamn things. But it's bullshit. You know? If they wanted to get us, they would've snuck up on us, right? A burglar doesn't ring the bell on his way in, does he? I think it'll be real interesting."

"Thank you, Mister . . ."

"Small, Ed Small. Small's Jalousies and Windows." He leaned toward the camera and waved. " 'When you think of windows, think Small.' "

A few people had stopped to watch the interview. Dan zeroed in on a woman with her son, eight or nine years old.

"What do you think about all this, young man?"

"About the monsters?"

"Le . . . roy," his mother warned.

"You think they'll be monsters?" Dan asked.

"They're *always* monsters," he explained patiently.

"He watches too much cube." His mother glared at the camera.

"Mother. They're always monsters because that's what people want. The guys who made this up know that."

The mother stared at her son. Dan cleared his throat. "So you think it's all made up?"

"Well, it's on the cube," the boy said, explaining everything.

Dan laughed unconvincingly. "Do you share your son's skepticism?"

"Not really, no. I'm hoping it will be something . . . really wonderful. What the man you just talked to said, that's true. If they meant us harm they wouldn't have announced they were coming."

"You don't think it could be a hoax?"

"No—it's already too big."

"Well, *I* think it's a hoax," the man behind her said. He was ebony black, shimmering skintights like rainbow paint on a weightlifter's body. "They had it orchestrated months in advance, maybe years."

"Who are 'they,' then?"

"Well, who do you think has the money? If it's not the federal government then it's a group of conglomerates working together—

assuming the last act of the farce will be a spaceship landing on the White House lawn."

A live one, Dan thought. He made the hand signal that instructed the camera to move in tight. "And what will the government or conglomerates gain?"

"More and better control over us. *Thought* control!" He held up both fists. "Watch and wait. These aliens will be presented to us as unassailably superior savants. What they say is true, we will have to accept as truth. Who could argue with creatures who came umpty-ump light-years to save us?"

"You have it pretty well thought out," Dan said.

"I used to be paid to think," he said. "Dr. Cameron Davisson, at your service. Ex–professor of philosophy at this august institution."

"Um . . . what do you do now, Dr. Davisson?"

"I try to serve as a bad example."

"Ah . . ." Out of the corner of his eye, Dan saw a vision of loveliness. "Ma'am? Pardon me, señorita?"

The woman stopped and looked at him. She was a classic Latin beauty—statuesque; haughty, aristocratic features. Ebony hair and skin like dark honey set off by a simple white dress that loved the flesh it clung to and partially exposed.

"I'm interviewing people here about the Coming."

"The aliens? I think it's marvelous. Have to get to work." She turned and walked away and even the camera stared at her. I wouldn't mind going to work with you, Dan thought, but he didn't know half of it.

Gabrielle

She'd forgotten to take the gel home with her and so that meant an extra fifteen minutes without pay at work, feet in the stirrups. So it didn't make any difference that she'd worn underwear. She couldn't have worn this dress without underwear, anyhow, and it was a hot-weather favorite.

Two blocks into campus, she turned into the building discreetly labeled IISR, the International Institute for Sexual Research. What a joke.

She took an elevator to the top floor and went into Lab 3 and locked the door behind her.

"Gabby? You're early." A bald man looked up from a machine.

"Forgot to take the gel home. Afternoon, Louis."

"Hi, Gab." A young man lounged by the window, naked, scanning a magazine about popular music. There was nothing unusual about him except for the length and breadth of his penis.

Gabrielle stepped into a small bathroom, where she hung up her dress and put her shoes and underclothes on a shelf. She urinated and tried to break wind, and the medical student in her wondered for the dozenth time what perversity of psychology and anatomy made it impossible for her to do it now and almost imperative later, horizontal and public.

Obeying state law, she didn't flush the toilet. She checked her makeup, carefully blotting the slight shine of sweat from her face and between her breasts. She tried to smile at her reflection and then left the bathroom and walked toward the table.

"Panty lines," the bald man said.

"Harry. I knew the gel would take fifteen minutes to set, so I allowed myself the exquisite luxury of underwear, okay?"

"All right. I guess they'll be gone."

"Maybe your customers *like* panty lines." She mounted the table with a gymnast's slow grace, her ankles landing precisely in the stirrups. "I bet you never asked."

"Artistic convention," he said with a straight face.

"Right." She picked up the large syringe next to the table and applied a liberal amount of lubricant to the nozzle, and then some to herself. She inserted the nozzle carefully, grimacing, and slowly injected the clear gel. If you did it too fast you left air bubbles in the vagina, which would be edited out later, but why make work for your boss? Even if he *is* a pig.

The gel provided a medium with the proper index of refraction. It smelled and tasted like diesel fuel and was about as hard to get rid of as a coastal oil spill. Fortunately, Gabrielle didn't have any lovers who might complain about it, just an uncritical fellow medical student with whom she shared occasional spasms.

She leaned back. "Louis, would you get me that pillow?" She took off her long black wig and smoothed on a cap of metal mesh, then put the wig back on. Louis was already wearing his neural inductor cap.

He brought over a firm cylindrical pillow and she put it under her neck and gave him a playful tug. He was semierect. "You see the stuff on cube about the aliens?"

"Yeah, I was watching it." He ran a finger lightly down her thigh. "Qué maravillosa."

"Hey," said the bald guy from behind the machine. "You come too soon and neither one of you gets paid."

They exchanged professional smiles. "I'll try to control myself, Harry."

"I'll try to keep my hands off him. What did you think?"

"Gonna be a long couple of months. Can't wait."

She nodded at the ceiling. "Anything could happen." She dipped a finger into the softening gel and spread it around her external genitalia. "You ever have Professor Bell?"

"No, I never took astronomy. I had her husband."

"I had her intro course some years back. Before medical school, of course." She circled her clitoris lightly.

"Good teacher?"

"Oh, yeah. A little nervous, but really sincere. Really wanted you to love the stuff. Too much math for me, though."

"Doctors just need to know how to add," he said.

"You have that right. How's her husband?"

"Kind of sweet. He starts out tough, but it's all an act."

"Big class?"

"No, a quartet. Six-week phrasing workshop a couple of summers ago."

Harry came over with a thing that looked like a cross between a snake and a telescope. "Take a reading." Gabrielle pressed both thighs with her palms and spread wide. He inserted the tube a few inches into her.

"Ow!" She jumped. "Easy on that thing. It's the only one I've got."

"Yeah yeah." He peered into the tube and turned a knob. "Squeeze." She did, grunting. "Again." He nodded and pulled the thing out with a little sucking sound. "Okay. Get it up."

Gabrielle grabbed the nearest projection and pulled Louis closer. She cradled his scrotum with the other hand. "So what's phrasing?"

"Basically timing."

"You're good at that."

"Thanks. It's . . ." He gasped and paused a moment as she took him into her mouth. "It's how you put your own interpretation on a piece of music. Of course, with a quartet, you have to all agree."

"Sounds difficult." She stroked him slowly, studying his progress. "This is the only instrument I ever learned how to play. Skin flute."

" 'Duet for skin flute and honey pot.' "

"Honey pot, yeah. Marry me and take me away from all this."

Harry rolled the lights and holo cameras in around them.

Harry explained the narrative, such as it was. They were in a rowboat near the shore of a small lake. Nine minutes into the sequence, another boat was going to approach. They'd try to get down and hide, but would keep fucking, and be caught at the last minute.

He turned on a flatscreen that showed what the actors on the actual boat were doing, so they could mimic the postures and timing. They didn't have to be too precise. The actors on the boat wore skinspray that conducted the feeling of rough wood and water splash. The somatic input from Gab and Louis would be edited in, combined into the main male and female tracks.

"Gabby, get on your knees and back up here." He unmounted the stirrups and pushed a button that lowered the platform a foot.

"Oh, goodie," she said, rolling over. "Arf, arf."

"We still have a little panty line."

"Oh, bullshit, Harry," Louis said. "You can make this look like we're in the middle of a rowboat, and you can't edit out a little panty line?"

"Just extra work. Take a couple of dips before we put the harness on."

They worked together well. Louis stood still behind her and let her control how deep, how fast. The external cameras caught it in every detail. He slid out of her and was so erect his penis slapped against his abdomen.

"Good, we got that," Harry said, and handed him the harness. Louis rolled it over his organ, a loose transparent condom covered with tiny wires. He tightened a collar at the base of his penis and pulled the lower part of the arrangement over his testicles. Harry lubricated a pair of sensors and Louis eased one into his own anus and one into Gab.

She sighed. "Well, let's move it." Louis inserted his decorated dick and they proceeded.

The virtual-reality recording equipment had been bought as part of a legitimate grant for the study of orgasmic dysfunction. Harry was not a scientist, of course; he was an *artiste*. The scientist whose department owned the equipment was willing to let it be used for artistic purposes twice a week, for an amount of money roughly equal to his IISR salary, before taxes.

Gab and Louis had the talent of being able to make their bodies ignore all the hardware. The customers on the receiving end were not so encumbered, of course; they just wore the neural inductor hats.

A lot of customers went to the same feelie twice, male and female, to see how the other half felt. Gab had tried it once, fucking herself, but partway through she took off the cap and left the theater, anxious and confused. That had been the semester she first did cadaver dissection, and although she hadn't been too squeamish about the woman's body, cutting it up didn't put her in much of a mood to look inside her own.

This was going to be a 2X deep feelie: two orgasms and the internal sensors. With only two climaxes, it might even have a plot, though the audience wasn't demanding. It would be called *Love Boat II*.

A commercial feelie wasn't exactly like "being there," perfect virtual reality, which was dangerous and illegal because of the drugs involved. People participating in *Love Boat II* would taste and smell and feel a simulacrum of what the four actors did, and some of them would experience orgasms along with Gab and Louis. The "deep" feelie part enhanced that; they could see what was going on inside the vagina, and for most people that made it work better. Other people went to the regular feelies, which were less anatomical but had more dialogue.

There was a countdown clock on the flatscreen that told them how many seconds to orgasm. Gab was looking at it in a mirror; they were facing each other now, lying in the bottom of the boat. At sixty seconds she squeezed his shoulder hard and gasped *for Christ's sake slow down,* and concentrated furiously on the names of the facial nerves and the cost of the textbooks this embarrassment was financing. When the clock allowed her to, she let go and quite enjoyed it, as usual. If she'd enjoyed it much more she would have pulled Louis off the platform, which would have been okay if he could manage to stay inside her.

Harry monitored the ejaculation on a small holo cube, and applauded lightly. "Excellent. Louis, pull out suddenly at minus twelve seconds." On the flatscreen, a rowboat with an elderly couple came alongside and overacted. The couple in the bottom of the boat sprang apart the same time as Gab and Louis. She laughed, out of breath. "My God; he's even bigger than you."

"Trick photography," Louis said, panting. Harry brought them a couple of large towels.

Gab dried off and went back into the bathroom and used the bidet. Then she douched with a solvent and used the bidet again, as hot as she could stand it. She inserted a special tampon and dressed.

Harry gave her a check for two thousand dollars. She said good-bye to the men and left. A fairly busy whore could make that in one night, she thought; four tricks. She'd given herself to a million men and women for that. But her cheapest text this semester had cost four hundred dollars. This took a lot less time than waiting on tables or typing.

Besides, a doctor ought to be objective about her body. "Temple of the Lord," her mother always had called it. If Mom knew how many people had worshiped at this particular temple, she'd have a heart attack and die.

She put on her broad-brimmed hat and went out into the sunlight. If a million people go to this feelie and half of them ejaculate twice, how much sperm is that? Half a million times five cc's times two . . . five million cc's. Five thousand liters. She visualized a quart jar full of sperm and tried to multiply that by five thousand. A roomful, anyhow.

A greasy ugly man leered at her and she looked away, suddenly nauseated.

‖‖‖‖ Ybor Lopez

Dios, Ybor thought, that beautiful creature has just now had sex, still radiating pheremones and sweat. He turned to watch her walk away, a little unsteady but still linda, dark skin visible under the white dress, white underwear accentuating the curve of her buttocks. He started to get an erection but the pain at the injection site wilted him. He would remember the sight and smell of her later, though, and put it to good use.

He went into Building 16 and stood for a moment in the air-conditioning, using his floppy hat to mop the sweat from his face and neck. Concentrate, now. Have to be quick and careful. Download the data and erase all links. He started reviewing the process in his mind as he hurried up the steps.

No one in the office. Lock the door or not? It would be a little suspicious, but the extra couple of seconds while the secretary rattled away would give him time to change what's on the screen. But the secretary wouldn't have any reason to be curious about what he was working on, and no one else was likely to come in except Dr. Whittier, his partner in crime. He left it unlocked.

He put a data cube in the desk niche and said, "Commence Minotauro." A blur of numbers and words scrolled up the wall. He took a keyboard out of the drawer and waited. A couple of times a minute, the scrolling stopped and a query blinked. He typed a quick word or number and the scrolling continued.

After about ten minutes, the wall made a sound like a tree frog and went blank. Mission accomplished. He put his thumb over the "off" button and said, "Review data, Aurora Bell."

Blocks of statistics, paragraphs of biography. "Faster, one hundred percent," Ybor said. He could read very fast with the drug's help.

Whittier was going to be disappointed. Dr. Bell either covered her tracks well or didn't have much of a past. Parking tickets and one for speeding. Now, this bit about her husband might be useful. . . .

The door made a faint *tick* sound and Ybor thumbed the display off. He half turned toward the door.

It wasn't Whittier; it was Malachi Barrett, the chancellor. He stepped away from the door and said, "Here." A uniformed policeman swiveled in with gun drawn; aimed, and fired.

Sergeant Rabin

It was a good clean shot, right into the biceps. The man was able to pull the dart out, but that didn't make any difference. He got partway out of the chair and then fell back, dazed.

"You are under arrest. Anything you say may be used as evidence. A copy of this proceeding will be provided for your defense attorney.

"Let it be noted that the drug 71 Tikan has been administered. Your testimony will be reviewed in that light.

"Ybor Lopez, you are charged with information theft and unauthorized decryption. Do you wish to deny the validity of these charges?"

Ybor tried to look up at him but his head slumped. Then his whole body sagged forward and he fell out of the chair.

Rabin kneeled down and turned him over. His eyes had rolled back so that only the whites were visible. He felt for a pulse under the jaw.

"What's happening?" the chancellor asked. "Does this usually happen?"

"No, sir. I think it's a drug interaction. Seventy-one Tikan is psychotropic, and if the offender has taken some other psychotropic drug . . . shit. There goes his pulse." He chinned a microphone switch. "Dispatch, this is Rabin in 16-dash-304. We have a code nine here, need help fast. Heart stopped." After a few seconds a female voice said they were on their way. Rabin had already begun cardiopulmonary resuscitation.

After a minute of rhythmic shoving on the man's chest, alternating with breathing into his mouth, he asked Barrett, "Sir, can you do CPR?"

"Uh, no. I'm afraid not." He made an ineffectual gesture with both hands. "I've been meaning to take the course. . . ."

Another minute. "Find someone who can. I may need help." It was hard work, and Rabin was out of shape. He'd heard of people having heart attacks themselves while administering CPR. He didn't want to be part of an ironic newspaper story.

Barrett didn't go straight out the door, but first stepped over both of them to take something off the desk. Then he went out into the corridor and started knocking on doors and shouting at people.

"Code nine" meant that a suspect needed immediate medical attention. Sometimes the rescue unit dragged their feet a bit, since suspects were usually guilty, and a dead suspect meant less work all around.

Rabin was starting to have chest pains, which he knew were psychosomatic, when a middle-aged black man kneeled down next to him. "Need help?" Rabin nodded and rolled away, gasping.

He leaned back against the desk and watched his replacement: slower, but pretty good, considering that he'd probably never done it on a live person before. Of course this person was only somewhat alive.

Not armed, at least not obviously. So why had he been ordered to dart him on sight? If he was dangerous, why risk sending the chancellor along to identify him?

Could the dart have been switched—did he inadvertently fire a killer dart rather than a talker? No, he'd loaded the weapon himself when the call came in.

The dart was on the floor. He leaned over slowly, still hyperventilated, and picked it up. The charge cartridge was green-blue-green, 71 Tikan. He got a plastic bag out of his utility kit and dropped the cartridge in and put it in his pocket.

Other evidence. He stood up slowly and checked the desk. A keyboard, but nothing up on the wall. No crystal or cube in the readers. A notepad and stylus. He pushed the "previous message" corner of the notepad and got a crude drawing of a naked woman and a neatly printed phone number.

He wrote the number down in his notebook. Ma'am, you're being investigated in conjunction with a serious information crime.

No, don't bother getting dressed. I'll just handcuff you to this bed here.

Chancellor Barrett stepped into the office. "Sir, what was it you took from the desk here?"

"Desk? Oh, nothing. Nothing . . . I was just checking the notepad there."

"But I—"

"Nothing, Sergeant Rabin."

"Yes, sir." The old bastard, it must have been a cube or crystal from the reader. Whatever this guy was working on.

It put Rabin in an interesting situation. Under oath, or drugs, he would have to testify that he'd seen the chancellor take something from the desk. Did the chancellor realize that? Was the chancellor corrupt enough to threaten his job? His life?

"I was mistaken, sir. I thought I saw . . . it was a confusing moment." The older man put a hand on his shoulder and squeezed, wordlessly.

The rescue unit, two men and a woman, came crowding in. They relieved the black man, ripped open the suspect's shirt, applied two inductor pads to his chest, and cranked his heart. He flopped around and coughed and retched. They had to repeat it twice before his heartbeat stablilized.

The woman stood up. "Should we take him to the cardiac ward or the secure ward?"

"Secure ward," Rabin said. "Have them find out what drug he's on. This was a 71 Tikan reaction."

"Probably a DD," she said. She made a gesture and her two helpers rolled the man onto a stretcher. They rushed him out the door.

The chancellor thanked the black man, Professor Pak, and ushered him out.

"Sir, if you don't need me, I'd better follow the ambulance."

"Of course, Sergeant. Thank you."

On the way to where he'd double-parked, Rabin called dispatch and said he was ambulance-chasing, headed for the secure ward at North Florida. He had to shout to be heard over the ambulance's shriek.

The historian

The sudden wail shattered his concentration. He watched the ambulance lift and sail down the street, followed by a squad car. What department was that building? Physics?

He capped the old-fashioned fountain pen and took a sip of his tea. He liked to work here, on the edge of the student food court, because nobody would sit down and say, hey, you writin' a book? There were distractions, but usually if it was sirens, they were of the female variety.

He opened the memorybook and typed in a date. It had every Gainesville newspaper from the Civil War onward. He reread an article for the dozenth time and continued writing:

> *The first battle was really no more than a skirmish.* ~~*Union forces*~~ *A raiding party of 42 cavalry rode into town, encountering no resistance.* ~~*Under orders*~~ *They posted guards on the streets entering G'ville, while the main body constructed a hasty fort of cotton bales on what is now University Avenue.*
>
> *Mrs. Dickison, wife of the cavalry commander, happened to be visiting Gainesville. She knew that there was a cavalry group camped [a few] miles away, at Newnansville. She wrote a note explaining the situation, and sent it via her eight-year-old son, who slipped by the Yankee picket, pretending to be grazing his horse.*
>
> ~~*A*~~ *The small Confederate force, led by Captain _____ Chambers, attacked the next morning, but were unable to break through the cotton-bale fortifications. The Union soldiers, armed with repeating rifles, killed one man and [many] horses. Chambers retreated with his wounded to a camp outside the city, but the Yankees*

decided to quit while they were ahead, and that night returned to their main group at Waldo. They torched a syrup warehouse, but left behind nearly a million dollars' [$85M in today's money] worth of supplies and provisions.

in October

It was a good month for oracles. The local one, Charles Dubois, wrestled with Scripture and calendar and proved that January 1 would be the two-thousandth anniversary of the Savior's Resurrection. And thus the occasion for our resurrection, if we first cleansed ourselves. They had to install outdoor loudspeakers at his church in Archer, to provide for the overflow of believers sitting in the gravel parking lot or seeking shade in the old live oaks.

Johnny Kale asked his hundred million followers to pray for guidance; this thing is "a sign and a portent" whether it comes from heaven or merely an alien civilization.

The American archbishop Philip Stillwell followed the pope-in-waiting in reverence. The Coming was still only a two-word phrase whose provenance was the realm of science, not spirit. The Ayatollah Bismahin dismissed it as a blasphemous hoax.

The tabloids, electronic and paper, had a field day. The big ones arranged among themselves to rotate points of view, so that at any given time there would be headlines to suit those who believed in the Second Coming as well as those who believed the government was out to get us all.

The stock market went into a two-day spasm and settled back

into a period of growth, slightly accelerated. RadioShack International coined money with an aimable radio antenna that you could point to any spot in the heavens, and pick up alien broadcasts. So far the aliens had only "broadcast" in a beam of light, but surely they'd discover radio before long. Outfits that sold survival gear also prospered; one called Take Control (actually a subsidiary of L. L. Bean) bought short-term leases in malls across America, selling complicated knives, solar collectors, dried ("L. L. Brand") beans, and five-gallon jugs of tap water.

There were the usual riots in the usual countries, controlled by the usual methods, which provoked the usual responses. But even the most coolheaded and rational looked toward Christmas and the New Year, and wondered if there would be a January, after the first of the month.

Things did calm down for Aurora Bell, after the first week or so. She became science coordinator for the Committee on the Coming, which involved little enough science, in the absence of any new data.

Deedee Whittier had a nervous month, wondering whether Ybor would keep his silence.

1 November

Ybor Lopez

Ybor woke to the chiming and looked at the clock set into the wall, as if it might reveal a surprise: 0700 1 NOV 54, one month after he'd been arrested.

He put his feet on the cold cement floor and rubbed his face. The walls were blue this morning. Powder blue or baby blue. It was better than the pink.

The other inmates were making getting-up noises. He added his bit to the symphony of splashes and flushes. Brushed his teeth; rubbed shaving cream on and rinsed off his stubble. He sat back down.

At least he had a measure of privacy, behind his white-painted bars, since Manny had walked. Manny, who until two days ago had occupied the cell across the way, was a wild-eyed kid from Ohio, come to Florida for the drugs. Wound up in this "pussy prison," no walls. Just a white line painted on the ground. Cross that line and they send you to a real prison. He'd rather put up with the bullshit, thank you.

So Manny might be in Raiford by now, four in a cell with murderers and rapists. Or he might be back in Dayton. He'd left inside a driverless bread truck. It probably took him exactly as far as the gate.

What to do for the hour before the door unlocked for breakfast? He was allowed to keep two books at a time. *Biophysics of Cell Formation* and *Don Quijote, Segunda Parte.* Neither one appealed this early.

He lay back down and tried to remember heaven. He would do his two years and go out and score again, if not José y María, then White Cloud or Vista Interminable, the other local sperm-based DDs. The very notion of rehab revealed their ignorance. Like being rehabilitated from being a twin. From being human.

There had been no physical withdrawal. He'd listened to the agonies men went through in the other cells, and felt compassion for them, but not empathy. His loss was deep and spiritual, like losing a parent or a brother. It didn't make him scream or cry or puke. It made him patient in his grief. If you lost a person, he was gone for good. Ybor could go to a lab and jerk out a few cc's of himself, and have his powerful brother back the next day.

Meanwhile he would measure out his days here, loneliness and labor, neither intolerable. He put in six office hours a day, working on the prison's computers, and then two "work" hours in the laundry or kitchen.

He was learning interesting things about the computer system. He couldn't erase the record of his sentence—that was backed up in too many outside systems—but his record here would be of a model "patient," who emerged drug-free and eager to face the world.

His life was his own the rest of the time, as long as he stayed inside the white line and returned to his "unit" after dinner. He read a lot in the library and, for a couple of weeks, watched the cube with the other patients. But the cube, which he'd ignored all his adult life, proved dangerously addictive. He'd left it for the others to enjoy.

So he didn't see the news. He probably knew less about the Coming than any adult in Gainesville. Which suited him. If Whittier hadn't gotten a hair up her ass about Rory Bell, he wouldn't be in here.

A metallic chatter broke his reverie. The fat trusty Bobón was rattling his baton on the bars. Behind him, a man who looked vaguely familiar—Gregory Moore, the court-appointed lawyer who had so successfully defended him straight into this bunk.

"What's with the beard?" Ybor said.

"Makes me look older," Moore said. It did; it was white, while his hair was salt-and-pepper gray. "I've come to take you to an interview." The trusty unlocked the door, and it slid up into the ceiling.

"Will it get me out of here?"

"Might get your sentence reduced. Your period of treatment."

"Yeah, treatment. I'm cured, already." He followed the lawyer out and walked down the corridor between him and Bobón. Carefully. The trusty's stick was a neurotangler, and he liked using it. It didn't hurt much, depending on how you fell, but could be embarrassing.

In prison movies, the other prisoners would hoot obscenities and bang their tin cups on the bars. At Alachua Rehabilitation Center, they had Styrofoam cups and a point system, and few serious criminals. Most of them glanced up momentarily from books or games, if they reacted at all to the parade.

"Left here," the trusty said, and Ybor followed the lawyer through an unmarked door he'd never seen open before. He'd thought it was a storage room. It opened into a narrow damp corridor as long as a cell was deep, ending in another unmarked door. The lawyer held it open for Ybor and closed it behind himself. On the other side, the trusty locked it with a rattling of keys.

The room was white and spotless, starting to brighten with light from a picture window facing the horse pasture to the east. A door to the outside was open, metal screens keeping the bugs out.

Three hard chairs faced a plain white table. He recognized the man behind the table, and was startled. They'd never met face-to-face before, but everybody knew who he was.

"Willy Joe Capra," he said. "You're the mob guy."

"You buy that shit?" He smiled. "There ain't no such thing as a *mob*."

"This is still a funny place to make your acquaintance." He took the chair directly in front of the man. Moore stood behind him, silent, until Willy Joe pointed to the chair on his left.

"I wouldn't call this place funny," Willy Joe said. "I was here, I'd just want out."

"Sí. It could drive you crazy." Willy Joe just stared. "Mr. Moore said you might be able to help me."

"Yeah. You help me, I help you."

Anything you want, Ybor thought. But he just nodded and waited. Looking at the screen door.

"At your hearing," the lawyer said, "you testified that you were working on your own. A 'fishing expedition,' you called it."

"The woman was on the news," he said carefully. "I knew she had lots of money, or her husband did."

"So you figured you'd find something and squeeze her," Willy Joe said. "Just like that. Nobody put you up to it."

"I do it all the time," he said, which was true. "Usually just for fun." So far, he hadn't implicated his boss, figuring that silence would pay off in the long run.

"That's what you said at the hearing," Moore said, "and voice analysis indicates you were telling the truth, or some version of the truth. It also says that you lied later, when you said you didn't find anything interesting—I think 'useful' was the word."

"Yeah, well . . . you know voice spectrum's unreliable. Not admissible in court."

"This ain't no court," Willy Joe said. "This is a fishing expedition, too. Look at the bait." He reached into a jacket pocket and withdrew a hypo popper.

"That can't be mine," Ybor said, but he felt sweat suddenly evaporating on his forehead. "Nobody can get in there but me."

He twirled the cyclinder, smiling at it. "I don't have to get into your private stash. Where do you think this shit comes from?"

"From you?"

"From a friend of mine. Not the guy you buy it from. What he's called, Blinky?"

"That's right, Blinky." He could smell his armpits now, sour.

"Blinky don't make the stuff. He just collects the juice and the money." He balanced it upright on the table. "Suppose I could get you this once a week. You spill your guts for that?"

"What . . . what do you need to know?"

"You been followin' this alien bullshit?"

Oh, shit. "Not much, no. I got busted the day it all started."

"But you do know the Bell woman was behind it," Moore said. "You were going through her files, and that pulled down the wrath of God, or at least the chancellor."

"So what did you find?" Willy Joe said. "What wasn't 'useful'?"

Damn. It wouldn't be enough. "Look. I'll tell you all I know. But you got to get me out of here."

"As if you were in a position to bargain," the lawyer said.

"I'm worth a lot more to you on the outside. I can get more information where this came from."

"Sure," Willy Joe said. "Like you'll get your old job back and they'll let you hack their computer."

"You don't understand jaquismo," he said quickly. "I don't have to be at the same computer."

"Just you let me know what you got. I'll decide how much it's worth."

"Okay." What's the best way to put it? "Dr. Bell and her husband . . ."

"Dr. Bell and Dr. Bell," Moore said.

"Yeah. They're living a lie. Covering up his past."

"He kill somebody?" Willy Joe straightened slightly.

"Worse than that. He got caught fucking a *guy*."

Willy Joe looked at Moore. "I told you he was a fucking mariposa." To Ybor: "This was after the law."

"After the state law. Before the federal one."

Willy Joe nodded. "This ain't much. I seen him hangin' around with Nick the Greek. If they ain't queer I ain't never met a queer."

"This wasn't Nick the Greek." Ybor paused long enough for Willy Joe to open his mouth. "It was a cop."

"A cop. Which one?"

Ybor stroked his chin. "Don't know yet."

"What is this 'yet'? You know it was a cop, but you don't know who?"

"That's right. I need more time on the computer."

"What did you find out?" Moore said.

Ybor stroked his chin harder. "You holdin' out on me," Willy Joe said quietly, "you don't get your DD. And I get you transferred to Raiford. You want to meet some fuckin' queers."

"All I know is the path of the data link, and the way it was stopped. And when and where he was picked up."

"Go on," Moore said.

"It was down at People's Park, three in the morning. Twelve April 2022."

"So what were they doin'? Blow job, cornhole?"

"The call-in didn't say. Just that it was a 547, sodomy. They identified Norman Bell, but the other guy didn't have an ID."

"So how you know he's a cop?" Willy Joe leaned forward. "Make it good."

"The whole record got erased, all the way back to the call-in. It was an 'administrative edit,' and the authorization came from a police-department internal-security unit."

Willy Joe tapped the DD popper on the desk, in a slow rhythm. "It got erased, but not to you."

"I saw the hole in the data. It's complicated. But there was an erased link to Norman Bell, and I followed it up to the hole, so to speak. From there, I just searched unencrypted chat mail for a half hour around that time. Found a guy who monitors police and emergency bands, and he was talking to somebody when the sodomy call came in."

"I don't see how the lack of data implicates a policeman," Moore said. "Sounds more like Norman Bell pulling strings. He has money, or she does."

"They did pull strings." Ybor allowed himself a smile. "Mrs. Bell did, anyhow. The cops were glad to take her money, but the erasure was complete a good eight hours before she paid."

"She didn't just pay," Willy Joe said. "Even a professor ain't that stupid."

"No . . . I just looked for a big credit transfer. The guy she paid was the police dispatcher's father. She bought a new garage door. But no installation fee. Like she put it in herself."

"That *is* interesting," Moore said. "The sodomy charge would ruin him, and she'd go down for buying off the policeman. So your next step would be to confront them?"

"Yeah, if I *had* a next step. I'd just found the garage-door thing when the cop stepped in and shot me. Son of a bitch."

"So if you was to walk out this door," Willy Joe said, "you'd get your shit together and then go hit up the Bells."

"Well, I guess not," Ybor said carefully. "Guess you'd want to do that."

"Smart kid," Willy Joe said to Moore. He tapped the cylinder with his finger and it rolled almost to the edge of the table. "Here ya go. Have a ball."

Ybor uncapped it hungrily and turned his back to the men. He almost caught his penis in the zipper, in his haste.

A sharp sting and the first real peace he'd had in a month. He felt the calm power glow through his muscles and organs.

He took a deep breath, and something rattled in his chest. He turned and sat down. A surge of nausea and twisting pain in his stomach. "What . . ."

Willy Joe

"Y'know, I think you made a mistake there. You're not supposed to shoot that in your dick."

"No, he isn't," Moore said.

Willy Joe stood up with a bright smile. "That's supposed to go in your *pussy!*"

Ybor was doubled up in pain. "Shit. Immune . . . system."

"Yeah, little mix-up. Sorry. Some girl musta got yours. No fun for her, either."

Moore stared at Ybor's convulsions. "They said it would be sudden and painless."

"One outta two." He picked up his cap off the floor.

He set the cap on his head and straightened it, looking at the mirror on the wall. He saluted whoever was behind the mirror, probably Bobón and the warden. "You wanta take it from here?"

Moore didn't answer at first. He was watching Ybor, who had fallen off the chair, rigid, and was slowly moving his limbs around, his jaw locked open in a silent scream.

"I said you wanna take care of it?"

"Sure," Moore said, not looking up. "Papers already made out. Bad drug reaction."

"I'll say." Willy Joe wrinkled his nose at the smell. "Think I'm gonna die some other way." He pushed the screen door open, stepped out, and took a deep breath. The golden pasture smelled wonderful, a mile or more from the early-morning highway fumes. He stepped over the white line painted on the sidewalk, the symbolic wall, and pulled out the antenna on his phone.

"Where you guys at?" he said. "Five minutes, then. Runnin' behind and we ain't even started." There was no anger in his voice, though. He selected a joint from his wallet and lit up, smiling, and walked into the trees to his left, away from the rising sun.

There was still a little mist close to the ground. The woods were dark, but he didn't need the flashlight he'd used coming in. He followed a path of pine needles, an exercise trail for the staff and a few trusted inmates.

In front of him, the darkness rustled, and he was down on one knee, pistol out. Shit! In the woods without a bodyguard. He hustled sideways, to crouch behind a fat twisted oak.

Silence. Just a squirrel or a bird. If someone was after him, he wouldn't make no noise, just wait. You never hear the one that gets you. But he strained to see down the dark path, looking for motion.

Too many people knew he was here, alone. Maybe that was not too bright. But you got to trust somebody. Or do you? His knee was getting wet. Noiselessly, he switched to a squatting position, still staring down along the barrel into the darkness. Come on, bright boy.

He heard the high-pitched hum of the car whine down as it approached, and the crunch on gravel when it parked on the shoulder a couple of hundred yards away.

He worried the phone out of its pocket, clumsy with his left hand, punched one number with his thumb, and whispered. "Car . . . Bobby, we might have a situation here. You and Solo get out of the car, get ready to cover me. It probably ain't nothin'."

He winced when the car doors slammed. Maybe that was good, though. He stepped into the open and walked down the trail, at first holding the pistol out. A squirrel scampered across the path, about where the noise had come from. He tracked it, leading just a hair, and then relaxed. He was holding the pistol loosely at his side when he came into the clearing and saw the big Westinghouse. He waved at Bobby the Bad and Solo, and pressed the pistol back into its holster. It clicked into place and he straightened his jacket.

"Problems, boss?" Bobby said. He had the partygun with its big snail clip of buckshot, ready to gun down an angry mob.

"Heard something. Guess it ain't nothin'. Darker 'n I figured." He opened the car door. "Let's get a move on. Fuckin' ATC." He was usually in and out of Nick's before the traffic control switched on.

The Westinghouse scattered gravel in a fishtailing U-turn and surged up the hill. "Get what you're after, boss?" Bobby said.

"Yeah. Had to pop him, though."

"What, the *lawyer?*"

"Fuck, no. The junkie." He carefully stubbed the joint in the ashtray. "He knew stuff. Can't trust a junkie." He studied Solo when he said that; no reaction. Could he really think that Willy Joe didn't know about him and his ice?

Most skaters don't think they're addicted. Let 'em go a couple of weeks without. Might be a fun experiment with Solo. Lock him up in that cabin in Georgia for about a month. Then come scrape him off the walls and see what he'll do for an icicle.

Almost twenty years' dealing and clean as a nun's butt. Marijuana and booze, that's nothing. Dropped heroin and cocaine cold turkey at the age of nineteen, when he started dealing for the Franzias.

There was no traffic until the Archer ring. As they went up the ramp they got the ATC warning chime. Solo let go of the wheel and punched in the four-digit code for Nick's restaurant, then two digits for "drop-off." Then he unfolded a Miami newspaper and resumed reading in the middle of the entertainment section.

The traffic wasn't too heavy, but this far out in the country, more than half the cars were gas or LP. The trees nearest the road were spindly and yellowish with pollution. Car owners inside the city limits had to pay an annual "green" tax if their vehicles weren't electric or pure hydrogen, so on still days the city could become an island of relatively clean air inside a doughnut of haze.

"So how'd you do him?" Bobby said conversationally.

"Did himself, fuckin' junkie. He gave me what I wanted, so I give him what he wanted. What he thought he wanted."

"You said he was José y María, right? He didn't overdose on a DD, did he?"

"Nah. There was some kind of mix-up." Willy Joe took the ampoule out of his pocket and held it up to the light. "These are his colors, but it wasn't his DNA. Can't trust nobody these days."

"Bet that was pretty."

Willy Joe shrugged and looked out at the scenery. Maybe it was overkill. No, he was a wild card. Blackmail's worth shit if you got too many people in on the secret. So now it would be just the three of them, and Moore would be doing most of the dirty work, anyhow.

"Wake me when we get there." He pulled his cap down and settled back into the cushions, shifting a little to the left so the holster didn't press into the small of his back.

He replayed the Ybor business in his mind. This might be really good. Maybe put the squeeze on both the queer and his wife? She's gotta know—hell, she paid off the cops—but maybe they don't talk about it. Shit like that happens with girlfriends all the time. Wouldn't hurt to try. Have Moore find out if they got separate bank accounts. Money come from her side or his?

Shouldn't've had that joint. Got to concentrate. Relax, then concentrate. He pulled up the armrest to his right and fished out the crystal Scotch decanter. Poured an ounce into a shot glass, took a sip, then knocked it back.

He closed his eyes and fell into a familiar dream, where he was sitting on a bench in a police station, naked from the waist down, handcuffed. People came and went and took no notice of him. Some of them were people he had killed, including the latest, Ybor, and the first, his father. He woke up as the limo surged left into the parking lot beside the Athens, the ATC guiding it through a hole in traffic just inches wide enough.

He blinked at the traffic gliding by. "What the fuck?"

"We're here, boss," Solo said. "Park or cruise?"

"You keep movin'." He opened the door. "I'll be on the curb, five or ten minutes."

"I should call Marlo's?" he said. "Tell him we'll be a little late?"

"Huh-uh. I mean it, five or ten minutes. We'll be there on the button." Smart-ass. It was true he was used to spending some time in Nick's, have a drink and go through the horse papers, dog papers. But he liked to hit Marlo right on time.

Odd to smell garlic instead of pastry, walking into the Athens in the morning. Three tourists at a front table, eating breakfast. Big omelettes with that Greek cheese.

And look who else. "¿Qué pasa, Profesor?"

"Same old," the professor said, and went back to his book. You're in for an interesting day, old man. Willy Joe waved at Nick, busy behind the bar, and dropped a dollar for the sports page.

He sat down at the bar and took out his notebook. Checked the trifectas first, no action. But there were two long shots that came in, ten across—over a thousand each! Nothing on the dogs.

Nick set down his coffee, pastry, retsina, and five-hundred-dollar bill. Willy Joe looked up. "Hey, Nick. Let me buy you one."

"What?"

He held up the retsina. "Eye-opener. Just hit two long shots for a grand apiece."

"Oh, hey. Thanks, Willy Joe." He poured a small one and went back to unloading the dishwasher.

It didn't take long to map out the day's bets. He wrote them down in neat columns and sipped the coffee and wine, ignoring the food. The way the guy died had kind of killed his appetite. He could still smell it.

He watched the limo go by twice—make 'em sweat a little—and then called his bookie with the bets and got up.

The professor gestured at him on the way out. "Buena suerte."

Yeah, good luck to you, too. You'll need it, mariposa.

Norman Bell

The little crook never came in except on the first of the month, Norman had noticed. Not an early-morning person; he always looked as if he'd been up all night. This morning he looked especially tense, even though he'd evidently come out ahead on his horses.

What could his world be like? Up all night partying? Hanging out with the other hoods in some pool hall or after-hours bar. He was so macho, maybe he was gay. There were still clubs, Norman knew, though he hadn't been into one in eight years, not since the federal law got pushed through. It was being tested for constitutionality in a dozen states—but not Florida, which had its own sodomy laws. Norman was not the crusader type, anyhow. And the clubs were for young people, alas. He'd feel like an old pervert.

They'd had a raid on one in downtown Southeast a couple of weeks ago. Norman had studied the coverage to see whether there was anyone he knew, and in fact there had been, but not among the men and boys arrested. One of the cops, Qabil Rabin. The one he'd been with when Rory found out. Though of course she hadn't been surprised.

Qabil was a strange and beautiful man, just a year or two out of the army when they'd met. He'd been an enemy POW, captured in Desert Wind. But the army found out he'd been pressed into the Iraqi force against his will, going along with it just to protect his family in Kurdistan. When they were liberated, Qabil wound up in the American army, a three-way interpreter.

He came to UF for political science, police-department scholarship, but he minored in music, and Norman met him in a cross-cultural composition workshop. One thing led to another. They'd been together for over a year, when Rory came home unexpectedly and found them—in the kitchen, of all places.

Norman had seen him now and then over the years, and they exchanged careful signals of recognition. He had a wife and at least two children now, and a uniform that probably restricted his sex life. He hoped things were going well with him. There had been something like love between them, despite the differences in age and culture.

Thinking of him brought an interesting melody back to mind, a Middle Eastern thing in a Phrygian mode. He jotted down a pattern of notes on the back page of the mystery he was reading (trying not to read who done it) and went up to pay Nick.

Nick poured a plastic bowl of soup for Rory and sealed the top. "Things quietin' down over there?"

"Not lately, anyhow. There's a news special tonight, a one-month update. All the networks, crazy."

"Yeah. Like a war ain't enough news for 'em."

"Not as long as we're not in it." Greece was, now.

Nick said something in Greek. "Grace a' God," he explained. "You say hi to the professor for me."

"Sure thing." Norman carried the soup out and secured it in his front basket, which had an adjustable holder for such things, and pedaled off.

He went a few blocks out of his way, to avoid traffic. Rory wouldn't be in the office till eight, anyhow. He passed Rabin's house without looking over at it.

Rory's car was in its spot at eight-oh-one. Norman locked his bike in the rack by three spots that had "Permanent Press" signs. He was not quite old enough for that to make him think of trousers.

There was nobody in the office. He put the soup container in the fridge with a note—"Albóndigas—no avgolemono today"—and hurried back to his bike. He wasn't avoiding Rory, but he wanted to get home and work on this Phrygian theme. While he pedaled, he searched his memory for a source besides the Middle East folk tune. Once he'd spent almost a week on a composition, and when he played it for Rory, she pointed out that it was a jingle from a beer commercial.

Home, he splashed some cold water on his face while the coffee reheated. Then he sat with the cello and played the theme in E and G and then settled on D.

He snapped on the Roland and keyboarded it, and worked out a preliminary pattern of chords and dischords. Then he set it to repeat, and played the cello along with it a few times. He turned off the machine and improvised for most of an hour, the coffee growing cold again while he was lost in thought.

He put the coffee back in to reheat again and with two fingers sketched out the elaborated theme, looking back and forth between the screen and the keyboard. He could midi it in straight from the cello, but knew from experience that it saved time to go through the Roland, since a note's duration was recorded more precisely, and you didn't have to clean up harmonics.

Sipping coffee, he played the twenty-four bars over and over, using a light pen to isolate four voices. He set the Roland to try different instrumentations, reluctantly admitting that the solo voice couldn't be a cello. Clarinet or even oboe. He played with the phrasing of the oboe and turned it into a parody of Rimsky-Korsakov, which he saved as "Joke 1." Then he returned to the original phrasing, dropped the solo an octave, and tried it with bassoon, and then bass clarinet. Odd but good. He saved it as "BC 1" and got up to stretch and walk around.

Tense. He locked himself in his office, undressed, and gave himself an erection. From a locked drawer he took a VR girdle and goggles and gloves, and a highly illegal, because it was homosexual, compact ring. It was called "Scherherazade"; he'd bought it because the boys reminded him of Qabil Rabin.

He set the CR on the stereo spindle and hurriedly fitted the girdle over his genitals, around his waist, and between his legs. He rolled on the gloves and slipped the goggles over his head. Put the earplugs in and said, "Go!"

It was a harem scene, seven young men lounging naked on silken pillows, chatting, sipping coffee from small cups.

There was a random function that determined which boy would show interest; if the customer wanted a different one, he could say "reset." Norman liked them all.

One of them looked at him and smiled, and said something in Arabic. He set down his coffee and gracefully uncoiled from his supine position, becoming erect as he walked toward Norman.

A part of his mind always marveled at the technology. The boy gently took hold of his penis and cradled his testicles, and drifted to his knees.

Norman stared at the top of the boy's close-cropped head as he gently fellated him. With a couple of words he could switch to anal sex, active or passive, but this was enough for him. He watched the other boys, having fun with each other while they watched him and his virtual partner. (That part felt fake, or at least too staged, since it was always the same, a kind of moving erotic wallpaper.) After a few minutes, he knew he couldn't delay any longer, or his body would lose the illusion and melt, so he pushed a couple of times and ejaculated. The boy stood up while the whole scene faded into gray mist.

He walked into the bathroom with his silly-looking garb and carefully unwrapped the girdle, everted, and scrubbed it. Then he patted it dry with a towel, folded everything together, and returned it to his hiding place. He lay down on the couch and asked the room for Rimsky-Korsakov, and closed his eyes for a few minutes.

He only half slept, thinking about the composition. If a bass clarinet was going to take the melody, he wanted another line, a bass viol in a slow pedal. Doubled with one of the violins here and there. A quiet percussion rattle, like a distant woodpecker, signaling the measures where the two came together, two octaves apart. And a metallic tapping, like a muted triangle, doing 5:4 against their 4:4.

He got up and dressed, running through the changes in his mind. He went back to the great room and snapped on the Roland, but then saw that the phone was blinking. The call hadn't come in while he was napping, thank goodness; he would have lost his train of thought. It had come while he had the earplugs in, getting blown by a ghost. Probably a middle-aged man by now, like Rabin.

He keyed in the bass viol and adjusted the second violin. He couldn't get quite the percussion he wanted, so he left it off and wrote a note over the staff. He'd call Billy Kaye this evening and have him send something over; he stocked a cube of foreign percussion effects. After he was satisfied that he'd written everything down, he went to the phone.

Two calls. The first was a man he didn't recognize. Row upon row of paper books behind him, matched leather bindings identifying them as Florida statutes. A rich lawyer, couldn't be good news.

It was worse than he could have imagined. He smiled politely and nodded. "Professor Bell, I have a client who has something of value to you: silence. About you and a certain policeman. We will be having lunch at the rear table at Alice's Tea Room at noon today. Noon. If you're not there, we'll go to the police."

"You've met my client, Guilliame Capra." That slimeball Willy Joe. "Surprisingly, he has many friends on the police force."

The man disappeared. Norman played it back and it didn't improve. He erased it and sat back to think, but nothing came. Nothing but rising panic.

He went to the kitchen and got a wineglass, then opened the wine cabinet and closed it again. Instead, he poured an inch of brandy. He sat at the breakfast table and took one sip. Then he poured it out and rinsed the glass. No answer there.

What a lovely world this was.

Maybe they were only going to threaten to expose him to Rory. Big surprise. It would take some playacting, but they could simulate an outraged wife and penitant husband.

But no. Not in this day and age. They would threaten his career and Rory's, too.

Could Qabil be behind it? No; he'd lose even more than them. His fellow officers would not be amused.

He'd talk to Rory after work. First find out what the blackmailer wanted. He realized he couldn't say within a million dollars either way, how much money they had. Better find out before lunch. He checked his watch; two hours.

He went to call the bank and remembered the second message. It was Rory, asking him to call. He punched index-1.

Aurora

Her personal line rang and she punched it. Norman returning her call.

"Company tonight, sweetheart. You remember the Slidells, from Yale?"

He nodded and rubbed his chin. "Vegetarians?"

"You're amazing. He's vegan, I think, Lamar. At least he wears an equals sign on a necklace, Church of Reason."

"Okay." He seemed distracted. "I was going downtown for lunch. Market's not open; I'll see what Publix has."

"No eggs or cheese?"

"Heavens, no. I wouldn't enslave our fellow creatures." He didn't smile.

"There's something wrong?"

"Bad morning. Talk about it later."

"We can talk now. There's no one here."

"No . . . no, I have to check some stuff out . . ."

"I mean, I'll have the Slidells with me when I come home."

"It's okay. Later." The screen went blank.

She almost called him right back. Something was really bothering him. But the other phone rang, her public line.

"¿Buenos?" She'd seen the woman before, but couldn't place her.

"Good morning, Dr. Bell. June Clearwater, mayor's office." Of course, the mayor had heard about the anniversary broadcast and wanted some "input." He wanted to be sure that Rory would mention Gainesville, she assumed. He came on-line.

"Mr. Southeby. 'Input'?"

He showed a professional number of teeth. "Rory. I just heard about your shooting schedule and wanted—"

"Hold it. You know my schedule and I *don't*?"

"The camera crew was just here," he said, a little defensive. "They were headed for you next."

"That's wonderful. They were supposed to call." On cue, the call-waiting icon strobed in the corner of the screen. "That's probably them. Talk to you later, Cameron." She punched control-#, to record.

It was Chancellor Barrett, his face all grim furrows. "Rory. Do you remember a young man named Ybor Lopez?"

"As in Ybor City? Sounds vaguely familiar."

"He used to work in Deedee's office."

"Used to . . . is he the one who got arrested last month?"

"That's right; data crime. He was nosing through your files, among others. He hasn't been in touch with you, then, since his arrest?"

"Not that I recall. He might have tried—I probably have five or ten people call this number for every one that gets through. I could have someone check the log."

"That would be fine . . . um . . . the police might be bothering you about this; they just called me. Lopez died in jail this morning, under suspicious circumstances."

"Oh, that's a pity. For a computer crime?"

"I don't know any details. Just thought I'd give you some advance warning."

"Thanks." All we need is a bunch of cops rubbing shoulders with the reporters. "I'll let you know if anything happens. Buenos días."

Chancellor Barrett

"Buenos." She broke the connection. Busy woman, that cube thing coming up tonight.

There was a maddening lack of information here. Before calling Deedee, he did a quick mental review of what had happened a month before:

He'd come back from that damned meeting, having asked Deedee to use Lopez to snoop on Aurora Bell. He was straightening up before lunch and a bright red flag came up on his screen: a security compromise warning. It said that Ybor Lopez was grinding away at the encryption of personnel files. So he didn't have as much jaquismo as Deedee had given him credit for.

Although he would have preferred to let Ybor toil away undisturbed, the cat was out of the bag, whatever that actually meant. So he called in a warrant request and said he'd meet the arresting officer down at the physics building.

Then the screwup with the stunning dart. He'd managed to pocket the ejected data crystal. The sergeant saw but shrugged it off.

There was nothing much on the crystal but universes of data about Deedee and Bell. For some reason, Lopez had been pursuing details about a garage door Bell had bought. If they'd come in a few minutes later, there might have been something interesting there. Lopez hadn't gone off in that odd direction for no reason.

He tried to visualize the Bells' garage door. Nothing unusual.

Barrett put his anachronistic glasses down and rubbed his eyes. Had he indirectly murdered this young man by asking Deedee to check up on Bell? He'd only talked to Deedee about it once, right after the arrest. Lopez hadn't had a chance to tell her anything.

His personal line chimed and he swatted the button. It was Deedee, her eyes red and streaming with tears.

Deedee

"My God, Mal. What have we done?"

"The police talked to you, too?"

"No—it's on the goddamned *news*. Somebody murdered him."

"What? The cop said—"

"Drug overdose; that's what the news said. But you can't overdose on a DD like José y María, and people who are on it don't *take* other drugs. They don't work. . . ."

"But why would anybody want to kill him? Just a hacker who wasn't as good as he thought he was."

"I don't know. Maybe he was hacking for someone besides me, besides us. And he found out something dangerous."

"Yeah. I doubt it was Rory Bell."

"The damned drug *might* have been involved. You don't buy it at Eckerd's." She blotted her eyes with a tissue. "If he had a source in jail, they could have killed him easily by putting poison in his dose."

"So maybe they were oversimplifying for the press, when they said overdose."

"Or covering up. If he was getting it in jail, he was probably getting it from the police."

Malachi winced. "Deedee! Maybe we shouldn't talk about such matters over the phone. Can I meet you somewhere?"

She looked at the clock. Lecture in ninety minutes, but she could do it in her sleep. "Down at the mercado? The coffee end? As soon as you can get there."

"I'll be right over." His image faded to black. She hung up and turned off the privacy shield and looked around; nobody else in the office. She got the makeup kit out of her purse and worked on her eyes and sharpened up the tattoo. It would take Mal ten minutes to huff and puff his way to the mercado.

Somewhat fixed, she grabbed a sun hat and her lecture notes and went down the hall to the stairs. A little exercise, not using the elevator, and smaller probability of running into someone.

It was already hot and muggy, under a sky like polished metal. She remembered a New York childhood when sometimes it would have snowed in October, at least by Halloween. But New York was hotter now, too. Her parents' weekend place on Long Island under water for the past decade.

She got an iced coffee from a black kid wearing an Italian peasant outfit, and sat at a picnic table in the shade, pretending to study her notes.

Poor Ybor. She already hated herself for having set him up for jail. And he'd been loyal during the trial, not implicating her. Had he kept that silence in jail? Did the people who killed him know that she was an accomplice?

Accomplice, hell. She was the criminal, and Ybor was just a convenient tool. Or she and Malachi shared the guilt; didn't he start it?

He sat down heavily across from her, mopping the back of his neck and his various chins.

"No hat, Mal?"

"Forgot it till I was outside. So it couldn't have been an overdose?"

"No; that's impossible with bioreflexive DDs. If you shot yourself up ten times, the effect would be the same intensity and duration as one dose. I suppose your penis would hurt more."

He made a face. "I asked for a copy of the police report. That's legitimate. We're still his employer of record. But I doubt it will have anything of interest."

"Better hope it doesn't. Anything of interest probably would point back to us. Or at least to me."

"It might be me as well. During the confusion of the arrest, I picked up the crystal he'd been working on. The policeman saw me do it, or do something, and asked about it later. I sort of bulled my way through it. But if that was on his report, they might come around asking questions."

"Probably not. A prison drug death, they probably just cleaned out his cell for the next guy, and closed his file. Could you read the crystal?"

Malachi nodded and wiped his face with the damp white handkerchief. "You're on there as well as Aurora. Did you ask him to do that?"

"No." That was interesting. "I suppose he was trying to find something on me, for future use. Did he?"

"Oh, I didn't read through it," he said slowly. "The file on Aurora is ten times as big; it took me a week of evenings. Nothing there, as far as I can see."

"You might not be devious enough. Let me see a copy."

He brought a cube from a side pocket and set it between them. "Take the original. I don't have any use for it."

She rolled the crystal between her thumb and forefinger. "I think this is where we vow not to betray one another."

"I trust you, Deedee."

"A good thing, too." She removed her sunglasses and looked straight into his eyes. "I could hang your ass so high. . . ."

"Is the coffee good?"

Deedee turned around, startled. It was that crazy woman who pushed the grocery cart around. "Yes. Yes, it's good."

"I'm sorry someone died." She leaned into the cart and rattled past. "Get my coffee, too."

⫿⫿⫿ Suzy Q.

Funny how you can always tell, somebody died and they both feel guilty. He's some bigwig, I seen him give speeches. She's a teacher and real serious about it. Wonder if they killed somebody like I killed Jack. Who would they both not like enough to do that? Maybe they're in love and it was her husband or his wife, or both. Where would you put the bodies nowadays? With that new mall over the swamp. On top of old Jack, him lying there looking up the little girls' dresses while they walk over him, and he can't do a damn thing about it.

That's a nice thought, him all bones but still can see. And a bone down there but no juice to go with it. He who lives by the bone shall die by the bone, or the frying pan. That was a mess on the rug, good thing we had so many cats.

Maybe he couldn't see so good, his eyes hanging out like that. I remember when I drag him from the trunk of the Chevy into the swamp, I almost turn him over so he look down into hell, then thought no, make him look up at God and Jesus and Mary. Now he looks up the dresses of little girls. That's funny. And here comes my favorite little girl, with her coffee and bread for me.

Sara

"Here you go, Suzy Q. Sweet stuff today; a couple of almond rolls left over."

"You sweet stuff you'self. Thank you kindly." She carefully lined up the rolls and coffee on the cart's fold-out shelf.

She was wearing several layers of clothes in the gathering heat, her face red and sweating. "You don't have to wear all that, do you, Suzy Q.? You look so hot."

She nodded. "I don' mind being hot, and it keep the rays out. Came down here to get hot, but that was before the rays. Don't want the cancer."

Sara adjusted her hat. "That's a point."

"You know," she went on, "I could leave the extra clothes some-where, and nobody would take them. I know that, even though the town's full of murderers, but the problem is, I might not remember where I put them. Come winter I'd get awful cold."

"It's already November, Suzy Q. It doesn't get real cold any-more."

She laughed, a nasal wheeze. "That's what they say, all right.

You watch out, though." She took a sip of coffee and pushed on. "Watch out for them murderers."

Always good advice, Sara thought, watching her rattle away, waiting for her to say it. She stopped and turned. "You know it snowed the day I was born?"

"No kidding!" Suzy Q. nodded slowly and pushed on. Sara went back into the place.

José was cross-slicing onions. "That's probably enough. It's too damn hot." The onion flowers really sold when it cooled off. This year, it looked like the aliens would get here before winter did.

And here comes Señor Alien himself, resident alien, Pepe Parker. "What'll it be, Pepe?"

"Café con leche, por favor." He sat down at the bar. "And a date, if you dance."

"What?"

"New club opening in Alachua tonight. Old stuff—tango, samba. New club, new girl, what do you say?"

She smiled and put a cup of milk in the microwave.

"Pepe, I haven't danced in years. I had an accident, and I'm still an operation away from the dance floor." The bell rang and she took the milk out. "Thanks for asking, though."

"Professor Bell told me about that . . . horrible thing. They ever catch who did it?"

"No." She stirred a heaping spoon of Bustelo into the cup and brought it over with the sugar. "I think I know. But I could never prove it."

"Gracias. Who?"

She looked around. The two customers had left and José was buried in his tabloid. She lowered her voice. "You're no Boy Scout, are you, Pepe? I mean, you know how the world works."

"As much as anybody, I suppose."

"We have to pay protection, to keep the café from getting gang-banged. Is that shocking?"

"No. Sad, but no."

"There's a slimeball comes in here at noon today, every first of the month, to pick up his five hundred bucks. He calls himself 'Mr. Smith,' but everybody knows he's Willy Joe Capra."

"He did it?"

She nodded. "Or at least knows who did it. He's made that pretty clear."

"And you can't go to the police?"

She shook her head wordlessly for a moment, and then knuckled at tears, her mouth in a tight scowl.

Pepe

He handed her the napkin that she'd just handed him. "The bastard."

She pressed it to her eyes. "I, maybe I should. But what I'm afraid of, I go to the police, they pick him up, he gets off. And a week or a month or a year later, I'll have another accident. During which, Willy Joe will be in church or talking to the Lions Club or something."

"The devil never forgets a face. People like him eventually get what they deserve."

"No." She balled up the napkin and stuck it in her pocket. "This is the real world, remember?"

Pepe poured sugar into his coffee and stirred it slowly. "Nothing people like you or me could do. Shoot the bastard, we wind up choosing the door."

"Instead of getting a medal." She wiped the clean counter in front of him. "You want something to eat with that?"

"No, thanks. Just had breakfast." He'd skipped it, actually, needing to lose a few pounds. He only had one suitcase of clothes, and wanted them to last another couple of months. The kilt and trousers were getting tight around the waist, and suspenders had gone out of fashion last year.

He drank the coffee fast enough to get a little buzz. It would be nice if he could do something about this Willy Joe character.

He allowed himself an adolescent fantasy about Sara's gratitude. But that sort of thing wasn't really in his job description.

He put a ten under the saucer and waved adios to Sara and her partner. Not for the first time, he wondered whether they had something going. Their mutual affection was obvious.

Her body would be unusual. But that could be an attraction.

In that erotic frame of mind, he stepped out of the café and stopped dead in his tracks, paralyzed by a woman. She was dressed like any other student, jeans and halter and sun hat. But she had a classic chiseled beauty and perfect carriage, and she radiated sex.

Gabrielle

It barely registered that the handsome Cuban took one look at her and stood like a deer caught in headlights. Whenever she walked through campus she was caressed by eyes. Did any of them ever recognize her from the films? Not likely. She'd only had face parts twice.

She hated physics, but couldn't put it off any longer. She had to take a chemistry elective next semester, and the only ones she could take required physics.

So they were doing fluid dynamics today. A doctor does need to know about fluids. In her other persona, she knew plenty about them. Semen stings your eyes and makes your eyelashes look as if semen has dried on them. But it was better than the fake stuff Harry sometimes squirted on her. Soap solution and glycerine and some white powder. It stung the eyes even worse, and made you smell like a cheap whorehouse.

That was one of her father's favorite observations: You smell like a cheap whorehouse. Just before she left home, she was able to make the obvious rejoinder: You would know, Dad, wouldn't you? Someday she'd have to find a cheap whorehouse and go in for a sniff.

One nice thing about physics was the building, air-conditioned to the max. She went through the door and it was like walking into a refrigerator. She put her books and hat down on a table and patted the sweat from her face and hair with a handkerchief.

A carefully beautiful woman walked in and gave her a familiar look: appraisal, hostility, neutrality. Blue cancer tattoo on her cheek, Dr. Whittier.

 Deedee

"Oh, hi. You're in 101."

The beautiful girl nodded. "Gabrielle Campins."

She put the name and the face together. Pre-med, having trouble with the math. "See you there."

Trying to act normal just after learning you killed a man. Killed him by blackmailing him into illegal activity. Directed against a friend and colleague.

The door to Rory's office was open. On impulse, she tapped and stepped through the little entryway. Rory looked up from a journal.

"Hi, Rory. You ready for His Holiness?"

 Aurora

"His *ass*-holiness. Ready as I'll ever be." They had a meeting with Reverend Kale and some of his minions tomorrow. "I heard about Ybor Lopez. I'm sorry."

Deedee trembled for a moment and a chill ran down her back.

Could there have been something between them? The phone chimed, saved by the bell.

"Gotta teach," Deedee said, voice quavering. "See you later."

"Hasta luego." She picked up the phone.

It was Marya Washington. Could they come by in twenty or thirty minutes? Rory said sure, and put the "Do Not Disturb the Bitch" sign on her office door. How much of an article could she read in twenty minutes?

She actually got through the first page of an *Astrophysical Review* article by a friend at Texas, who had found a consistent correlation between galactic latitude and duration of one class of short-term gamma-ray bursters. That could imply local origin; at least not extragalactic. Or hopeful mathematics, anyhow.

Security called up and she took the sign off her door, and ushered in the young woman and her "crew," one man shepherding three cameras. "So welcome to Gainesville, Marya. How's New York?"

"God, don't ask. It's a miracle we got out." A two-day blizzard had just stopped. "We were able to get an old chopper into JFK this morning. Otherwise we'd still be in traffic. If you can call something 'traffic' that doesn't move."

The cameraman suggested where to place the cameras and Marya nodded. "I know there aren't any revelations," she said, "but do you have anything new? Or that I can pretend is new?"

"Any time now," the cameraman said. "Just be natural, ma'am; we'll edit later."

"Well, Marya . . . this isn't *new* exactly; it's from last week. But I'm not sure anybody got the whole story."

"You mean the bounce-back from the thing."

"Exactly." How to phrase this diplomatically? "You reported it, and so did others. But it was more important than you gave it credit for being."

She smiled. "Okay. Words of one syllable?"

"We sent them a message and they sent it back. Can I say 'message'?"

"So far so good."

"It came back with absolutely no distortion. We couldn't do that. Period."

Marya shut her eyes and pinched the bridge of her nose. "Yeah, right. I remember." She waggled a hand in front of one of the cameras. "Off the record, Rory, we couldn't really punch that up."

"They intercepted a signal that was 'way blue-shifted, in a relativistically accelerated frame of reference. They recorded it and rebroadcast it with exactly compensating distortion. The signal we got back was *absolutely* the same as the one we'd sent."

Marya laughed and shook her head. "Jesus, Rory. Would you come join the world for a minute? The real world?"

"Okay." Rory smiled, too. "So you couldn't 'punch it up.' "

"Look. It's worse than that. We have to think of *counter* story. We run your version and three out of six tabloids are on us like clothes from Kmart. 'We got exactly the same signal.' So where do you think they'll say it came from? Outer space?"

"Of course it came from outer space."

"No way in hell. It came from *you*."

"What?"

"You're trying to stay in the spotlight. So you generate a story."

"God, can you *hear* yourself? That's so ridiculous."

"It's not, Dr. Bell," the cameraman said. "People want to think conspiracy. Want to be on the inside. You can sell any goddamn thing if it's against the establishment."

"*I'm* the establishment?"

"You're authority," Marya said. "Bobby's right. Best way for you to get that story out would have been to let somebody else announce it and you hotly deny it."

Rory realized she was standing, and sat down. "It's so *Alice in Wonderland.* So what do we do?"

"Just what we've done here. We didn't punch it up, so when we repeat it next week, it's backstory. It's routine, so it must be true."

"*That's* when people point out how important it is," Bobby said. "Do it all the time, in politics."

"As if I, or we, didn't understand how important it was at the time."

"You don't have to go that far," Marya said. "Just don't punch it up for now, and later it'll look like you've been cautious. Conservative."

"Okay. You're the boss."

Marya smiled and nodded to the cameraman. "Good evening. It's exactly one month since the discovery of the Coming, and so we've left the blizzards of New York to revisit Dr. Aurora Bell at the University of Florida. . . ."

Marya

The interview went pretty well, though they had to ask Rory to repeat some things in simpler and simpler terms. They got out by ten, though; only fifteen minutes later than they'd expected.

And about two minutes late on the parking meter. Marya saw the big white tow truck from half a block away, checked her watch, and broke into a run.

It was a heavy-duty floater with a bed big enough to hold a large passenger car. It could park parallel to a car and, using a kind of built-in forklift, pick it straight up and haul it aboard in no time.

Marya got to him just as he was raising the car. He was a young black man. Her intuition weighed charm versus indignation as she ran up to the driver's-side window. "I'm sorry, mister. I got held up just a minute or two."

The man looked down at her wearily. "You're gonna get held up, you oughta park on campus. Park on the street and I get the call soon as your time's up, automatically. You didn't know that."

"No. I'm from New York."

"Well, enjoy the sunshine. You can pick up your car at the police lot anytime after twelve. Bring four hundred bucks and be prepared to spend a couple hours."

"Oh." She smiled. "The press card on the windshield doesn't . . ."

He gave a little start of recognition. "No, Miz Washington. Nobody escapes the wrath of the Gainesville Police Department."

The cameraman had caught up with her. "Couldn't we just pay the fine here, and be on our way?"

"What, is that the way they do it in New York?"

"No," he said. "In New York we pay a little extra."

"Like five instead of four," Marya said. She folded up a single bill and offered it.

The driver looked up and down the street, and then pushed forward on a big lever between the seats, and the car eased back down to the ground. He took the bill and slipped it into his shirt pocket.

He picked up a wand from the dashboard. "Give me dispatch."

Rabin

Sergeant Rabin walked up to the dispatcher's desk. The woman was grinning and shaking her head while she talked. "Yeah, some of those meters. It's a crime. Hasta luego." She took off her headset and tossed it on the desk. "Those tow-truck guys make more than the mayor."

"You know it. Got a gun for me?"

"Down here." She opened a drawer and lifted out a white box labeled EVIDENCE. "What's the story?"

He opened the box and took out the pistol. "Murder weapon, probably. Tossed in Lake Alice." Bright chrome revolver, maybe fifty years old. "Some kids in a biology class saw it in the shallows and fished it out."

He pointed at the short barrel, a duller metal, slightly rusted. "This is cute. Forensics says it's a homemade barrel, smooth bore, a little bigger than the .44 Magnum bullet."

"So you couldn't trace it?"

"Maybe, but it doesn't make sense. We find a .44 bullet in somebody that doesn't show any trace of rifling, we know it came from this gun."

"Have a body?"

"Not yet. But this thing wasn't in the water more than a day or two. So we're looking."

"Buena suerte."

"Yeah. Meanwhile, I get to take this around to the local dealers and pawnshops, see if anyone says, 'Oh, sure, I sold that to John Smith last week.' "

"Sounds like a fun job."

"I think 'shit job' is the technical term. But maybe I can do some Christmas shopping in the pawnshop. Buy the kids a couple of matching pistols."

"Start 'em out right." Rabin had four-year-old twin daughters. The phone rang and he waved good-bye.

There were two pawnshops just a few blocks down Sixth, so he decided to leave the squad car and walk. Get lunch down there, too.

It wasn't the best part of town, but they didn't put pawnshops in the high-rent district. Or police stations. It amused him to walk along in uniform and watch people's expressions. Trying to look innocent was a real strain on some of them.

There were two large shops next door to one another. He went to the farther one first; the owner was a likable enough guy.

He stepped into the cold air. They probably kept the airco cranked up to minimize the attic smell, mildew and dust. Gun oil and furniture polish. Rabin was fascinated by the places, but not the weapons counter. All the biographies scattered around. Life stories, death stories. Complete tool sets, well-used musical instruments, fancy camera and cube sets. You got so little on the dollar for them, their owners had to be dead or desperate. Or thieves.

The bell when the door closed brought the owner out of a back room. "Qabil. What can I sell you? Can I buy your gun?"

"Yeah, and my thumb, too." His weapon was keyed to his thumbprint. "Check this out?" He put the box on the glass case full of handguns.

"Evidence, eh? What happened?"

"Some guy's going around killing pawnshop owners. What you think?"

He picked it out of the box gingerly and rubbed his thumb along the base of the butt, where the serial number had been ground off. "Cute barrel. Not exactly a sniper weapon."

He clicked the cylinder around, peering through. "Ruger stopped making these in the teens. I see 'em now and then."

"Bet you do. That was before they started isotope IDs."

"Tell me about it. I don't think this one came through the shop, I mean with the original barrel and number. Don't see many chrome-plated ones, in any caliber."

"You think the chrome plating was factory?"

He took out a pair of magnifying glasses and slipped them on, and peered along the weapon's edges and surfaces. "Yeah. Guarantee it." He took off the glasses and set the gun back in the box.

"What else?"

"You fished it out of the water, but it hadn't been in there long. Allow for that, and the gun's practically new. Probably stolen from some collector. Must have been. That's where I'd start."

"What's it worth?"

"Actually, nothing. Without the barrel, I wouldn't touch it. Obvious hit weapon. If it had the original barrel, four or five grand. Before its little bath."

"On the street?"

"Maybe a grand, maybe five hundred. You oughta ask the guy next door about that."

"Think I will." Rabin closed the box and tucked it under his arm. "Thanks, Oz. You've been a help."

"Sorry I couldn't ID it. Buena suerte."

"Buenas." When he opened the door the sun was so bright it made his eyes water. He crunched through the gravel parking lot and walked up the unpainted wooden stairs to the next place.

The door opened with a surprise like a slap. Norman Bell!

Norman

His heart stopped and restarted. "Qabil. I . . . I don't know what to . . . buenos días."

"Uh . . . buenos. How've you been?"

"Fine . . . just fine." Could he be in on it? No, he'd never. "I saw your girls a couple of weeks ago. They're growing fast."

"They do that." There was an awkward silence and he held out a box. "Got to see a man about a gun."

"Oh. Sure." He held the door open. Rabin stepped through and then stopped.

"What are you doing here? Slumming?"

"I come by every now and then, looking for old guitars and such. Nothing today."

He nodded. "I see your wife on the cube all the time. She looks good."

"Oh yeah. She's fine." The one time they'd met had been strained. In the kitchen, she with wide eyes and he with mouth full.

"Take care," he whispered with tenderness, and turned toward the gun rack and counter.

Norman finally shook off his paralysis and walked down the stairs. If Qabil had come in a couple of minutes earlier, he would have interrupted an illegal transaction.

The pawnbroker wouldn't say anything. He was guiltier than Norman. Selling a pistol without waiting period or ID check.

It had to be a coincidence. Rabin wouldn't be in on a thing that would cost him his job and family and put him in prison for ten or twenty years. As if a cop would last even one year in prison.

Norman stood at his bicycle and considered waiting for Qabil to come back out. Tell him about the threat and enlist his aid. He couldn't do anything legally without throwing his life away. But maybe he would do something illegal.

Maybe later. First he'd talk to the lawyer and his gun-toting pal. Maybe they'd have a shoot-out there in front of the lunch crowd, and simplify things for everyone.

He clipped the bag onto his handlebars. It was awkwardly heavy, with the snub-nosed revolver and box of bullets. Had to find someplace private to load it.

He went a couple of blocks uptown and locked his bike outside a pool-hall bar where he'd never been. Just as soon not be recognized. He unclipped the bag and walked into a darkness redolent of marijuana and spilled beer.

There were no other customers yet. He walked past the rows of shabby billiard tables to the small bar at the end.

There were three crude VR games along one wall, at least twenty years old, and a century-old pinball machine, dusty and dark, glass cracked. A sign on the wall said NO FUCKING PROFANITY/¡NO USE PALABRAS VERDES, CARAJO! under a shiny holo cube of the president, all brilliant smile, a helmet of perfect hair guarding both of her brain cells.

The bartender was out of sight, rattling bottles around in a back room. He called out "¡Momentito!" and it actually was just a moment.

He was a big black man with startling blue eyes, obviously Cuban. Bright metal teeth. "What'll you have?"

"Draft Molly. Use your bathroom?"

"Sure. Ain't cleaned it yet."

Norman was prepared for an odoriferous hell, but it wasn't bad in that respect. The urinal was a metal trough that evidently dispensed a powerful antiseptic. There was blood on the floor, though, and a smeared handprint of dried blood on the stall door.

He opened the door and didn't find a body, so the previous night's activity had probably been conflict resolution rather than murder. He locked the stall and sat down and opened the bag.

He'd bought an old-fashioned revolver for reliability. It had been so long since he'd fired a gun; more than thirty years. In 2020 he'd killed a couple of dozen men for the crime, he always said, of wearing the other side's uniform. Something he'd had in common with Qabil, though their wars were a generation apart, and he was technically the enemy.

In Norman's mind, there were no enemies in war. Just victims. Victims of historical process.

Heavy blued steel. He fiddled with a mechanism on the side and the cylinder swung away. He slid six fat cartridges into their homes and snapped it shut.

He could just put the muzzle in his mouth and, again, simplify everything. Sure. Then Rory would have to identify the rest of his body, and Willy Joe and his pals would just shift their focus to her.

Besides, simplifying was against his nature. He resealed the cartridge box and considered what to do with the nineteen remaining rounds. If it were combat, you'd want them as handy as possible. But he couldn't imagine a situation where he'd have the opportunity, or necessity, to reload. He knew that Willy Joe carried a weapon; that was part of his swagger. Maybe his lawyer was armed, too, or there would be bodyguards.

He'd survived two bullet wounds, lung and leg, in the war. He might survive another. But the real lesson from the experience was to aim for the head.

They were experimenting with brain transplants. In Willy Joe's case, anything would be an improvement.

He considered throwing away the nineteen cartridges here, where another patron could make use of them. But with his luck the police would find them instead, and they'd trace them back to him. Assuming he survived lunch.

The rational part of him knew there was little danger; he was useless to them dead. But part of him would always be in the desert, fighting men with guns, and he wasn't going to face one unarmed.

Besides, Willy Joe didn't strike him as particularly rational. He put the bullets back in the bag and took out the light plastic holster. He set the revolver on a shelf and read the instructions, then opened his shirt and twisted the holster back and forth rapidly. It warmed in his hands. He carefully positioned it under his left arm and pressed it into place. It stuck like glue, but would supposedly peel away painlessly. He slipped the gun into it, the weight strange but reassuring, then flushed the toilet (a flagrant violation of the law) and returned to the bar.

The bartender had waited for him to come out. He cracked the tap slowly and filled a frosted mug. "Y'know, I got a memory for faces. You ain't been in here before, but I seen you someplace."

"That's not surprising. I've lived around Gainesville for forty years." The beer was a new kind, bland but with a little catnip bite. Ice-cold, though, and welcome. "Good. Norman Bell. I'm a music teacher and musician."

"Sí, sí. I've seen you on the cube with your wife, Professor Bell. What you make of all this stuff?"

"Well, I sort of have to go along with the wife. Preserve domestic tranquillity."

He laughed. "I hear ya."

"She makes a good case, though. New Year's Day is going to be interesting."

"Little green men on the White House lawn?"

"Probably something even weirder than that. Something we can't even imagine."

The bartender poured himself a small glass of beer. "Yeah, I was reading . . . like why don't they send a picture? They afraid of what we'd do?"

"What my wife says, they have no reason to be afraid of us for anything. They could fry the planet if we made a threatening move."

"Jesus."

"But there are any number of innocent explanations. Maybe they don't send pictures because there's nobody aboard; it's just a robot that's programmed to wander around, listening for radio waves. That's what Rory thinks. My wife."

"That was in the article. Also maybe they're like invisible. Made of energy."

I've had students like that, Norman thought. "I don't think there's anything mysterious about it. They know a lot about us, evidently, and don't want us to know too much about them. That's what a military operation would do."

"So we can kiss our ass adios."

"Not necessarily. We don't know anything about their psychology. They might be following some kind of a ritual. Or keeping us in suspense as a kind of joke. Who knows?"

"Yeah, I guess." He wiped the bar slowly. "You do any gettin' ready for it?"

"You mean emergency preparations?" He shrugged. "Just what we have on hand for hurricanes. Plenty of water and food. I'm more worried about people panicking than aliens."

"Me, too. You ought to go down to the pawnshop and get a gun."

Norman jumped. "¿Cómo?"

"What I did. Somethin' a guy at the bar said. 'Ammunition will get you through times of no food, but food won't get you through times of no ammo.' The guys with him thought that was muy chistoso. Then one of them whispered something and they looked at me and laughed again. Them's the kind I went out and got the gun for."

"Claro. You must have some rough customers here." Norman nodded toward the bathroom. "Looks like you had a big fight back there last night."

"Oh, mierda. They bust it up?"

"No, just blood."

He nodded philosophically and picked up a bucket. " 'Scuse me."

Norman finished his beer and pondered leaving a tip. No; the guy didn't need any more surprises this morning.

Back in the sunlight, he clipped his bag to the handlebars and looked down, out of the glare: a storm drain. There was nobody in sight, so in a quick motion he pulled out the box of ammo and tossed it into the drain.

It was as if a weight had been lifted from him. Odd. He supposed the act confirmed that the gun's function was purely defensive.

He checked his watch. Twenty minutes, and the restaurant was ten minutes away at a slow pace. Do you show up early for a blackmail lunch, or late, or on time? He decided on time would be best, and took a detour down by the student ghetto, a part of it that still had trees and shade.

This was where Qabil had lived when they met. He'd gone to his apartment a couple of times, though the house was less risky. Unless your wife came home early.

Alice's Tea Room probably had its share of clandestine meetings. The only expensive restaurant in a block of student eateries, it had what they used to call a "shotgun" shape, a long rectangle with one row of tables.

They were at the farthest table, and the two nearest them were empty, with "Reserved" signs. Otherwise the restaurant was full.

The maître d' approached and Norman pointed. "Joining that party."

The walls were decorated with mediocre-to-okay paintings by local artists. It occurred to Norman that this was an odd choice for a supposedly clandestine meeting. If the bartender at that pool hall had recognized him on sight, what were the chances no one here would?

Pretty good, actually. The bartender was a fluke; besides his students and the Hermanos crowd, there weren't too many people in town who would know him.

The lawyer, if that's what he was, and Willy Joe and another man, a small skinny weasel with a sallow complexion, watched him as he walked down the aisle. He sat down wordlessly.

The sallow man thrust out a hand. "The bag." Norman slid it over. "I smell gun oil."

Norman tried to keep a neutral expression while the bodyguard, if that's what he was, zipped open the bike bag and sorted through its contents. "It's valve oil you smell, genius. I'm a musician. I was cleaning a trumpet." They might know something about his sex life, but he doubted they knew which instruments he played. Definitely not trumpet.

"It's okay, Solo," Willy Joe said. "Professor wouldn't bring a gun in here." The man zipped up the bag slowly, staring.

He slid it across slowly. "What outfit you with?"

"What?"

"You've killed people, maybe lots." He was almost whispering.

"It's in the way you walk, the way you're not afraid. So you were a soldier?"

This man was dangerous. "Hundred and first. Second of the Twenty-third. But that was a long time ago."

"You killed men, Professor?" Willy Joe said conversationally. "As well as fucking them?"

Interesting that he didn't know that elementary fact. "As I said, a long time ago, both."

The lawyer leaned forward, and he did whisper: "There's no statute of limitations on being a faggot."

Norman felt heat and a prickling sensation on his palms, the back of his neck, his scalp. Adrenaline, epinephrine. He knew his face was flushed.

If they hadn't been in a crowded restaurant, at this moment he might find out how many of them he could kill before he died. Certainly one.

"There ain't no need to be insulting, Greg," Willy Joe said. "Let's not use that word."

"I apologize," he said. "This is a financial proposition, not a moral judgment."

Norman sat completely still. "Go on."

"We know that your wife knows," the lawyer said. "She paid off the police." He looked up as a waiter approached.

"My name is Bradley," he said. "For today's specials, we—"

"I want the special," Willy Joe interrupted. "We all want the special."

"But we have four—"

"We want the first."

"The grouper?"

"Yeah. What kinda wine goes with that?"

"I would suggest the Bin 24, the—"

"Bring us two bottles of it. Pronto?"

"Yes, sir." He hurried away.

"You was sayin', Greg."

The lawyer paused, staring at Norman. "To be blunt, it's your wife's money we're after. Her inheritance."

"We have a joint account."

"We know that, of course. But your wife seems to have enough on her mind right now. So we thought we'd approach you instead."

"She'd lose her job," Willy Joe said. "Even if she didn't go to jail, for buying off the cops. And you and your boyfriend would get Raiford for sodomy. Separate cells, I think."

"You might live through it," the lawyer said, "but he wouldn't. A fag . . . a homosexual cop in Raiford."

"They'd use him up real quick," Willy Joe said.

One chance for the offensive. "I don't think you've thought that through, Willy Joe. Qabil has a lot of friends on the force." He saw the man's eyebrows go up and thought, My God, they didn't know his identity. But he pressed on. "And he's a family man, cute kids; everybody likes him. You send him off to certain death in prison— yourself not a man well loved by the police—and what do you think his friends are going to do to you?"

"I got friends in the police, too."

"It just takes one who's not your friend, but is a friend of Qabil's. You may have noticed that the police kill criminals all the time, in the course of their duties. If one of them killed you, he wouldn't go to jail. He'd get a promotion."

"This isn't about Qabil," the lawyer said. "It's about you and your wife. Your wife's job and money."

"Oh, really. You can expose me as a homosexual without naming my partner?"

"This Kabool ain't the only one you done," Willy Joe said.

"Oh? Name another." Norman stared into the little man's face. "Give me one name and I'll write you a check." There were no others, not in this state, this country.

"You're a piece of work," the lawyer said. "You take a false premise and build a considerable edifice of conjecture."

"Oh, I'm sorry," Norman said. "That's your job."

"You can't fuckin' turn this around," Willy Joe said.

Norman stood up. "Why don't you discuss the ramifications of this," he said quietly. "Your life expectancy after you condemn a cop to death." He picked up his bag.

"Sit down," Willy Joe said.

"See you here tomorrow, same time."

"I can have you killed," he said in a harsh whisper, theatrical.

Norman looked at the sallow man. "You, Solo?"

"Nothin' personal." He smiled a genuine smile. "See you soon."

Norman turned to go and almost ran into the wine steward. He snatched one bottle out of the ice bucket. "This one's mine, thanks."

He heard Solo laugh as he walked away. "Balls. You got to admit he got balls."

Southeby

"Norman!" Odd to see his neighbor at a fancy place like this.

"Mr. Mayor." Norman saluted with his left hand and strode toward his bike.

"He looks familiar," his companion, Rose, said.

"Aurora Bell's husband. We're neighbors."

"They let you bring your own bottle to a place like this?"

"I guess." He held the door open for her. Nothing wrong with the mayor having lunch with his university liaison. He didn't know that most of his office knew exactly what their relationship was, and thought he was a fatuous old fool. Some of them had an even lower opinion of her, for being able to stand him.

Southeby stiffened when he saw Willy Joe Capra at a far table, along with that slimeball Gregory Moore and some other gangster type. Capra locked eyes with him and gave a small nod.

"Right this way, Mayor," the maître d' said, and led them back to a table distressingly close to Capra's. Southeby took the chair that would put his back to them.

A waiter came with menus and took their drink order. He asked for lemonade, though he could have used something stronger. She ordered E.T. Lager, a new local brew.

"That any good?"

"Probably not. I just want to see the label." She lowered her voice. "You know those guys?"

"Not to speak to, except the oldest one, Greg Moore. Used to be public defender. Now he works for the little wop, Capra, who's got Mafia connections. The third one, I don't want to know."

He hadn't noticed that she flinched at the word "wop." Blond and blue-eyed, three of her four grandparents had come from Tuscany. "He's the one the petty cash goes to?"

"Jesus, Rosie!" He took a leatherbound notebook out of his jacket pocket and riffled through it.

"Really, I'm curious," she said, just above a whisper.

"Who told you this?"

"You withdraw it for 'office supplies.' That's a lot of staples, Cam."

"Okay. It's a kind of insurance. For the building, not for me."

"What?" The waiter brought the lemonade and beer. The label was a movie poster from the twentieth century, a goofy-looking alien with a glowing fingertip. He poured the beer. It was pale green, and probably glowed in the dark.

The waiter left. "You didn't work here four or five years ago. We used to get trashed all the time—graffiti, broken windows. Gang stuff."

She nodded. "So they could get their jail time."

"Verdad. A new gang member would confess and get his week in jail. Rite of passage. But it was costing the city a fortune, and the cops were powerless. You catch one in the act, hell, that's what he wants.

"So Capra moves in. The gangs stay away from any building that has his mark."

"Or else . . . what?"

"That's another thing I don't want to know. A few days after Capra started marking buildings, the leaders of three gangs disappeared overnight. Never came back, good riddance."

"He killed them for *vandalism?*"

"Had them killed, probably. And probably not 'for' anything, except to show what he could do if they didn't cooperate."

She stared at him in silence for a moment. There was a heated argument going on *sotto voce* at the gangsters' table. She shook her head. "God. This town."

"This town is peaches and cream, honey, compared to—"

The waiter had returned. "May I . . . are you ready to order? Ma'am?" His voice was a little loud and nervous as he glanced at the other table.

"Jimmy!" Willy Joe shouted. "Cancel them specials. We gotta leave."

"As you wish, sir," the waiter said. The three of them shuffled out from behind the table, and left in a little procession: Willy Joe striding in the lead, the pale hoodlum following, and then the lawyer.

Gregory Moore

He stopped to shake the mayor's hand. "Cam. Long time no see."

"We seem to travel in different circles now," he said.

"It's all circles, isn't it? 'What goes around comes around,' my dad used to say."

"Your father was a good lawyer."

"So are you, Cam. Señorita?" She nodded at him with a curious smile, and he followed Solo out the door.

"You're pals with the mayor?" Solo said, opening the car door.

"Not exactly 'pals.' Remind me to wash this hand."

"He's a asshole," Willy Joe said, getting in, "but he's *our* asshole."

The doors slid shut and the air conditioner's roar abated. Solo, behind the wheel, pushed a button. "Address for Norman Bell."

"This is lunacy," Moore said. "Isn't one murder a day enough?"

"He can't *fuck* with me that way!"

The car told Solo the address. "Go there." It pulled away from the curb, hesitated, and slipped into the traffic.

"Plenty of people saw us together. Saw him leave."

"Shut up, okay? Just gonna check the fuckin' thing out."

"Just promise me you won't—"

"I don't promise you or nobody a fuckin' thing," he said quietly. "But Solo ain't gonna kill him. Just rough him up a little. Put the fear o' God into him."

"Jesus. Listen to yourself."

Solo turned around to face them. "Boss, I don't think he's the kind of guy you just push around. . . ."

"That's right, you don't *think*! You don't *think*! You just do what I tell you."

"What do you mean, Solo?"

"I mean beggin' your pardon, Boss, but God knows I met all kinds a tough guys and phony tough guys, inside and outside. He's not phony, and he's pissed. I think he'd just as soon kill any one of us as look at us."

"You've got a fuckin' gun. How's he gonna kill you?"

"You buy that shit about the trumpet oil?" Solo put a finger beside his nose. "Hoppes No. 9, I've smelled it all my life. He's got a gun, all right."

"So he's got a gun. He's a faggot professor twice as old as you."

"Push the info button for me, Solo," Moore said. He did. "Public records, military. Norman Bell."

"I'll need a service number," the car said, "or current residence."

"Gainesville, Florida."

"Norman Bell volunteered for the draft during Desert Wind, in September 2031. For his service in the 101st Airborne Division, he was awarded the Silver Star with two clusters and the Purple Heart."

"Silver Star," Solo said. "Two clusters. Some faggot."

"So? So you afraid of him?"

Solo didn't move. "I'll do what you want."

"I want."

Moore kept an eye on the road. There was a bike lane. But Bell probably would take a less direct route, avoiding traffic.

"He probably has a burglar alarm. House full of musical instruments."

"Solo can take care of a burglar alarm."

"Yeah, or run like hell."

Moore shook his head. "You ought to wait until he's home, if you have to do this. Knock on his door and push your way in."

"Excuse me, Mr. Lawyer. We already gone over this in the restaurant."

"It's an unnecessary—"

"I don't got a replay button. You clear on that?"

This could get them all into trouble. Too many people in that restaurant saw the four of them together. "It's going to be an interesting trial. Calling the mayor as a witness."

"Shut the fuck up. The mayor's fuckin' ours. Besides, he came in after the professor left."

"This is going too fast."

"Sometimes you gotta *live* fast. We got a chance for perfect timing here. Get them both, get the money, get the fuck out."

After they dropped Solo off, he was going to go confront Aurora Bell. In theory, by the time she called home, her husband would be sufficiently intimidated. They would empty their bank accounts into Willy Joe's coffers.

Again in theory, the Bells couldn't call the police. This Qabil Rabin was still on the force, Willy Joe had said. But what if the jealous wife was not exactly fond of her husband's boyfriend. Or her husband, for that matter. This whole thing could blow up in their faces.

The car turned right and went uphill for a couple of blocks, through a quiet residential neighborhood. Then left and right and they pulled up in front of the Bells' house, a large rambler with conservative but well-maintained landscaping. There was nobody in sight.

"No burglar-alarm signs," Willy Joe said. "People who got 'em advertise it."

"Yeah; like me," Moore said. "Someone *stole* my sign."

"Move it," Willy Joe said. Solo opened the door and got out.

Solo

He stood for a moment with his hand on the door. "Call you tonight, Boss, or come by?"

"Call." He shut the door and the car glided away.

Solo stood for a moment, feeling exposed and perhaps betrayed. What the hell was Willy Joe's game this time? A test? A sacrifice play?

You couldn't just walk out on him, crazy and vindictive fucker. Solo fought the reasonable impulse to call a cab and go straight to the airport, sighed, and turned on his heel. Shit or get off the pot.

He went up the walk briskly, checking his watch for the sake of unseen neighbors. The place was a perfect design for breaking in; a small atrium hid the front door from the street.

The atrium was cool and smelled of jasmine. He went straight to the door and rang the bell, getting his story ready in case there was a servant or a robot.

No answer. He looked around carefully for security cameras. If there was one, it was pretty well hidden.

The double lock was a Horton magnetic dead bolt and a plain Kayser underneath. He took out a plastic case of tools and threaded a probe into the Horton and pushed a button. It sometimes got the combination right away; sometimes it took a few minutes. With two mechanical picks, he unlocked the Kayser in seconds. Then the Horton gave a solid snap. He pushed the door open.

He stepped into the anteroom and eased the door shut. Books, paper books, from floor to ceiling! This might work after all; these people had real money.

The Horton lock snapped and he looked back at it—hell, it was a keypad on this side. He'd have to find another way out.

He took one step and a voice in every room said, "Hello? Who's here?"

Shit. The place did have a system. "Professor Bell," he said, and the system answered "okay"—but of course it was already calling the police.

Quickest way out. He ran into the kitchen. The door to the garage was also a keypad. There was a glass door and a stained-glass window looking out into the atrium. He picked up a heavy bar stool and swung it against the glass door; it bounced back, nearly dislocating his shoulder. He threw it into the stained glass, which crashed in a glittering rainbow shower, and jumped through the hole into the atrium. He rushed to the walk, paused to smooth his jacket and his tie, and started striding toward town, casually but fast.

Hope the dispatcher's not too swift.

Rabin

"Units seven, nine, and twelve. I have a 217 at 5412 NW Fourteenth Avenue. Who wants to pick it up?"

Allah, Rabin thought, that's Norm's house. What's going on?

"Take it?" his partner said. "That's like eight blocks."

"Wait and see if there's a closer pickup." Seconds ticked by, and no other unit responded.

"Come on, Qabil. We could use some laughs."

"Sure. Let's take it." Two-seventeen was B&E, usually no big deal. Except when the house being broken into belongs to your fellow sodomite. Sweet Allah!

"Unit nine on the way," his partner said, and switched to manual. The car surged into the middle of the street, and traffic parted in front of them like the Red Sea for Moses. Qabil checked to make sure his pistol was on "stun." He was tempted to accidentally switch the dart selector to "lethal." Whatever this guy might say was unlikely to advance his career.

He allowed himself one long moment of reflection. That had

been a turning point in his life—as large as being a soldier; larger than the POW camp. He went straight after the wife caught him with "Normal Norman," at least straight enough to collect his own wife and kids. Love is love, though, and lust, lust, and a man can't help being what he is.

"Perp shot," the radio said, and the monitor showed a picture of a well-dressed man swinging a bar stool at a glass door. The image ratcheted forward and rotated, to give them a full-face portrait of the man.

"We have an ID," the radio said. "Suspect did six months Raiford in fifty-two, accessory to extortion. Two juvies, B and E and A and B. He has a Georgia license to carry a concealed weapon, supposedly in three states. Dolomé Patroukis, street name Solo. Consider him armed and dangerous."

"Well, hello," his partner said. The suspect was loping down the sidewalk toward them, on the other side of the street, hands in pockets. No other pedestrians in sight. "Guy can't even afford a car."

He turned on the lights and pulled over to the curb, traffic weaving, and bumped up onto the sidewalk. The man crouched as if to run, and then stood up with his hands over his head.

"I'll take it." His partner got out and walked toward the man while Rabin unclipped the detector from the visor, then opened the door and stood behind it, peering through the detector tube.

"David!" he said. "Left armpit!" He and David both had their stunners out in an instant.

Solo stood on his toes, reaching high. "Hey! Hey! I got a ticket! I'm a private investigator!"

"Yeah, sure." David reached into the man's jacket and pulled out a light automatic. "You got a Georgia ticket outta some cereal box. You got the right to remain silent anything you say may be held against you this encounter is being recorded and encrypted and will be acceptable as evidence against you."

"I don't say nothing until I talk to my lawyer. Not meaning to be disrespectful."

"Like I say," David said, "everything you say is evidence. Everything you don't say, too."

"You can call your lawyer from the station," Rabin said. "First we're going back to the place you were trying to rob."

"Hey, I didn't take nothing."

David took him by the shoulder and steered him toward the car. "Keep talking. You were a Jehovah's Witness, or what?"

"I got lost, I was confused. Went to this house to ask directions, and then this voice starts up."

He pushed him down into the backseat. "Put your wrists on the armrests, please." He did. "Close." The armrests handcuffed him. "So then you had to break your way out."

"Man, it locked me in! What would you do?"

"Oh, I'd probably call nine-one-one. But then I'm a cop. I have the number memorized." He eased the door shut and went around to the driver's seat.

Rabin had just finished calling it in. He turned around and studied Solo for a moment. "So whose house was it? What were you after?"

"I don't know. Like I say, just wanted directions."

"Bullshit. We have you on a previous B and E."

"What, bacon and eggs?" Rabin just smiled as the car bumped over the curb and eased into traffic. "Look, I was just a kid. The judge said that was goin' to be erased."

"Probably on the condition of good behavior. Assault and battery isn't such good behavior."

"That was juvenile, *too*! You never got into a fight?"

"No, as a matter of fact. Not until the war."

Solo was staring at his name badge. "Oh."

"That's right; I was on the other side. And here I am, a towelhead, arresting you. Is this a great country?" They pulled into the driveway at 5412.

David said "release" and helped Solo out of the car. He chinned the microphone on his lapel. "This is Eakins. You got the owners on this B and E?"

"Not yet," a distant voice said. "One's at lunch, the other's in transit."

"Keep trying." He inserted a probe like Solo's into the Horton lock. Both locks snapped open instantly. "After you." He pushed Solo inside.

"House," Rabin said, "this is the police."

"I know," the house said.

"Did this man take anything or do any physical damage to you?"

"Yes, he broke a stained-glass window. The replacement cost will be six thousand four hundred and fifty dollars."

David whistled. "Felony property. You should have done a different window. Or even used the door."

"Like I said. The house locked up."

"Hello?" someone said from the hall. "Police?"

||||| Norman

A police car in the driveway and the door wide open. The holster with its illegal weapon felt heavy as a stone.

Then *he* almost turned to stone when he saw Rabin. And then he recognized Solo. His voice almost squeaked. "What's going on here?"

"I'm Lieutenant David Eakins and this is Sergeant Qabil Rabin. We apprehended this man fleeing after a robbery attempt."

Solo looked straight at Norman. "I'm tellin' you I didn't rob nothin'. It was all a big mistake. I got trapped in here and panicked."

"Have you ever seen this man before?" David asked.

"I'm not sure," Norman said. "He looks familiar."

"I don't know him from Adam," Solo said. "It's like I said—"

"Shut up," Eakins said. "After he set off the alarm, he couldn't bust through the plastic doors, so he broke your stained-glass window to escape. The house says it's worth six thousand four hundred and fifty dollars."

"More than that," Norman said slowly. "The artist was a friend, and he's dead now."

"Ten grand," Solo said.

Norman looked at him. "What?"

"Look, I don't know much about law, but if me and him agrees, can't we like change venue from a criminal offense to like a civil one? Him bein' the only aggrieved party."

"I don't know," Eakins said. "House, did you follow that?"

"Searching," the house said. "*Mason* versus *Holabird*, 2022. If both parties agree on the settlement and there is no objection from the state."

"Fifteen thousand," Norman said.

"Twelve!" Solo said. "If I even *got* twelve." He pulled out his wallet and riffled through the bills, extracting the brick-red ones. "Nine . . . ten . . . eleven. I got eleven and some change."

"That's a lot of money for an innocent bystander to be carrying around," Rabin said.

"So my family don't believe in banks. That a crime now?"

"He was armed," Eakins began.

"Legal!" Solo said, holding out his wallet. "Look! I got a god-damn permit."

Eakins waved him down. "You can get those permits in any truck stop in Georgia. What I mean, Professor Bell, is that his intent here might have been to do you harm. I wouldn't be too quick to let him buy his way out of it."

"That's a good point," Norman said.

"He has a jail record," Qabil said, "down in Tampa."

"I was a *kid*," Solo said. "Look, let me use the phone. I can make it twenty. Like I say, I'm a private investigator. I can't take no jail term on my record. Adult jail."

"This is getting kind of complicated," Norman said, taking a calculated chance. "I don't know. Twenty thousand would more than replace the window. But it's not as if we were poor. Maybe I ought to let you guys have him, for my own safety."

"What, your *safety*? I don't mean you no harm."

"He doesn't have another weapon?"

"Not of metal," Rabin said. "I scanned him outside."

"Tell you what," Norman said, taking the phone off his belt and handing it to Solo, "you guarantee me that twenty thousand, and then you and I will have a little talk. Agreed?"

Solo gave him a look he'd seen over many a poker table: What the hell do you have in your hand? "Yeah, sure. I can use your john to make the call?"

"Be my guest." Solo went down the hall toward a bathroom.

"I think you're making a mistake," Eakins said. "This jerk's a career criminal if I ever saw one. He just hasn't been caught before as an adult."

"Or he's been caught," Norman said, "and bought his way out of it. Like now." He looked toward the bathroom. "You've got his weapon—I mean, you can keep it?"

"By all means," Rabin said. "We have to send it to Jacksonville for an FBI check. That's a federal law, and his change of venue doesn't mean anything with them."

"Why do you want to talk to him?" Eakins asked Norman.

"I don't know. As you say, he probably didn't walk in off the street. Maybe I can find out what's going on."

"We're paid to do that, sir," Eakins said. "If you really don't need the money, let us take him downtown. He's a felon now, and we can use drugs to make him talk."

That would be really great. "He's a felon but he's a human being. If I decide to change the venue back—"

Solo came back up the hall and handed Norm the telephone. "We done a direct credit exchange," he said. "Check your amount at the credit union. You're twenty grand richer."

"Thought you didn't believe in banks," Eakins said.

"Got friends who do."

Norman took out his wallet and thumbed his bank card. He didn't actually remember how much had been in his liquid account, but $38,000 did seem like a lot. It was there; he held up the phone to the police. "Any trouble, I'll call you guys. Thanks."

"I wish you'd reconsider," Eakins said, but they both headed for the door.

"What about my gun?" Solo said.

"You'll get it back eventually," Rabin said. "Just come by the station next week." He gave Norman one long look as they left.

When the door clicked, Norman said, "House, we want privacy. Turn yourself off for thirty minutes, or until I push an alarm button."

"Very well."

Norman went to a sideboard and poured himself a glass of red wine. "You have a lot to explain. You can start with Sergeant Rabin."

"Somebody else did that. Or else it was an accident. Surprised *me,* that's for sure."

"I wonder. I saw him earlier today, myself."

"Small town."

"Not that small." He picked up the glass with his left hand and took a sip, staring at the man. "Did Willy Joe send you here to intimidate me?"

"No more questions," Solo said, and stepped toward him. He froze when Norman pulled out the big revolver.

"Just a few." He pointed the muzzle to the left. "Out in the garage."

Solo had his hands up, walking slowly backward. "What's in the garage?"

"Just easier to clean up. This is loaded with crab rounds, the kind that spin like a drill and pop out tiny claws when they hit. I think they make an awful mess."

"Jesus! Hold on. What I do to you? I mean, the window, yeah, but—"

"Open the door there." The garage was large and neat, two bicycles hanging from ceiling hooks, an orderly wall of tools over a workbench.

"It's not what you did to me, or even what you intended to do to me. Have a seat."

The only chair was a stool by the workbench. Solo climbed up on it.

"When I was a young man I killed twenty-five other young men, just because they wore a uniform different from mine. Slightly darker skin. Whereas you broke into my house with the intention of terrorizing me, and destroyed a work of art that was dear to me."

"I'm sorry about that. I'm really sorry."

"It's hard for me to express how unimportant your feelings are in this matter. I'm just weighing practicalities."

"It sure as hell wouldn't be practical for you to kill me." Sweat was popping out on his face. "You don't fuck with Willy Joe."

"You may overestimate your importance to him. You haven't demonstrated a high degree of competence in this matter." Norman set down the wine and propped both elbows on the workbench, holding the pistol with two hands, steady on Solo's heart. "And don't even bring up the police. They'd thank me."

"Now that isn't so. You'd go to trial, and they'd find out about . . ." Norman pulled the hammer back with a loud click.

"You're in an unenviable situation right now. You know I'm a homosexual, and could ruin my life with a word. You're of no value to me, alive. Dead, you would be a powerful warning to Willy Joe."

"You don't know him. He's crazy. He'd come kill you."

"He might try. I'd still have five crab rounds left."

Solo looked right and left, head jerking, about to flee. Norman's finger tightened on the trigger.

Solo stared at the tool rack. "Wait. I got a good idea."

"It's about time."

He reached slowly toward the tools. "Con permiso. I take this hatchet and—"

"Stop it!"

"Okay, okay!" He froze in position. "I was gonna say, like I chop off one of my fingers. Tell him you made me do it, at gunpoint."

"You'd do that?" Of course it could be grown back, for a price.

"I just want to walk outta here, man."

Norman considered it. "Use the hammer." He pointed with the pistol. "The iron mallet there. Break your gun hand, the right one."

"I'm left-handed."

"Then I'm doing you a favor. Do the right." He'd reached for the tools with his right hand.

He slowly removed the hammer from the hook and hefted it, not looking at Norman.

"Don't even think of throwing it at me. Bullet's a lot faster." He raised his point of aim to the man's face. "Now put the mallet in your left hand and put your right hand on the anvil—"

He'd already put his right hand on the table, fingers splayed, and with his eyes closed, chopped down with the mallet. It smashed the knuckles of the first and second finger. The mallet clattered across the table, and for a moment he cradled the broken hand silently. Then he sank to the concrete floor, keening, and rolled into a ball.

Norman cringed, but kept the gun pointed at him. Then an old and remorseless feeling crawled over him. Go on. One round. Simplify your life.

The phone on his belt beeped. He stepped back into the kitchen, closing the door, keeping an eye on Solo through the window.

He clumsily extricated the phone with his left hand. "Buenas."

"Sweetheart, what's going on there?" Rory said. "I got back from lunch and there was a message from the police. We were broken into?"

"It's more complicated than that. The burglar was actually a blackmailer. He knew about Rabin."

||||| Aurora

"Rabin?" She put two fingers over the speaking end of the wand. "Would you excuse me? This is personal."

"Of course. I can get back to you later." The man who'd been waiting for her got up and left. A local politician, she'd thought, or some kind of lawyer, holding a business card.

"It's not something we should talk about over the phone," he said.

"That's right."

"The situation's more or less under control."

"You paid?"

"Not exactly. Check our balance. I'll explain when you get

home. Right now I have to fix a broken window, before the bugs get in."

"Broken . . . okay, later. I'm on camera in ten minutes. Adios."

Pepe was leaning on the door. "Who was that?"

"On the phone? Norman."

"No, no. The suit who was in that chair and just now left without saying anything."

"He didn't say who he was?"

"That's why I'm asking *you*, Hawking. He must have walked in while I was in the john."

She waved it away. "Probably some studio guy. You ready for this?"

"I'm ready, yeah. You could use some makeup, though. You're bright pink."

"Just let me get my breath." She crossed the room and got a cup of ice water, then sat back down and tried to breathe normally. Break-in, blackmail.

"You don't look too good. Want me to get Marya and reschedule it?"

"No, look . . . our house was broken into; there was a message from the police. But I talked to Norman and he says things are under control, whatever that means. A broken window, but I think the only breakable windows in the house are the stained glass ones in the living room and kitchen."

"Hope not," Pepe said. "They're beautiful."

"And irreplaceable, literally. They were by old man Charlie what's-his-name, died a couple of years ago." She massaged her temples. "I'll be all right."

Pepe checked his watch. "Why don't we go down early? Get a Coke from the machine."

"Marya says that's a bad idea. You might burp."

"So they edit it out."

"It's *live*, Pepe." She got up. "I'll risk it, though."

He ushered her through the door. "Burping on camera will make you seem more human."

"Oh, please." They walked down the corridor to the converted lecture hall. Just outside it, Rory stopped at the machine, slid her credit card, and got them a Coke and a root beer.

Marya was helping a cameraman arrange an improvised drape over a whiteboard, for a backdrop. They exchanged hellos.

"Look," Pepe said. "You don't need me here. Why don't I run over and see whether I can help Norm?"

Rory hesitated. "Help him?" She looked disoriented. She was always a little nervous with the cameras, even with nothing else on her mind.

"The broken window? You know, rain?"

"Oh, sure." She shook her head. "Sí, por favor."

||||| Pepe

On his way down the hall, Pepe called for a cab to meet him across the street at Burgerman's. Before leaving the air conditioning, he buzzed Norm.

It rang ten times before he answered. He was curiously hesitant; but said sure, he could use some help; come on over.

There were two cabs waiting, illegally parked on the grass strip in front of the fast-food palace. He asked them and the second cab said it was his. He gave it the Bells' address and settled back for the short ride.

This was a complicated business. He knew what role Aurora was supposed to play in the Coming, but Norman was an unknown factor. On the other hand, there was a personal side to it. Norm and Rory were more than just his friends.

Two years before, he had made a real error in judgment, and wound up deeply involved with an undergraduate who turned out to be an extremely competent and calculating bitch.

He had considered himself sophisticated; well schooled in the nuances of American society, but she was more sophisticated, and had set him up and knocked him down.

They'd had sex once, and she had pictures of it. Pictures of them doing something that was technically illegal in the state of Florida. And she just an innocent girl, ten years younger than him.

All she wanted was a passing grade. But she hadn't done any of the work.

Just an innocent girl with a hidden *camera*, Rory and Norm pointed out, when he confessed to them over dinner at their place. And forget about the oral sex law; the house did a quick search and found that the law had never been enforced against heterosexuals except in connection with actual child abuse. This child was nineteen, going on forty.

They got a copy of her transcript and made a few very discreet inquiries. It turned out that at least three of her high grades were gifts of love, with the help of a camera. One of the men, who had since left the university for a private firm, was eager to testify against her, before the dean, a jury, a firing squad, whatever.

Rory did some administrative shuffling and made herself the girl's advisor. Then she called her in for "counseling" and presented the evidence, and told her she could either take an F and leave the university, or go to jail for extortion. She left.

That had not just saved his academic life. Even if the girl's threats were empty, any kind of adverse publicity could have cost him his blue card. It would be hard to monitor the Coming from Cuba.

As the cab turned onto Fourteenth Avenue, he saw another cab parked in front of the Bells' house. A man in a suit, with a bandaged hand, got into it. The cab pulled away and Pepe's U-turned to take its space.

He verified his credit number and went up the walk. When he stepped into the atrium, Norm opened the door and said, "Buenas."

"So who was the guy with the bandage?"

"That's a long story"—Norman let him in—"and a short one. The short one is that he's the man who broke the window."

"The burglar? Why don't the cops have him—you just let him go?"

"The cops were here. Turns out you can settle out of court, on the spot. He offered twenty big ones, more than twice the replacement cost."

"Must be a lot of money in his line of work."

"Whatever that is. Let's measure the thing." Pepe followed Norm into the kitchen, where he rummaged through a couple of drawers and came up with a tape measure. The broken window was 80-by-160 centimeters.

"I've got some one-by-two-meter pressboard," he said. "It's ugly, but it'll do."

They went into Norm's neat garage. The neatness made Pepe uneasy. His own garage, under the apartment, was a collection of random junk. There was actually room for a car in this one.

Norm went to a rack that was mostly woodite and pressboard, but did have a few actual boards of fragrant pine. He tugged on a big sheet of pressboard. Pepe stepped over and helped him with it.

The house chimed and said the privacy period was almost up. Norman asked for another thirty minutes. He worked silently for a few minutes, using the tape and a T square to measure out a rectangle on the pressboard. They carried the board over to the table saw.

On the workbench next to it, an iron mallet and a splatter of blood. Norman saw Pepe staring at it. "That's part of the story, the long story."

"You want to tell it?"

"Not really, no." They wiggled the board and the table saw's guide until it was exact, the saw blade's kerf on the waste side of the drawn line. They cut off an eighty-by-two hundred rectangle, and then cut that to size.

"You don't have to answer this," Norman said suddenly, "but we were talking a couple of years ago, after Rory went to bed. Talking about sex, homosex."

"I sort of remember that. We'd had a bit to drink."

"A lot." He stamped the board on the table twice; then went over the cut edges with a rag. "You'd done it, you said."

"Well, it's not a big deal in my culture," he said, trying to separate Cuba from the place where he actually grew up. "Older men think it's scandalous, effeminate. But they probably did the same thing when they were boys."

"Boys," Norman said, rubbing the board with the rag.

"It's just play," Pepe said. "You nortes are still Puritans."

"Some." Norman smiled into space. "Some of us are still boys."

"¿Cómo?" Pepe said. "Still boys?"

"I've been homosexual since before you were born. Rory accepts it."

Pieces falling into place. "And that's what the man was here about?" He looked at the blood spatter and trail. "The man with the bandage."

"Blackmail. You can imagine how long I'd have my job if it came out."

"Rory, too," Pepe said. "The way things are."

"Exactly." He put the board under his arm and Pepe followed him into the kitchen.

"So the blood? The guy's hand?"

The board fit the space exactly. "Hold this in place?" Pepe held it while Norman went through drawers, and finally found a thick roll of white tape.

"You know a guy named Willy Joe Capra?" He pulled out tape to match the top and tore it. It had an unexpected smell, raspberry.

"No, never heard of him." Not until this morning, from Sara.

"You're lucky. He's our friendly local Mafia connection."

Pepe went all over cold. "Jesus, Norman. What did you do to his hand?"

"Oh, that wasn't Willy Joe. That was his bodyguard, or something." He pulled out long strips for the vertical sides. "His name's 'Solo'; I guess that's why they sent him after a musician."

"And what did you do to him?"

"He did it to himself. I suggested he take a hammer and apply it to his gun hand."

"Madre de Dios." Pepe lowered himself to sit on the windowsill, a foot off the floor. "And where was his gun?"

"The police took it from him."

"The police who were just here?"

Norm nodded. "They have some sort of scanning device."

"I've seen it on the cube."

"They didn't use it on me. When this fellow threatened physical violence, I pulled out my own gun."

"You carry a *gun*?"

"Not under normal circumstances, Pepe; haven't since the army. But I knew who I was dealing with."

"Let me get this straight. You pulled a gun and said, 'Let's go out to the workshop and smash your hand.' "

"No, that was his idea. He offered to take a hatchet and chop off a finger."

"But you, you decided to be nice to him?"

"Well, he could have a new finger in a week. Actually, I think he wanted to use the hatchet on me."

"And lose all that blackmail money?"

"I don't think their brains work that way." Norman went to the refrigerator. "I don't understand them any better than you do. Want a Coke or something?"

"Something stronger. Early as it is."

"Me, too. White plonk?" Norman pulled out a ball of white wine and squeezed them two tumblersful. "Look, we'd had a meeting. Willy Joe and some lawyer and this bodyguard. A lunch meeting. They told me what they knew, and it was correct."

"So how much did they want?"

"Well, I don't know. I got up and walked out."

Pepe kneaded his face. "You have a death wish, Norman?"

"Sometimes I think I do. Or at least place a low value on survival. Con permiso." He picked up the buzzing phone. "Buenas— oh, it's you." He pushed a red "record" button on the side.

"That's not possible. We're having company over for dinner tonight, and I—

"I suppose you might." He listened, shaking his head. "Just you and Capra. And we talk outside the house, on the sidewalk, not inside." He pushed the "end" button and looked at the phone.

"That was the bodyguard?"

"No, the lawyer." He drank half the glass of wine and replayed the conversation.

Capra congratulated Norman on being cute ("qué guapo") and

gave the phone to the lawyer. He said the rules were different now, Norman having upped the ante by using violence. They had one more thing to show him, and if they couldn't do business then, they would reveal his secret in time for the evening news, and just be done with it.

Come to Capra's house, 211 SW Third Avenue, at five, prepared to make a million-dollar credit transfer. Otherwise, they'd come join him and his company for dinner, and make it a really interesting party.

"Southwest Third. Wonderful neighborhood," Pepe said.

"If you're in the market for dope or prostitutes," Norman said. "I never have one without the other, myself." He drank some wine. "Showdown, I guess."

"You sound like you're looking forward to it."

He smiled. "An end to it, possibly. Don't tell Rory anything. I'll go ahead and fix dinner, and leave her a note."

"What, 'Go ahead and enjoy dinner; I'll be back after I shoot some blackmailers'?"

"It won't come to that. Don't worry."

"You want me to come along with you?"

"Thanks, but no. I'll probably just give them the million."

And then they'll just leave you alone, Pepe thought. "Of course I'll keep your secret. But I think you're making a mistake." A mistake that could derail everything.

"I have a few hours to think on it. Maybe I'll come up with something."

Pepe had a few hours, too. He finished his glass of wine. "Well, I've got to run. Fill me in on it tomorrow?"

"Sure," he said. "Mañana. Hasta."

"Mañana." Pepe left through the front door, trying not to hurry. Another piece had fallen into place, something in the back of his mind ever since Sara had mentioned Willy Joe Capra's name.

Norman

Norman watched him leave. *Fill you in on it if I'm still alive.*

Well, he could distract himself for a while preparing dinner. He hadn't gone to Publix after lunch, as promised. What could he conjure up out of the pantry for a couple of cheeseless, eggless, milk-free vegetarians? He turned the house back on and asked for random Vivaldi, music for vegetarianism.

He studied the orderly array of boxes, cans, and jars on the pantry shelves, and perhaps *was* inspired by the music: Italian bean pie—a layered terrine of bean purees; red, white, and green. When you sliced it, it looked like the Italian flag.

Taking the three cans from the pantry, he asked the house for the recipe, and it appeared on the screen above the range. "Larger," he said, not wanting to use his glasses.

He peeled and sliced potatoes and put them on to simmer, and then worked on the three colors of beans, sautéing them variously with onions, garlic, and shallots, and then setting them aside to cool. By then the potatoes were done; he tossed them with herbs Provence, olive oil, and white wine from the grocery-store ball.

He started to pour himself a glass, but then realized this might be the last wine he would taste in this world. He went to the top of the rack and pulled down a '22 St. Emilion, maybe a week's salary in a bottle. He pulled the cork and poured a third of the bottle into their largest balloon glass, then carefully preserved the rest of the bottle with nitrogen and knocked the cork back in. The Slidells were pleasant, but they weren't close enough or important enough for a '22 Bordeaux.

Everything had to cool for a while, so he turned off the music and carried the wine into his studio. He tuned the cello and ran through the latest partita he'd been developing for *The Coming*, but he was too distracted to work on it. He turned on a new book of old European folk dances and sight-read his way through Spain and Portugal, sipping wine between pieces.

The house reminded him when it was 1600. He carefully spooned the layers of the terrine into a loaf pan, then drained the wine and oil from the potatoes and tossed them with a grind of pepper, a sprinkle of vinegar, and a little more herbs Provence. He put it all in the refrigerator and left Rory a note saying he was out; if he was late for dinner, make their traditional lettuce-and-tomato salad, minus the goat cheese, God forbid we should exploit goats.

He put on a jacket against the afternoon cool and locked up, went into the garage, slid the heavy gun into its holster, and pedaled away.

Plenty of time. He dawdled at the park's exercise trail, watching young and old run and jump and heave and stretch. He should get back into that. Maybe tomorrow, if there is one.

He pedaled slowly along the mile-long green belt, and then picked up speed as the traffic alongside him slowed, grinding into downtown. Comtemplating a new life rule: "Never be late for a gunfight." Noting that Willy Joe and the lawyer would assume he was armed, so would be protected by armored clothing. Get close enough to shoot for the head. Get Willy Joe and then the lawyer, if you live long enough. Was this the wine speaking? Or just the war. Both, probably.

But the gun still felt like a burden. Not a partner, as it had in the desert. You might just pay them off, and save the killing for later, if they came back for more. When. They would be sure of themselves, then, and more vulnerable.

A few blocks from the house, a fire truck screamed by him, then an ambulance, and then another fire truck. There was a wisp of black smoke ahead of him, and then a column.

He stopped at Fourth Avenue, a block from Capra's house, which was now burning like a bonfire. He took from his bike bag the monocular he used for birds, to verify the address.

Medics and police were moving a small knot of onlookers away, off the sidewalk, to make way for the ambulance gurney. Lying in front of the house, there was a man in a chair, evidently tied up, covered with firefighting foam. They finished cutting him loose, and he stood, shakily, and they eased him onto the gurney.

It was Qabil. They rolled him toward the ambulance.

No meeting tonight, no shoot-out. Norman reversed his bicycle on the sidewalk and sped home.

He got there just minutes before Rory pulled up with her guests. He reluctantly turned off the cube—no news bulletin yet—and met them at the door.

Lamar and Dove Slidell were both astronomers, out in New Mexico now, classmates and pals with Rory from graduate school. Evidently they'd already said all there was to be said about the Coming, and knew that Rory would just as soon talk about anything else. So it was mainly gossip about mutual friends, and job comparisons. The Slidells worked on a mountaintop where you could actually see the stars. In Gainesville, the night sky was bright gray soup.

Norman tried to appear interested, and accepted the compliments for his cooking, and drank somewhat more wine than the others. Finally, his phone rang, and he excused himself to take the call in the kitchen.

It wasn't the blackmailers. It was Qabil.

"Look, I know you've got company. I shouldn't be recorded coming into your house anyhow. But we have to talk before I go to work in the morning."

"Where are you?"

"Down on the corner, where the street splits. Blue Westinghouse with silvered windows."

"I'll be there in a minute." He pushed "end" and thought for a moment, and then rushed back into the dining room.

"I have to run out for a bit, student emergency. Kid's got an audition tomorrow, broke an A string. Sounds like he might need some serious hand-holding, too."

"Which student?" Rory asked.

"Qabil. Just down the street." She nodded, wordlessly, and forced a smile.

Norman got a string from his study and said "back in a minute," and went out the door and down the street.

The passenger door opened as he approached. He slid in and closed it.

One side of Qabil's face was blistered, covered with a transparent gel. His right hand was bandaged.

"What happened?" Norman said.

"I'll get to that. First would you tell me what the fuck is going on?"

"The basics . . . Willy Joe Capra was going to blackmail me. About you and me."

"That much I know. He told me in some detail, after he kidnapped me from my own goddamned driveway. Then that Tampa thug Solo, you broke his *hand*?"

"In a way, yes." Crickets loud in the darkness. "I held a gun on him and he did it himself."

"A gun. You've been leading an interesting life, since we parted."

Parted. Norman tried to keep emotion out of his voice. "What did those bastards do to you?"

"Do to me? What the hell did you do to *them*?"

"Me? Nothing. Just the hand."

"Norm, you can tell me. If you can trust anybody in the world with this, it's me."

"I was supposed to meet them at five. I talked to the lawyer, Moore; he said they had something to show me."

"Yours truly, Exhibit A. So what the hell did you do?"

"I didn't do anything. I got to about a block away and saw that the place was burning to the ground. I saw the medics cut you loose from the chair, saw you could walk, and got away as fast as I could." He shook his head. "I'm sorry. I got you into this. I don't suppose there's any way to cover it up now."

"Wait. Before we talk about covering up. You didn't kill those shits?"

"I didn't kill anybody. I was ready to, but . . . the fire. I saw you and figured it was a police thing."

"No . . . whatever that thing was, the police don't have it. I'm getting debriefed tomorrow, and I'm not sure what to say. You didn't *do* it?"

"What was it? Some kind of firebomb?"

Qabil touched his face gingerly. "The three guys just blew up. I saw it happen. I haven't said anything to anybody, just that there was a fire. But I saw it all."

"They blew up?"

"A window broke, a window behind me. The Tampa scumbag, Solo, raised his gun—it was already in his left hand—and started to stand. Then he just burst into flames."

"Jesus. Like a flamethrower?" Norman had seen them in use, and he still had dreams about it.

"No—it was like he exploded from the inside out. Not his clothes, his flesh. Then the other two. One, two, three. Staggering around like something out of a movie. Then their clothes started to burn. Capra had a gun in a holster in the small of his back, and the rounds cooked off.

"He fell into the drapes, and they went up like tinder. Some of the furniture was smoldering. Then fire running out of their bodies like burning oil. I was able to half stand up, tied to the chair, and had to kick my way through the front door, fell down the steps, and knocked myself silly. Some civilian sprayed me with a fire extinguisher, maybe saved my life."

"What the hell could do that? Make people burst into flame like that?"

"I was hoping you could straighten that out. Some new military weapon or something."

"Come on, Qabil. I haven't held a military weapon in thirty years."

Qabil nodded and then had a coughing spasm that ended with a stifled retch. "The smell was disgusting. You know I'm forbidden pork. When human flesh—"

"I remember, Qabil." He shook his head hard. "It must have been a Mafia thing. Or a gang thing."

"Well, the gangs . . ." He cleared his throat. "The gangs don't have any reason to love him. But they run more to baseball bats and knives. If they had burst-into-flames ray guns, we'd all be in real trouble.

"I thought about the Mafia. But why would a hit man kill three hoods and leave a live policeman as a witness?"

"Maybe he didn't know you were a—"

"I was still in uniform. But maybe, maybe that was the point. Maybe they want us to know they have this ungodly weapon. Willy Joe was not some godfather type they had to assassinate in a dramatic way. Just a bagman with delusions of grandeur."

They listened to the crickets for a minute. "What can make a body burn up?" Norman asked. "We're mostly water, aren't we?"

"Yeah. Crematoriums need a really hot fire to get things going. But we've both seen what napalm does."

"That's adding fuel. You said these guys just started to burn from the inside out."

"I saw that clearly. Their clothes weren't even on fire, not initially. Then *everything* was on fire."

"There've been cases of spontaneous human combustion."

Qabil laughed one "hum" and touched his cheek. "That always turns out to be nothing. Some old person or drunk, or drunk old person, falls asleep smoking. They die without noticing they've died. After they've smoldered awhile, fat starts to drip out. They burn like a candle then. Like an oil lamp."

"What about the water, then?"

"I guess it's like the water in a green stick of wood. If it's hot enough, the wood burns anyhow." He scratched his head. "But this was nothing like that. They didn't smolder or anything. They just ignited, like they were made out of gunpowder."

Norman sat straight up. "Oh, hell. It's obvious."

"Enlighten me."

"It's a *police* weapon. They knew you were—"

"No, hold it. We don't have anything remotely like that."

"Not that *you* know of. But let me finish. If the whole story came out, if any one of those three lived, there would be hell to pay. A homosexual policeman, a faggot's wife bribing a cop, the Mafia involved—hell, they'd use atomic weapons to keep that under wraps."

"But nobody knows. It's buried so deep—"

"Willy Joe found out."

Qabil shook his head hard. "If the department knew, I'd have been eased out a long time ago. Believe me; I've seen it happen. We use administrative procedures long before we resort to supernatural weapons."

"You once told me there was no such thing as 'supernatural.' If something happened, it was part of Allah's design, and therefore natural."

"Touché. And mystery is part of that design." He shook his head, smiling at the thought. "So think of this as a murder mystery. Weapon, motive, opportunity."

"The weapon, table that. Except to note that the person using it probably knew he was in no danger from his targets, once he pulled the trigger.

"The motive. Well, Capra probably has more people in this town willing to kill him than anyone else but the mayor. Right now you're the prime suspect, but I'm the only one who knows that, and if you say you didn't do it, that's enough for me. Who else? Did Rory know you were headed for a meeting with Capra?"

"No; I didn't want to involve her." *Jesus! It was Pepe!* "Besides, she was on camera all afternoon. Perfect alibi."

"And nobody else knew."

"No, of course not," he lied. Could Pepe's research have some kind of weapons application? Something developed from those gamma-ray bursters? Norman didn't know much about it. Maybe a burst of gamma rays could catch someone on fire.

"So what about opportunity? Usually linked to motive and weapon. If this is just a criminals-killing-criminals thing, the timing of it has to be explained."

"Because it's so propitious?"

He nodded. "And risky. In broad daylight, in a neighborhood full of criminal activity, someone sneaks around behind a house, breaks a window and kills three people inside, setting the house on fire, and walks away."

"There will have been witnesses."

"Most likely, but not models of good citizenship. And they probably don't want to get on the wrong side of whoever did this. Would you?"

"But wait. There's going to be a record of your having come to my house and catching this guy, Solo, Willy Joe's right-hand man. Then you wind up in a house with both of them dead."

"True. Except, as far as I know, there's nothing in police records linking the two. That would have been a real red flag. He was ID'ed as an out-of-towner." He breathed out, a loud puff. "We may get lucky. That fire was so intense it probably didn't leave anything useful, DNA or skeletal remains."

"Which might in itself be suspicious."

"It happens. They had all kinds of weapons in the war that made it impossible to identify remains. Usually intense heat and chemical action." He tapped his lower teeth with a thumbnail. "It's an angle. A possible angle."

"That someone in the military wanted to get rid of Capra?"

"Or someone with access to sophisticated weapons. I mean, suppose I just tell the truth, the part of it having to do with the weapon. Make the military connection, if no one else does."

"But then what puts you there, watching it all? Tied to a chair? Why did he kidnap you?"

"I've already got that part worked out. Fortunately, my partner and I are part of an observation team tracking drug distribution, designer drugs, inside the city limits. Capra was in it up to his elbows.

"I already told the patrolman at the hospital that's what happened: they'd followed me home and snatched me, and once it was dark they planned to kill me in a dramatic way. That much is true. But it wasn't for being on the drug task force."

"Yeah." Norman touched his hand. "Sorry I got you into all of this."

He said something in Arabic. "What will be will be. This is not something either of us had any say in. And the evil are punished, for a change."

"Funny attitude for a cop."

He smiled and nodded. "You better get back. I'll be in touch if anything happens."

Norman couldn't think of anything to say that wasn't a variant of "I hope I don't hear from you," so he just shook hands and headed back toward the house.

Should he confront Pepe with what he knew? Or just leave well enough alone. Curiosity versus gratitude, with a sprinkling of fear.

When he came back into the dining room, they were clearing away dessert.

"He didn't need the string?" Dove Slidell asked.

"What?" Norman was still holding his prop. "Oh, no—he'd found one by the time I got there. We just tuned up and went through a few difficult passages."

"Is he going to be all right?" Rory asked, trying to keep the quaver out of her voice.

"He'll be fine. I think he can go the rest of the way alone."

She nodded slowly, her eyes on his. "We're going to pick up some coffee at Nick's and go check the observatory. I won't even ask. You need your beauty sleep."

"Actually, I have to work for a bit. Started a new direction on the second partita."

"Well . . . party away." They said their good-byes.

||||| Aurora

She told the car to go to Nick's place. "He'll probably be sawing away at the cello if I get home at three."

"Hard to live with an *artiste?*" Dove said.

"Hard to live with somebody who doesn't keep regular hours. As if *I* did!" She turned around in the driver's seat. "But Norm's really odd. He never sleeps more than a few hours at a time. Naps now and then, no particular schedule."

"Like Edison," Lamar said.

"No lightbulbs or phonograph. But he's a heck of a good cook."

They murmured assent. "You'll be glad when this thing's over?" Dove said. "Get back to doing actual research."

"Not as much of that as I'd like. 'This thing' has kindled a new interest in astronomy in the young. I've bowed to pressure and agreed to take on two sections of elementary."

"That's a lot of kids."

"Fifty apiece. But I get two new grad assistants, so I just have to lecture."

"The rest of your load stays the same?" Lamar asked.

"Yeah, but it's not bad. A graduate seminar and a small class on nonthermal sources. And I'm getting a good bonus for the two extra sections.

"I've always enjoyed elementary. I just don't look forward to being spontaneous with the same lecture, three days a week."

Dove nodded. "I had to do two sections a couple of years back, when that boy genius from Princeton jumped ship. It's a strange sensation."

The car pulled up in front of Nick's, and the three went in for their coffee: burned, sweet, and rich.

Nick waved at Rory. "Just a second, Professor." She'd phoned in the order, not sure how late he stayed open.

She said hello to the only other customer, not certain whether she knew him. She'd seen him before, writing by hand in a bound journal.

The historian

He nodded back at Professor Bell. She would be in the last chapter.

He returned his attention to the book, up to the 1990s now.

In August 1990, Gainesville had a week of horrid fame, all over the world. Over the space of forty-eight hours, a madman captured, tortured, mutilated, and killed five students.

The bodies were rent with sixty-one slashes and stab wounds.

He carefully cleaned them up afterward—even the girl whose head he sawed off and placed at eye level on a bookshelf, for the police. Then he arranged the bodies into obscene positions.

The perversion eventually proved his undoing: he left semen at the scene, and its DNA identified him with no doubt.

He'd been free for months, before being arrested on another charge. A quarter of the student body had left in fear, or in response to parents' fears. The town was haunted by terror: gun sales sky-rocketed while real estate plummeted. It was a good time to buy property in the student ghetto; a bad time to live there.

in November

Alarming hair growth had continued in young white males since August, when a musical mime group, the Epileptics, had been briefly popular. What caught on was not their semirandom twitching, now admired and imitated only by the very young, but their odd facial hair: each of them had a braided rope of beard growing from one cheek, and were otherwise clean-shaven. Of course it would take years to achieve a really long rope, but many adherents had managed four to six inches. They dyed it odd colors and some waxed it with a heavy pomade, so it lolled from the cheek like a spare penis, much to the delight of their parents.

Two movies inspired by the Coming appeared. *Second Coming* was aimed at the Christian audience, and succeeded; *To Serve Man,* blatantly stolen from a century-old "first contact" story, did not do quite as well, once the joke of the title became common knowledge.

Europe treaded further down the path to open war. Every member present in the German parliament died on 17 November, victims of a swift bioagent that turned their bones to jelly. No one claimed responsibility for the massacre. The next day the Eiffel Tower came down, four people freighted with high explosives sacrificing themselves simultaneously, at the monument's four corners.

No one took credit for that, either. Official denials were discounted by most German and French citizens, as was the sober assertion that a third party was likely responsible for both atrocities; someone who would benefit from the two countries destroying one another.

Both armies massed along the border, doing maneuvers.

Insect restaurants opened all over California, Oregon, and Washington State. One chain, Eat More Bugs, was openly xenophobic, relating bugs with the Coming—cows and pigs and chickens are your relatives; eat something alien.

Most of the survival stores were failing. People who stocked up on water and bullets and nitrogen-preserved beans only went to the store once. So it was one month of huge profits followed by bankruptcy. Some of them hung on grimly, hoping for bad news. But there was no news from space; just the unchanging signal.

Norman told Aurora a version of the truth that did not include Pepe or weapons of incredible ferocity. The police investigation of the murder/arson did not publicly acknowledge that the bodies had been burned beyond even molecular recognition. The station scuttlebutt was that Willy Joe had arranged the arson to make it look as if he had died, a cover for disappearing out of sight. That was consistent with Rabin's fantastic testimony and the absolute lack of organic residue: the "men" who were holding him hostage were just convincing dummy robots, loaded with something like thermite. It would have been an expensive masquerade, but well within Willy Joe's budget, or at least the budget of his bosses.

Rabin had one more clandestine meeting with Norm, where they discussed the unlikelihood of that explanation. Of course, Rabin had gone along with it during the investigation, because it turned the spotlight away from him: Willy Joe had only picked up a cop so he would have an unimpeachable witness to his dramatic "demise."

Norm and Rabin stropped Occam's razor and concluded it must have been some clandestine military device that had fallen into the hands of an enemy of Willy Joe's. Norm was still thinking privately about gamma-ray bursters, but he left well enough alone there.

(An aspect of it that no one else was privy to was that the chief of police had a cousin in Washington who was high up in U.S. Army weapons research. He said there was nothing in the arsenal, or even on the drawing boards, that would do what Rabin had described. So it must have been fake.)

1 December

 **Aurora**

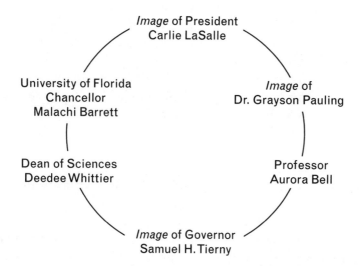

Image of President
Carlie LaSalle

University of Florida
Chancellor
Malachi Barrett

Image of
Dr. Grayson Pauling

Dean of Sciences
Deedee Whittier

Professor
Aurora Bell

Image of Governor
Samuel H. Tierny

"This should be entertaining." Rory snapped off the screen.

Norman was in the supplicant's chair. "Well, *I'm* impressed. The leader of the Western world up at nine." He sipped coffee.

"Oh, since eight at least, putting on makeup." Rory leafed through a thin stack of papers and slid them into a plastic portfolio. She reached for his cup. "May I?"

He pushed it an inch toward her. "No sugar."

"I stand in awe of your willpower." She took a sip. "Ugh. Delicious."

"Take it along."

"They'll have some there." She gave him a good-bye peck and took her jacket off the peg. "Wasn't it raining out?"

"Stopped before I left." She'd come to the office about four and saw lightning over the horizon. Crazy weather.

The elevator had a sharp scrubbed smell; first of the month. She put the scruffy jacket on over her businesslike meet-the-president dress, feeling bohemian. But who in Florida bothers with fancy cold-weather clothes?

The sky was gray with fast-moving clouds, the air damp and cool. It might rain again. She hurried along with the students hustling to their nine-o'clocks, some of them resolutely wearing shorts. Maybe they didn't *have* anything else.

She got to the conference room early and was startled to see the president already there. "It's just a test holo," Deedee said from the other side of the room. "Coffee?"

"Half a cup, sure." The holo looked absolutely real. Its eyes seemed to follow you. "I wonder how much science the holo knows. We could just go ahead and get started."

"Ye of little faith." Deedee handed her a plastic cup as she sat down, and took her own place across the table. "Let's hope it's just a pro forma pep talk."

"Not a funding cut," Rory said. "That's the first thing that occurred to me."

"It's been a real windfall for you guys."

She blew on the coffee. "You know it. Half our salary load this semester's covered by the federal grant. Of course it's generated a lot of paperwork. People trying to justify their ongoing research in terms of the Coming."

"I didn't hear that." Chancellor Barrett walked into the room.

"I didn't say it, Mal." She smiled at him. "I was temporarily in the thrall of millennial demons."

"That was *last* month." He poured some coffee and squeezed past Deedee to get to his assigned chair. "I hope we won't have to address the spiritual side of it this time."

"God willing," Deedee said.

"Amen." The meeting a month ago with Reverend Kale had been harrowing. You were either with him or against him, and he had come to the meeting knowing that it would be a confrontation with his strongest enemies.

He tried to turn it into a ground-shaking media event, but fortunately, the press was tired of dealing with him. So it was a lot of sound and fury and no airtime.

There was a soft gong and the president came to life, a few inches higher, her hair unchanged but her blouse lavender instead of teal. Governor Tierny and Grayson Pauling appeared at the same moment. The governor had a green suit with a red tie, Christmas coming. The science adviser always wore gray. This morning, his skin seemed a little gray.

"Good morning," the president said, as if she meant it. A smile that revealed just a trace of her perfect teeth. "Let's get right down to business." She reached outside of the holo field and someone handed her a leather folder.

Rory had expected the Oval Office, but this was some other room, oil paintings of the presidents looking down from windowless walls.

"This is top secret. You may not discuss it with the media. A few days ago, the secretary of defense asked me to convene a secret cabinet meeting."

"Oh, no," Rory said, at the edge of audibility. Pauling looked up at her, but the president didn't seem to notice.

". . . about our preparedness for what amounts to an alien invasion. Clearly, we are not prepared, he admitted, but just as clearly, we can be."

She looked around the room as if daring anyone to speak. "We reviewed your testimony on this, and the corroborating testimony of the National Science Foundation and the American Association for Science—"

"The Advancement of Science," Pauling corrected.

"Thank you, Grayson. Simply put, we felt that you were well meaning but wrong. This is actually a political issue, not a scientific one. I mean, we wouldn't know about the danger without you scientists, true. But it is a political problem with a political solution."

"Which is to say military," Deedee said. "Ms. President."

"Strategic. There's a time-honored distinction."

"Strategic, until you push the button," Pauling said. "Then it's military."

"And the reason for strategic preparedness is to prevent war."

"Ms. President," Rory said, "what are you going to use to scare these space aliens with? Nuclear weapons?"

"Better than that." She pulled a diagram from the folder. "Though it uses a nuclear weapon for fuel."

The diagram was just a polar view of the earth, with a dotted orbit surrounding it, about four thousand miles up. There were three equidistant Xs on the orbit.

"Each of these three shuttles has a one-shot maser, microwave laser, generator. It turns the power of a hydrogen bomb into a single blast of energy powerful enough to vaporize anything. At any given time, two of the three will cover any approach to Earth."

"Boy, I hope they don't have four ships," Rory said.

"What?"

"Ms. President, if you were going to invade another planet, would you send just one ship?"

"Well . . . I'm sure we can put any number of these things in orbit. . . ."

"*On* orbit," Pauling said. "And there are only three. Two of them aren't even—"

"You're always saying that, Grayson. As if you could be on an orbit the way you're on the street. I suppose we should make more."

"You can't," he said. "Even if it were legal—and it's not; they would be in violation of international law—you can't build these things in a month, no matter how much money you throw at the contractors."

"I think there may be more someplace," she said expressionlessly.

"I don't suppose they ever pass over France or Germany," the chancellor said.

"Several times a day," Pauling said.

"But that's immaterial," the president said. "These point up, not down. And we've worked out the international aspects. The UN Security Council will be part of the decision-making process."

"They point whichever way we want them to," Pauling said. "And the UN's big red button doesn't have to be connected to anything."

The president sighed. "You've always been such a good team player, Grayson. Until this thing came up."

Pauling faced the others. "I was the only cabinet member not in favor of this scheme. But then I'm the only one who knows an electron from his asteroid."

"As I said, it's no longer a scientific problem. The science has been solved. But we still have our people to protect." She was trying to look presidential but was obviously pissed at Pauling. He had probably said he was going to behave.

"Have they been orbited yet?" Rory said, avoiding the in-orbit/on-orbit controversy.

"No, Dr. Bell, they're undergoing checks. They'll go up next week."

"No matter what our advice is," Deedee said.

The governor cleared his throat and spoke for the first time. "Dean Whittier, with all due respect, the president and her cabinet have considered the scientific aspects of this along with all others—"

"And come up with the wrong decision!" Rory snapped. "This is like children setting up a practical joke to surprise Mommy when she comes through the door. She is not going to be amused."

"I have been assured that there is no conceivable defense against these weapons."

"Oh, please. The Praetorian Guard was invincible in its time, but one soldier with a nineteenth-century machine gun would destroy them in seconds."

The president stared for a moment, perhaps listening to someone offstage explaining what the Praetorian Guard was. "Science is on my side here, Professor. This energy beam goes at the speed of light. Do you know of any way to detect it and get out of its way?"

"No, but neither do I have a spaceship that can go the speed of light. If I did, I'd probably have something to protect myself against twenty-first-century weapons."

"Exactly my point last night," Pauling said. "The only thing we know about these creatures is that their science is beyond our comprehension."

"You may be committing suicide for the whole human race," Rory said. "Or murdering the human race out of ignorance and hubris."

"This is not just a bad idea," Deedee said. "This is the worst idea in history."

The president's famous temper finally boiled over. "Then history will judge me! Not a roomful of professors!" She disappeared, along with Pauling. The governor faded out with a fixed smile pasted on his face.

It was just the three of them, spaced around a plain round table.

Rory sipped cold coffee. "I think she has a thing about professors."

"Professors tend to have a thing about her," the chancellor said.

"We don't have to keep this secret," Deedee said. "We ought to get the word out before the administration does."

Mal shook his head. "She said it was top secret."

"I don't have any clearance," she said. "Do you?"

"I can probably get Marya Washington," Rory said. "She's not exactly pro-administration." She took a phone out of her purse and punched two numbers. She nodded at a robot voice. "Tell Marya that Rory Bell, down in Florida, has to talk to her immediately. Big scoop." She pushed the "off" button. "Big scoop of something."

"I need a real cup of coffee," Deedee said. "Go by Sara's on the way back?"

Mal checked his watch. "You two go. I still have time to show up at a budget hearing and surprise some people." He smiled and the smile faded. "Let me know if you need any help, Rory. With the cube people or Her Nibs."

"Thanks, Mal. I may need you to back me up on what the president said."

"Count on it." He looked at Deedee. "See you Saturday?"

Deedee

"With bells on." The chancellor nodded, snapped his attaché case shut, and left.

"Hobnobbing with the greats?" Rory said.

"He's a tiger in bed," she said hoarsely. " 'Administer me! Administer me!' " They both laughed. "It's something the provost dreamed up. They've invited all the four-point seniors to a barbecue with all the deans and Mal. Should be fun, if Mal and I aren't in some dungeon in Washington, along with you."

"Any bets as to who he'll show up with?"

"I don't gamble with love." There was a faint rumble of thunder, and she held up an umbrella. "Beat the rain?"

They didn't. Halfway to Dos Hermanos the skies opened up. The umbrella kept their heads dry, but not much else.

Dos Hermanos was warm and crowded. They sat at the bar and ordered cafés con leche.

"So it's us against the president of the United States," Deedee said. "Where do we go from here?"

"You know, she didn't say why she called the meeting," Rory said. "She must have known what our reaction was going to be. So what did she gain by letting us know before a general announcement was made?"

Deedee shook her head. "Maybe it was Pauling who set it up. She pretty much does what her cabinet tells her to do."

"Yeah, Snow White and the Fourteen Dwarfs. The executive

branch has seen better days." The coffee came and Rory stirred in a spoonful of sugar. Deedee just sprinkled a little cinnamon on top. "I wonder," Rory continued. "What if you could get someone to claim that this was a declaration of war, and need the approval of Congress?"

"Well, she owns the House, except the Greens. Put the House Greens with the Senate Democrats, you'd at least have some noise. But I don't think you can declare war against a vessel—or a message, which is all we really have."

She held the coffee cup to warm her fingers and sniffed deeply at the cinnamon. "I think the key is going to be education, or propaganda. Your newscaster is probably our most powerful weapon. If the gallups tell LaSalle not to launch the things, she won't."

Pepe burst through the door, drenched, holding a soggy newspaper over his head. "¡Hola!" He dropped the paper into the recycle bin.

There were no seats at the bar. He stood between them and ordered a double espresso.

"How'd the meeting go? Is Fearless Leader smarter in person?"

"A regular Hawking," Deedee said, and in low voices the two of them summed up what had transpired.

"I wouldn't be too worried," he said. "She's just putting on her 'woman of action' hat. France is going to raise holy hell, and Russia, too. She'll never get the Security Council behind it, and she knows that. She's posturing. Campaigning."

"Wish I could be sure of that," Rory said. "Sounds too sophisticated for her." Her phone rang and she plucked it out of her purse. "Con permiso. I have a call in to Marya Washington." She pushed the "record" button. "Buenos?"

Her jaw actually dropped; sharp intake of breath. "Did you record it? I'll be right over." She folded up the phone and put it away. "That was Norman, at the office. There's a new message from the aliens. A long one."

They left three coffees steaming on the bar.

Norman

He thumbed in a blank crystal and made another copy, for safety's sake. Then he sat and read the message on the wall:

We will arrive on Earth exactly one month from now, landing at Cape Kennedy 1200 Greenwich Standard Time on January 1. We will use the old shuttle landing strip. Please make sure it is clear and smooth.

We have a message that must be delivered in person. Recognizing the need for some ceremony, we will stay for a short time. Soon after landing, though, the runway must be clear for our departure. The nature of our message will make it clear why timing is crucial.

If we are delayed, your planet will be destroyed.

If any action is taken against us, every human being on Earth will die, whether we survive or not.

Our intentions are peaceful, but we know your nature well enough not to come unprotected. We will provide a small demonstration of our power as we approach, by destroying the martian moon Phobos. Be sure that there is nothing of value on that moon by Christmas.

We do come in peace, and we bring a message of hope.

Norman grinned. The third partita would be Christmas hymns, combining and then clashing, building to chaos and silence.

He would write the fourth partita after he heard what they had to say. If composer and audience were still alive.

Rory came bustling in with Deedee and Pepe, all of them drenched. They stared at the message, wordless. The phone chimed, over and over. Someone important, or the secretary would just file a message.

Still looking at the writing on the wall, Rory groped behind her and found the chair at her desk. She sat down slowly and pushed a button. "Buenos."

"I don't know how you did it." President LaSalle's face on the screen was blotchy, livid. "But it's not going to work. We will have those weapons in orbit in a week."

"Ms. President," Rory said, "I just saw this message one minute ago for the first time. I assume it did come from the spaceship?"

"That's what the NASA people say. But the timing is too perfect. I don't know how you did it, but you did it. And it's not going to work."

"Why don't you ask your NASA people how I could manage that trick?" she said slowly. "I assume they picked it up on the Moon as well as here. So by simple triangulation, you can tell how far the message has come. It was probably sent before we began to talk."

"Impossible," the president said, and disappeared.

"Pepe, go check on the Moon?" The phone started chiming again. Rory shook her head and stabbed the button.

It was Marya Washington, her face distorted and bouncing around the screen. "Rory, I'm in a cab to JFK. The station's putting me on their own plane; I'll be down in Gainesville"—she looked at the inside of her wrist—"in maybe ninety minutes. Can we have lunch?"

"Uh . . . sure. We have a lot to talk about."

"That Mexican place on Main Street? At twelve o'clock?"

"Yeah, fine."

"Good. Más tarde." The screen went blank.

"What the hell was that all about?" Norman said. "The prez?"

"That's what our meeting was about. She wants to orbit those killer satellites. The secretary of defense's idea, I take it. But all the cabinet's behind it, except Pauling."

Norman let out a little snort. "I guess this means we won't be invading France. Just frying it."

Pepe was mopping his long hair with a paper towel. "Surely she'll reconsider after she calms down." He gestured at the screen. "Or wiser heads may prevail."

"Wiser heads better get her out of office," Deedee said. "The woman is seriously bent. She sees everything in terms of conspiracy."

"Yeah," Norman said. "Poor old Brattle."

"Who's Brattle?" Rory said. Everybody looked at her.

"Undersecretary of defense," Norman said. To the others: "She doesn't listen to the news."

"She had him charged with sedition," Deedee said. "Sedition! 'Moderation' is more like it. But he's being investigated by a closed committee. Essentially under house arrest."

"Well, she can house-arrest me." Rory smiled at Norman. "At least I have a good cook. She's going to be terminally pissed off after I talk to Marya."

"Don't do that," Pepe said. "You mustn't do that. Not yet."

"Somebody has to stop her."

"Somebody will. In Washington."

"You sound pretty confident. For someone who's usually nothing but sarcastic about government."

"Just give it a day or two, and see what happens. If you violate the president's trust, you'll be out of the game completely. And you probably *will* go to jail somewhere."

"I think he's right," Norm said. "Where there's a loose cannon on deck, you want to be belowdecks."

"So what do I tell Marya? I left her a message that we were conferencing with La Presidente this morning."

"Just tell the truth," Pepe said. "That important matters were discussed, but you were sworn to secrecy."

Rory shook her head. "We're talking about the survival of the whole human race, versus my going to jail."

"Just give it one day," Pepe said. "See what Washington does. If they conceal it, hell, you'll give Marya even more of a story."

"I think he's right," Deedee said. "Another couple of days won't make a big difference. Stay out of jail and hold on to your professorship. That's my strategy."

Norm nodded at the screen. "You'll have plenty to talk about. I mean, now it really *is* an invasion from outer space."

"I'll do something useful," Pepe said, "besides checking the

Moon. See whether we can calculate how big a boom it would take to blow up Phobos."

"It's just a little pebble, isn't it?" Norm said.

"Compared to a planet," Rory said. "About twenty kilometers in diameter?"

"You're asking me?" Pepe said. "I'm not a planet guy. But that's twice as big as Mount Everest is tall. Think about a bomb that could level Mount Everest. Then multiply it by eight; two-cubed."

"Considerable bang," Rory said. "Interesting that they chose the larger one. If memory serves, Diemos is only half its size."

"I'll go see if I can find Leo." Leo Matzlach was their Mars expert. "Maybe I can get you a number before launch."

"That would be good," Rory said. "Anything concrete. We're not exactly in a data-rich environment."

Running out, Pepe almost collided with the chancellor.

|||||| Malachi Barrett

"Sorry." He dodged the young man, then walked into the office and exchanged greetings.

"Dr. Bell," he said to Norman, "I have to speak with your wife and Dr. Whittier in private."

"No problem." Norm got up and stretched. "Guess our lunch date's off, anyhow."

"Unless you want to be interviewed," Rory said.

"No; think I'll go home and play." He jerked a thumb in the direction of the wallscreen. "That gives me an idea." To Mal: "Stopped raining?"

"For a while." He brushed a few drops from his shoulder.

"Try to beat it home." Norm scooped up his bicycle helmet and left.

"This changes things." Mal dropped heavily into the chair Norm had vacated. "A direct threat."

"Her Nibs called right after the message came," Deedee said. "She thinks it's a fake, and Rory's behind it."

"Well?" Mal said.

"Well what?" Rory said. "Is it a fake?"

Mal shrugged. "Tell me it's not."

"Mal . . . okay, you've got me. It's a fake. But since it came from beyond the solar system, I had to send the message *before* we met with La Presidente. So I'm not only a traitor, I'm a fucking *clairvoyant!*"

Mal raised a hand. "Okay, sorry. I hadn't thought of that."

"You're one step ahead of Fearless Leader," Rory said. "She not only didn't think of it, she doesn't *believe* it. I don't think they covered that speed-of-light stuff at her finishing school."

"So you think she's going to go ahead with orbiting those weapons?"

"Seems likely. She has a testosterone problem. And she has the backing to push it through."

"They would probably work, though, wouldn't they?"

"What, the weapons?"

"Yes. I mean, there are thousands of satellites up there. Surely the aliens couldn't tell that three of them were weapons."

Rory paused. "Maybe they couldn't, especially if the weapons were disguised as other kinds of satellites. Though their positioning would be suggestive, suspicious." She rubbed her still-damp hair. "Besides, suppose there's more than one alien vessel? They seem to know a bit about human nature. Maybe they know us well enough to send a decoy first."

"Which could be behind the Phobos demonstration, too," Deedee said. "If it *is* an actual invasion, they may be sending a decoy in to provoke us and test our resources."

"Well, if it is an invasion, we can save our H-bombs. They can stand back a ways and throw rocks at us, at $.99c$."

"Another thing the president seems not to believe," Mal said. His own background was in psychology and sociology, but he knew enough science to grasp that.

"And she doesn't want to listen to the one person who keeps

telling her the truth," Deedee said. "Poor Pauling. He'll be out on the sidewalk before long."

"Replaced by her astrologer," Mal said.

"She has an *astrologer*?" Rory said, wide-eyed.

Mal shrugged. "Might be tabloid nonsense. Maybe she does chicken entrails instead."

"So what do *your* chicken entrails say?" Deedee said. "Rory's talking with Marya Washington at noon. We've been telling her to keep it under her hat, at least for the time being."

"I would, too. The president was unambiguous about that. 'Top secret,' she said. Though I'm certain she's about to reveal it herself. Maybe not until after the launch."

"She thinks these aliens aren't watching our broadcasts?"

"She doesn't think very far beyond the nearest camera lens, and this morning's gallup numbers. And she knows the people are going to eat this up."

"The people," Deedee said. "The only thing wrong with democracy."

The phone chimed and Rory thumbed it. It was the departmental secretary, looking strained. "Dr. Bell, I'm sorry to interrupt. But I have calls stacked up from all over the world. If we could schedule a press conference . . ."

"Okay, let's say fourteen hundred. Do you have Marya Washington's phone number?"

"Right here."

"She'll be landing here in a half hour or so, I guess with a small crew. Call her first, set up a time and place, and then contact everyone else."

"Okay, will do." The screen went blank.

"You always play favorites like this?" Mal asked.

"I guess I do. She's well informed and fair."

"She probably doesn't have a quarter the market share of CNN."

"I should care? The news gets out." The phone chimed and the screen flashed INTRADEPARTMENTAL. She pushed it.

Pepe: "Okay, I called the Moon and they confirmed. And the choice of Phobos is no mystery. It's cracked. There's a crater, Stuckney, that's a third the size of the moon itself, and it damn near blew the thing apart. Fractures radiate away from it; you just have to shoot a bomb down into there, and finish Mother Nature's job for her."

"So how big a bomb?"

Pepe shrugged. "Pick a number. Leo guessed a hundred thousand megatons. Give or take a factor of a thousand."

Rory laughed. "Well, that's precise enough. A hundred million megatons it is. Thank Leo for me—you want to come to this interview?"

"No; God, no. Earthshaking stress isn't in my job description."

Pepe

"Buenos." He pushed the "on/off" button on the pay phone and looked around the library. This was as good a place as any to wait for the news to break.

News. He hadn't been keeping up. He sat down at a console and called up *The New York Times,* and toggled back a couple of days.

That must have been when the president first got a hair up her ass about the orbital weapons. She was evidently a pawn, or a rook anyhow, in the current Defense Department power struggle—a schism between those who wanted to ally with Germany and Russia, and the isolationist/pacifist/Francophile set, who wanted us to sit back and watch.

If we stayed out of it, France and her allies would prevail; the eastern coalition was about to spin apart into impotent factions. But with our killer satellites always within a few minutes of Paris and Lyons, coupled with a commander-in-chief who was pro-East and prone to dramatic gestures, Paris had to stop and think: We could be vaporized.

Washington was thinking, as well. Not talking yet, waiting for the White House's lead.

It was like watching an ant colony scurry around, oblivious to the larger world around them. The Defense Department seized on the threat of the Coming to justify "weapons of mass destruction" in orbit. Thinking that when the alien hoax petered out, the weapons would still be up there. Pointed down, at Paris and her allies.

One microsecond blast from them, and Paris would be a postmodern Troy. There was a great city once, under the rubble and ash.

He knew it wasn't going to happen. The Defense Department might have a lunatic at the top, appointed by a fellow lunatic, but that was not going to last.

Poor Brattle. He was not even a liberal, but he was on talkshows and the gallup preps, talking about how futile and dangerous it would be to mount a campaign against these aliens: "If they come in peace, fine. If they come spoiling for a fight, we can't match their high-tech weapons. But we can resist them on the ground. They'll find we don't make good slaves."

Brattle was an intelligent man, but he was too straight and plainspoken to be undersecretary of defense. He was obviously under fire—under arrest!—because he had stood up to the president and his boss over the satellite scheme.

Pepe knew they wouldn't get three to orbit, and surely the president and her cabinet did, too. The maser weapon only existed as one demonstration model, and it would take a half-trillion dollars, and a lot of luck, to put three in orbit before the New Year. But even the demo could destroy Paris, and the other two could be dummies.

All of them pointed toward Earth.

"Hello, stranger." It was his girlfriend, Lisa Marie. "You've been awfully busy lately."

He liked her a lot, pretty and dark and quick, but he had been easing away from her, knowing he'd have to leave soon. "Yeah. Aliens this, aliens that."

Lisa Marie

"You still have to eat, though." She watched him carefully. "It's almost lunchtime."

He looked at his watch and hesitated. "Sure. You mind going to Dos Hermanos?"

"Love it. I'll buy you a taco."

He laughed, picking up his umbrella and book bag. "Where I come from, that would be an indecent proposition."

She knew that. "First things first, guapo."

She was glad for the light rain, holding on to his arm and huddling together under the umbrella as they walked across campus. He told her about the unsettling new message.

"Was the wording strange? I mean, did it sound like it was written by a human being?"

He put on a strange accent. "We come in peace, Earth beings. Lay down your weapons and take off your clothes."

She copied it: "And climb please into these pots of hot water. Bring vegetables."

He shook his head, smiling. "They may fry us. But I don't think it will be to eat us."

"You really think we're in danger?" They stopped at a fenced-in pond and watched an alligator watching them.

"Maybe not so much from them." He looked thoughtful and chose his words carefully. "Our own response might put us in danger, though. LaSalle is such a dim bulb, and she's not exactly surrounded by geniuses. Then we have the Islamic Jihad and the Eastern Bloc. Any one of them could try to knock the aliens out of orbit. Or nuke them when they land at Kennedy."

"There's a pleasant thought."

"Yeah—if LaSalle says she's going to stay home and send the

vice-president, I'm out of here. I don't want to be a hundred and sixty kilometers from ground zero."

"I've got a car," she said seriously. "The trunk's already full of food and jugs of water." She shook her head. "And a gun and ammunition. My father brought it all down a couple of weeks ago. 'Better safe than sorry,' he said. I don't think beans and rice and bullets are the answer."

"But you do keep them in your trunk."

"Yeah, but like you, I'm not so much afraid of the aliens. What I'm afraid of is gangbanging and looting. Like back in twenty-eight, all the grocery stores in flames."

"You weren't alive in twenty-eight."

"Born in 2030. But my parents would never shut up about it."

The air in Dos Hermanos was warm and heavy with spicy cooking smells. It was early, but they got the last table. Pepe waved to his boss and a black woman who looked familiar.

Something in his manner worried Lisa Marie. He seemed to be studying every customer in the café as they were led to their table and seated. Looking for aliens, maybe.

"Is something wrong?" he said.

"I was going to ask you the same thing. Just the message, though?"

"Yeah, just. I wonder how many people here haven't seen it." He pointed to the cube over the bar, which showed the message on a flatscreen with a commentator being earnest in front of it. You couldn't quite read the words or tell what he was saying, over the café hum.

She glanced at the menu but didn't really read it; she'd eaten here a hundred times.

"It's early," she said, "but you want to split a bottle of wine? Celebrate your aliens?"

He shook his head. "Like to, but it's going to be a busy day." The waitress who came up was the owner of the place. "Buenos días," he said.

Sara

"Buenos. Your aliens are at it again."

"Why does everybody call them 'my' aliens? They're Rory's aliens."

She looked over at their table. "Her newsie didn't waste any time getting down here. She called in a lunch reservation from her corporate jet, la-di-da."

"Sure glad I'm an overpaid academic," Pepe said, "and don't have to flit around the world at somebody else's beck and call." He ordered chicken fajitas with a double espresso and milk. His girlfriend, Lisa what's-her-name, got a Cuban sandwich and half carafe of white wine.

She was headed back to José with the orders when she heard the shrill emergency whistle from the cube. *"¡Silencio!"* she shouted. "Everybody shut up a minute." She cut her eyes to the cube and saw the unthinkable.

It was a long shot of the White House. One end of it was rubble, gray smoke and orange flames.

"We don't know what's happened," a tight, panicky voice said. "One minute ago, something . . . some explosion . . . we don't know!"

His image appeared in the corner, the normally unflappable Carl Lamb. "Word just coming in." He put his hand flat against his left ear.

"Oh, my God. The president is dead. Most of her cabinet, too. The vice-president, he, he's . . . he was in another room but he's badly hurt. There's an ambulance floater—there; there, you can see it." On the cube, a white floater overshot the flames, spun around, and settled down behind the smoke.

"All the Secret Service can say is it didn't come from outside. It was a powerful bomb that went off in the cabinet room.

"It was an emergency meeting, called about the aliens, the new message. What the Secret Service wonders is how could anybody know they'd all be in that room at that time?"

She sat down in the nearest empty chair, which was Rory's table. "The aliens . . . they couldn't've done this?"

Aurora

"I don't . . . No. No, of course not." Though it was certainly handy for them. She looked over at Pepe, the only other person here who *knew* how handy. He was looking at her.

A young man ran outside to vomit, falling to his knees on the sidewalk. Rory's own stomach twisted. Her head felt full of light, as if she were going to faint. Still staring at the screen, she reached across the table at the same time Marya did. Her grip was firm and dry but she was trembling.

"This couldn't be a movie or something?" Sara said. "This can't be happening."

Marya gulped. "A *War of the Worlds* thing, Orson Welles? They wouldn't do it, they couldn't."

Rory could only shake her head. She tried to say something but her mouth and throat were suddenly dry. She took a sip of water and it was like glue. Was she going into shock?

"Jesus," Marya croaked. Her dark skin was gray, bloodless. "It's like a palace coup. Who's left?"

Her phone buzzed. She took it out of her purse, listened for a moment, and said, "Okay." She put it back. "They want me to stay here," she said quietly.

There was a murmur of conversation. Two or three people were sobbing.

"Wait," the commentator said. "There is what? There is a message. Our station, many stations, received it right after the tragedy."

He looked off-camera and nodded, openmouthed. "This is Grayson Pauling, President LaSalle's, the late president's, science adviser."

Pauling looked tired and miserable. "Good morning. I have a grave duty today, which must be explained.

"It has been obvious for many months that our president is mentally ill, profoundly so. It has been a source of amusement in Washington, and a weakness for the brokers of power to exploit.

"The union has survived mentally ill and incompetent leaders, and it might have survived Carlie LaSalle, but for the Coming. Especially in light of this morning's message.

"Ms. LaSalle, with the very active cooperation of the secretary of defense, proposes to orbit killer weapons that will supposedly destroy the aliens before they have a chance to land. This would be suicide, genocide . . . there is no word for it. The destruction of our entire species.

"She does not truly understand the amount of power these aliens have demonstrated. To the extent that she does understand, she sees it as a challenge to her own power. It is not. It's just a statement of fact."

He looked down and sighed, and then looked into the camera again. "When I was a young man, I was a military officer. Often I had to order men and women into action, knowing that some of them would die. I often went along with them, and the possiblility of my own death—sometimes what I saw as the certainty of my death—was of no consequence, compared to the responsibility I felt for them. The guilt, perhaps.

"So today I'm going to die, and in the process, sacrifice the lives of many people who didn't even know there was a war. I'm sorry. My sorrow is no comfort to those of you who are going to lose loved ones. But we'll all be dead in one month if I do not do this.

"When I turn off the camera and set the delay on this message, I will leave for an emergency cabinet meeting set for noon. In my briefcase, I have twelve pounds of C-9, a powerful plastic explosive. When I am in the cabinet room with the president and the secretary of defense, I will open the briefcase and we will all die, as well as others, who are innocent bystanders. Collateral casualties, as they say.

"I have always liked Carlie LaSalle, in spite of her craziness, perhaps because of it, and now I am repaying her trust with murder. History will vindicate me, or at least admit the necessity for this, but that gives me no satisfaction this morning." He reached out of the cube and turned off the camera.

Rory found her voice. "What happens now?"

Marya shook her head. "Pray the vice-president survives. The speaker of the House makes Carlie LaSalle look like a Phi Beta Kappa."

"Who would've thought it," Sara said in a stunned whisper. "Here in America."

"Yeah, America. I wouldn't've predicted LaSalle, either." Rory shook her head. "Washington's a zoo." Carl Lamb was back on the cube, saying that the vice-president was being rushed to Walter Reed, but was not expected to live.

"It makes a kind of sense," Marya said, rubbing her chin hard. "I mean story sense. Grayson Pauling always was a wild card. You know he was DDT in Desert Wind?"

"No," Rory said, staring at the cube. "What's DDT?"

"It's a unit of the Special Forces they call 'Department of Dirty Tricks.' Unconventional warfare; I forget its actual name. He never talked about it; claimed he wasn't allowed to. But that may be how he knew how to build a bomb he could carry into the White House."

As if to back her up, the cube showed a gray positron scan of the briefcase. "Even cabinet members are checked when they enter the White House," Carl Lamb said. "Grayson Pauling appeared to have nothing but books and papers."

A security guard came into the cube, the side of his head bandaged, blood drops on his tunic. "Maybe we shoulda wondered about those books. Why would someone carry big books into a cabinet meeting?"

Lamb made reassuring noises. "His mind was made up this morning," Rory said. "He might have done it without the new message, eventually."

"This morning." Marya stared at her. "That meeting."

They looked at Sara and she got up. "Yeah, I got to go."

Everybody was hypnotized by the cube, but Rory lowered her voice to a whisper anyhow. "He was openly rebellious and she was really pissed off. It looked as if she'd allowed him to be in on the conference call if he promised to behave. But then he wouldn't go along with the party line."

"This is the scoop you called about?"

"Yes. The president was going to authorize three orbital weapons: masers powered by H-bombs. Pauling seemed to think they would wind up pointed the wrong way. Toward France."

"Ah. That's the DOD connection."

"What?"

"He said on the cube he was after the secretary of defense as well as the president."

"He did, right. Another interesting thing . . . the president cut him off, but I think there's only one of these masers. I guess the other two are decoys."

"I don't know how much of this I can use. Though I appreciate knowing it."

"What could they do to you?"

"Cut me off from Washington sources, at the least. Haul me up in front of a security committee—hell, they've got the undersecretary of defense under house arrest."

"Isn't he the *secretary* now?"

She shook her head. "Doesn't work that way. The president, whoever that may be, appoints a new one. If he can find anybody at home—I suspect half of Washington will be out beyond the Beltways before quitting time."

"France might do something?"

"More likely the Jihad. But we have lots of enemies who can see that it would be a good time for a couple of strategically placed bombs. Convenient to be out of New York, too."

"Sleepy college towns have their advantages."

"This one, I don't know. The way the Jihad rails about the Coming, they might be able to spare a bomb for here or the Cape. As long as they're bombing."

"You're not kidding?"

"Just professionally paranoid. Look at that. They kept turning rocks over until they found him."

Carl Lamb was standing on the Capitol steps next to Cool Moon Davis, who looked like a ninety-year-old Native American who had just been dragged out of a deep sleep. He was only seventy-two, actually, but had had an eventful life.

"Speaker Davis, do you have any words for America at this tragic time?"

He looked up into the camera, eyes dull, and straightened up slightly when his earphone started feeding him lines. "I've always admired Carly Simon—Carly LaSalle, that is, for her spirit and her dedication to American ideals of America. Like all Americans I feel a deep lens of sauce, I mean sense of sauce, and a truly deep outrage at this crime against the Republic. The crime of assassination."

"He came up with that himself," Marya muttered.

"Thank you, Mr. Speaker. We . . . uh . . . we have a link to Walter Reed, and the vice-president, I mean President Mossberg, wants to address the nation."

He looked bad, his chest a tight wrapping of bloodstained bandage, arms inert at his sides, breathing tube taped to his nose.

His normally clear voice was gravelly and nasal. "The doctors say I have a good chance of surviving, but I have spent most of my life in the company of professional liars, and I can see through them." He coughed violently, and a nurse cut off the view for a moment.

"I am ordering that an election be held as soon as possible after my death, and I'm sure Mr. Cool agrees." He spoke slowly, teeth clenched. "The nation faces—the world and this nation face an unprecedented historical challenge one month from now. We need a leader in place who is . . . is not Cool Moon Davis." He grimaced and his head lolled to one side. "Am I still alive?"

"Your brain is alive," a male voice said. "Not much else is."

"Thank you. In fact, I believe that you could pull a random citizen off the street and find him or her better able to deal with this crisis than Representative Davis. Or the late president, for that matter. Forgive me for speaking plainly, but—" The cube went dark, and faded back in with Carl Lamb and Davis, both looking a little pale.

"We seem to have lost—"

"The vice-president," Davis cut in, "has not been sworn into office . . ." He paused, listening. "And cannot yet speak as president. The laws of succession are plain, and there is no need for a special election."

"Chief Justice West is hurrying to Walter Reed as we speak," Lamb said. "He was en route to New York when this disaster struck."

|||||| Miguel Parando

The bartender realized he'd been cleaning the same glass for several minutes, ever since the emergency signal came from the cube. Someone broke a rack with a loud crash.

"Hey!" He spun around. "You show some respect?"

It was Leroy, a tall white guy, dealer. "I'm payin' for this table by the hour. You show me some respect." He lined up an easy shot and hit hard with a lot of draw, *whack*-thump, and the cue ball glided back to its starting place. "She was the worst president we ever had. So somebody finally punched her fuckin' ticket. What took so long, is what I wonder."

"You a hard fuckin' case, Leroy. She was a nice lady."

"Nice lookin'," said a short fat man at the bar. "I wouldn't go no farther than that. People in Washington didn't think much of her."

"You think much of them?"

A woman in a sparkly silver shift, blue eyes and black skin like the bartender's, smoothed a hundred-dollar bill on the bar. "I'd like a whiskey, Miguel." She put another bill on top. "And anybody else who wants one."

"When did you start drinkin', Connie?"

"Just now. A little ice?"

Leroy came up, emptied his glass, and put it on the bar. "I'll have one for her vaporized ass."

"Somebody gonna vaporize *your* ass someday, Leroy," Connie said. "You ought to get in some other business. The people you run with."

He pointed up at the cube, which was back to Cool Moon Davis. "Not as dangerous as those guys." Miguel poured four glasses, one for himself, and slid them over. "Or the frogs, if it's them that did it."

"That would be crazy," Miguel said. "The French don't want us in the war."

"So the damn Germans."

"Doesn't have to be a foreigner," Connie said. "People in this room who'd do it if the price was right."

"Ooh-woo." Leroy sipped the neat liquor. "My ears are burning."

"It's a hell of a thing," the short man said. "No matter who gets it. It's not American."

"Is now," Connie said. She looked back at the cube as it switched back to the Walter Reed hospital room.

‖‖‖‖ "Bobón" Mitchell

The cube room at the prison was crowded and silent, both rare. The warden had given permission to open the cells so that everyone could get to the news. Bobón and three other guards covered the doors, armed with tanglers, but nobody was going anywhere.

Bobón was still sorting out the murder he'd witnessed this morning. Not the first one, but Ybor was just a nice kid who hadn't hurt anyone. Why'd the warden have to drag him in there to watch? And now this damned thing.

Maybe it was all just a long nightmare. Maybe he would wake

up and it would just be another morning. But he'd felt that way before, and it never worked. Just in stories.

Why did so many people feel so bad about the president? Well, she's pretty and smart and powerful, and maybe people who like one don't like the other.

At least she never could of felt anything. That boy this morning went through all kinds of hell before he died. He couldn't get it out of his head.

The inmates knew. The way they looked at him, it's like they thought he did it. Not this time. Towelheads, watch out, though.

Davis had shut up and they switched to a local reporter.

Daniel Jordon

"—here at the International Plaza, we'd like to get the reaction from some of the students here, pardon me?"

The young man turned around and revealed a diamond-shaped scar on his cheek, a member of the Spoog gang. "I ain't no student fugoff," he mumbled in passing.

Great assignment. "Young man, could you give me your reaction to the tragedy in Washington?"

He was small and frail and red-eyed. "I really don't know anything. Was he crazy? He must have been crazy?"

"Some people have said he never got over his experience in the Gulf," Daniel prompted.

"I had an uncle there, and an aunt, and there's nothing wrong with them," he said, looking intently at the ground, and wandered away.

A pretty young woman approached, tailored suit, smile. "Pardon me, ma'am, could you—"

"No! Leave me alone!" She whacked him hard on the shoulder with her heavy purse, aiming for his head.

Like a message from the gods, a little voice in his ear said, "Switching to network in five."

Aurora

"Twelve pounds of C-9 is enough to demolish a good-sized house," a man in army fatigues was saying, the smoldering ruins in the background. "That was probably in case he got stopped at the door."

"Pauling might have used a little less explosive," Marya muttered *sotto voce*, "if he'd known he was going to give us Davis on a platter."

"Who's next in line if Davis dies?" Rory asked. "He looks like he'd blow over in a strong wind."

"Cabinet members, I think. It's not my beat. Maybe the president of the Senate, R. L. Osbourne. She's better than most."

As they found out in a few minutes, though, Senator Osbourne had been in the meeting room and was among the dead. So were the chief of staff, the attorney general, and the UN ambassador, as well as the administrators of Defense, Energy, the CIA, FEMA, and NASA. LaSalle liked to have all her cabinet together when she made her pronouncements, watching them for shifts of allegiance.

There would be a fundamental realignment of power in Washington, as soon as everyone came back. Marya had been right about the exodus, politicos prudently putting some distance between themselves and ground zero. Of course, the explanation was that they wanted to be with their families in this time of tragedy, and their families happened to be out of town, or at least were able to catch up with them there.

The vice-president didn't live through the hour. They watched the chief justice swear in Cool Moon Davis, inside a fast helicopter headed for Camp David. Then they saw a few minutes' coverage of the traditional riot in Washington, confined to a few blocks downtown, the looting and arson quickly discouraged by armored shock troops from the D.C. Police department and an air-mobile civil disturbance unit from the National Guard. No soldiers or police were hurt.

"I'm going to watch the rest of this at home," Rory said. "I feel like people are looking at me. You're welcome to come along."

"Thanks," Marya said. "I wouldn't mind getting away, either. Of course they'll call as soon as I get my shoes off."

They stopped by Pepe's table on their way out. "Don't bother coming in tomorrow," she said. "It'll just be chaos. I'll call if anything comes up."

Pepe

"Thanks, Rory." They nodded at each other for a moment, not able to say anything, and she left with the newsie.

"Will you come stay with me tonight?" Lisa Marie said hoarsely. "I just can't . . ."

"Sure." He was holding her hand, and briefly clasped it with his other. "Nobody should be alone now."

"I never even liked her," she said. "Did anybody you know?" Pepe shook his head. "But this is too horrible."

"It's not like America," Pepe said. "I guess it is *now,* but it's the sort of thing that happens in little dictatorships. Despot of the month."

"I wonder whether that old man will be able to hold things together." Davis was standing in a press room now, his hand to his ear, relaying his staff's answers to questions.

"He won't have to do much. I don't suppose he's made an unassisted decision in the past decade. If we make it through the next few hours, things will get sorted out."

"You think the Islamic Jihad might . . ."

"If I were him, I'd be more worried about the Democrats than the Muslims. They probably have a competency challenge all worked out. If I were them, I'd wait a decent interval, and give him a chance to do some really unforgivable things. Then start the impeachment process, more in sorrow than in anger."

She tilted her head at him. "You really know a lot about American politics."

"More than I do about Cuban. I had to study it for the blue card, and got kind of fascinated." He made a mental note to watch his step, not reveal too much sophistication. Lisa Marie was no danger, but there would be a lot of press and government around soon.

"Your aliens." She pointed at the cube.

Davis peered intently. "Would you repeat the question?" A reporter asked whether he intended to follow LaSalle's aggressive strategy toward the Coming.

He looked at her with robotic blankness for a long moment, an expression that was already familiar. "I don't want to say anything specific about that. Anything at all."

Aurora

"Anything at all. My people are looking into it." It was curious to hear Davis's voice coming out of her office. She thought she'd locked it. Rory had dropped by with Marya to see whether Norm might be there, not wanting to bike home through the rain. Inside, there were two strangers watching the new president on the wall cube.

"Hello? Can I do something for you?"

The short one clicked a remote and the president disappeared. They were in identical government-gray suits. The short one was bland, normal looking, but the other was over seven feet tall, his white hair trimmed to within a millimeter of his skull. She had seen him around, the past month.

They both produced identification. "I'm Special Agent Jerry Harp of the CIA," the giant said. The other identified himself as Howard Irving, FBI.

"You didn't just fly down," Marya said. "You've been here awhile. You were both at the—"

"We have no business with you, Ms. Washington," the FBI man said. "We would like to speak with Dr. Bell alone."

"I don't think so," Rory said. "This is my office, and I say who stays or goes. Unless I'm under arrest."

"We're only concerned about national security," the tall man said in low, measured tones. "Some of what we have to ask you about cannot be made public. Not yet, at least."

"I'll be down in the lounge," Marya said to Rory. "You've got my number."

"This won't take long," the FBI man said.

Marya said, "Sure," and he closed the door behind her.

"You talked with the president and Grayson Pauling this morning," the tall man said.

"Along with the governor, the chancellor, and the dean of science. I'm the small fish in the pond. Why aren't you talking to them?"

"In due course," the FBI man said. "This is like interviewing witnesses to an accident, or a crime scene. Best to get their separate impressions, before they talk to each other."

"Why don't you just play back the crystal? Surely they keep records."

The FBI man shook his head. "It was profoundly encrypted, scrambled. If you made a copy, you'll find it's just white noise."

"Unless you made an audio recording, independent of the VR projector/receiver," the CIA man said. "You didn't do that, did you?"

"In fact, it didn't occur to me. I'm really more of an astronomer than a spy." She sat down behind her desk and looked up at him. "How could they do that, though?"

"You question the president's right to—" the FBI man started.

"No, no—I mean *physically*. The signal had to be decrypted on this end. Why couldn't we make a crystal of it then?"

The tall one stared at her for a moment before answering. "That was from my shop. Before you spoke to the president the first time, we modified the equipment in your room. I don't understand the electronics, but if the signal from the White House is scrambled, you only see a transient virtual image. The signal that gets to the copy head is still scrambled.

"Of course the sound waves do exist. So an audio recorder that wasn't plugged into the system would have picked it up. A videocam would've gotten the sound, too, though the only image would be of you three actually in the room." He grimaced. "If we were as sneaky as people think we are, we could have bugged the room when we installed the rescrambler."

"But you didn't think we were that important."

"We didn't know the president's science adviser was a lunatic," the FBI man said. "We might have kept closer tabs on him."

"I'm not sure who the lunatic was," Rory said. "I'll leave that up to the history books."

"You don't mean you condone this mass assassination."

"Howard," the CIA man said, "let's not—"

"I don't *condone* it, but I can appreciate why the president's behavior drove Pauling to desperate measures."

"So you would have done it, too?" The FBI man was reddening. "If you could have killed the president, you would have done it, too?"

"That's a ridiculous question."

"Howard . . ."

"No, it's not! If you could have killed the president, would you?"

Rory considered refusing to answer. "It honestly wouldn't have crossed my mind. I would have liked to sit with her and talk, woman to woman. She was dangerously wrong."

"Dangerous enough to die?"

"Pauling thought so." She looked up at the CIA man. "So what do you want from me? It's been a long day already, and I want to go home."

"Just a description of what passed between the president and Grayson Pauling. There weren't any other administration people there, were there?"

"Not in view. Unless you count the governor of Florida. He was a better team player than Pauling. She used that term when she got exasperated at him: 'You used to be a team player' or something."

"They argued in front of you?" the CIA man said. "Please start at the beginning."

Rory went back to the original bombshell, LaSalle essentially saying that the secretary of defense had come up with this great idea. The conversation, or argument, had only lasted a few minutes, and she was pretty sure she remembered it accurately.

"So if you were to sum up Pauling's attitude, his mood?"

"He was quiet and patient. Quietly exasperated, like a teacher or a parent. Which drove LaSalle to the outburst of temper that ended the conversation."

"Quietly insane," the FBI man said.

"Why don't you go talk to the governor?" Rory snapped. "He'll agree with you, and then we can all go home." She turned back to the tall man. "I've heard that people often become remarkably calm once they've made up their mind to commit suicide. He must have known about the noon meeting; I suppose he may have already decided he had to die."

"And destroy the government." The CIA man shook his head. "You may be right. In another hundred years, maybe less, people will see this as an act of supreme sacrifice."

"Maybe one month," Rory said. "When the aliens don't destroy us out of hand."

"Which they may still do." He checked his watch. "Almost time for Whittier, Howard."

"What, with her you made an appointment?"

He nodded. "We don't have a key to *her* office," the FBI man said.

She followed them down the hall and turned into the lounge, where Marya was watching the cube, by herself, snacking on cheese and crackers from the machine.

Marya

"That didn't take long." She offered Rory some cheese and crackers.

Rory shook her head—"No appetite"—and got a ball of juice from the wall dispenser and poured it into a plastic cup. "Not much to tell them. That conference this morning didn't go five minutes, and that's what they were interested in—evidently the White House scrambling is pretty sophisticated; the CIA didn't have a clue what went on, and they're the ones who installed the descrambler here."

"You told them the truth, of course."

Rory eased back onto a worn couch. "Yeah, that our late great president was a demented fruitcake, which seems to have been news to the FBI man."

"They ask you about Pauling? That's what CNN's obsessing on now."

"A little. The CIA guy even admitted that someday he might be seen as a hero, a martyr."

"That's not what they're saying here. They've dug up men and women who were in the service with him, going on about how fanatical and unpredictable he was."

"That's probably why LaSalle picked him. Like unto like." She took a sip of juice and frowned at it. "Warm. He didn't come on that way, though. He was the reasonable one, trying to keep dear Carly from courting votes by destroying the human race."

Marya looked at her watch. "They want me to do a five-minute spot sometime today. It won't be live; we can wait awhile."

Rory dumped the cup in the recycler next to the couch. "Crew downstairs?"

"Better be."

"Let's just do it and go put our feet up at my place. Turn on the cube and watch Washington get nuked."

"Is there anything you don't want me to ask you?"

"No." Rory stood and stretched. "God, no. I have a feeling truth is going to be in short supply for a while. Anything we can do to keep Davis from launching those weapons, we ought to do."

"They didn't tell you not to talk about this morning?"

"I don't really give a shit. What can they do to me?" She pushed open the door. "Rhetorical question. They can pull off my toenails and make me eat them. But I don't think they will."

They took the elevator down to the first floor, where two cameramen were watching CNN on a small portable cube. "Let's gear up, guys. Five-minute spot."

She looked at the large flatscreen that provided the interview backdrop. It had the logo of the Committee on the Coming, two concentric *C*s with a question mark inside. "Don't want this one, Deeb. You got one of the White House ruins?"

"Just take a minute. I'll run back and snatch one from CNN. You want to thumbprint it?"

"Sure." When the picture appeared, Marya put her thumb in a box in the lower right corner. A list of options appeared and she touched the first one, onetime reproduction rights. It chimed and the list and box disappeared.

Rory was already seated at one of two black leather chairs that faced one another across a low table in front of a blue screen. Marya whistled at the cameras. "Position A, all three." She stepped aside while one of the small cameras rolled onto its mark. The man who wasn't Deeb set down glasses of ice water.

She dropped into the other chair and looked at herself in the screen, patting her hair reflexively. She could be a frazzled mess and the editor would automatically fix the image. "No pressure, but let's try for one take and bust outta here. Deeb, when I look at you, maybe four minutes thirty, we want the logo back, and then segue into the deep space shot."

"Got it," he said. "Editor on line now."

"Good." She took a page of scribbled notes out of a breast pocket and smoothed it on the table. She looked at the wall clock behind Rory. "Eight seconds." She shook her head. "No, wait. Cameras off. We're two minutes from the hour. Rory, if I can clear it, do you mind if we go live?"

"I'm a teacher. I usually go live."

She smiled and pushed a button on her phone. "Fez, this is Marya. Scramble." She pushed another button. "Loud and clear. Look, you got the feds there? Figures. Look, I've got a White House angle that we don't want reviewed; they'd gut it or even cancel it." She nodded. "Dr. Bell down here talked with LaSalle and Pauling this morning. Can you give me five live ninety seconds after the hour?" She laughed. "Owe you one, babe." She set the phone down and looked at the cameraman. "You didn't hear that, right?"

"Hear what?" Deeb said.

"Yeah, well, go take a leak for about a minute. Be back by two." They hustled out. "Rory, the broadcasts are going through a White House censor with a five-second delay. What they can do in New York is accidentally push the wrong buttons and leave the room. So this interview, scheduled for seven, comes in live instead, on a circuit that's not controlled by the White House remote.

"I don't know how long we'll have before they're able to cut us off. So I'll ask the most important questions first."

"We might not even get on," Rory said. "This room is probably bugged by the CIA."

"Hmm. They probably wouldn't have anybody live listening in, though. We'll find out." The two men came back in and she whistled the cameras to start. She looked at the main camera. "We're going to take five minutes, commencing fourteen-oh-one-thirty."

Rory twisted around to look at the clock and then settled into an interviewee posture.

Marya faced the camera and her expression became serious, then grim: "Good evening. This is Marya Washington coming to you from Gainesville, Florida. This afternoon I talked with Professor Aurora Bell, who is chief administrator of the Committee on the Coming.

"This morning, Dr. Bell had a VR conference call from the White House. Were there other witnesses to the call, Professor?"

"Oh, yes. The governor of Florida, the chancellor of this university, and . . . another professor. And science adviser Grayson Pauling."

"Did anything happen between the president and Pauling that might have presaged today's tragic events?"

"In retrospect, yes." She shook her head at the memory. "She blew up at him. At all of us, actually."

"What did you say?"

"LaSalle talked about orbiting three antimissile weapons, to destroy the alien spaceship if it made a wrong move. I think it was the DOD's idea, but she was behind it a hundred percent.

"This was *before* the new message came in. Even so, we argued that it would be suicide. The aliens' technology is so superior to ours that we would be like mice attacking an elephant. Ants."

Rory's phone was buzzing; she took it out of her pocket and skimmed it across the room.

"And Pauling was on your side?"

"As any reasonable person would be. She was annoyed at him, and then openly angry. Pauling implied that the rationale for orbiting these weapons was to have them flying over Europe. Over France, in case we did decide to enter the war. If the war happens."

"Do you agree?"

"I don't know much about politics. If I were French I'd be nervous. But the issue isn't Earth politics."

"Especially in light of the new message."

"If they believe it. The president didn't."

"You know that for a fact?"

"Oh yes. She called me back, right after the new message came out."

"Really!"

"She was mad as a hornet. 'I don't know how you did it, but it's not going to work.' "

"Well, the timing is interesting."

"Yes, but nobody on Earth could have done it. The signal started our way long before the conference call."

"We're off," Deeb said. "We had a second of white noise, and they cut to a commerical."

"Well, shit. Erase it back to Dr. Bell saying 'conference call,' and we'll continue as if nothing's happened. Okay?"

"Sure," Rory said. "It might be aired eventually."

"By historians."

"In five," Deeb said, holding out five fingers and folding them one at a time.

"Well, suppose the president were right, and it was a hoax. The hoaxers—one of whom would have to be you, or someone else who witnessed the conference call, could have had the second message made up long ago, and just signaled for it to be sent."

"But not from way beyond the solar system. It would take more than a day for the signal to get there, and more than a day for the message to get back. Parallax on the signal—comparing the angle of it from two different positions—proves how far away the aliens are."

"But a really paranoid person would point out that we have to take your word for that—yours and some other scientists' on the Moon. They could be in on it, too."

Rory smiled. "You could have said that, a month or two ago. But now it's close enough for two sites on Earth to triangulate it. It's a little fantastic to think of a conspiracy involving every astronomer in the world." Off-camera, Marya nodded to Deeb.

"Don't think nobody will suggest it, Dr. Bell. So . . . would you have any advice for President Davis?"

"Only the obvious: listen to the experts. LaSalle's problem, and finally her undoing, was that she surrounded herself with yes-men, and then followed their advice when they parroted her views."

"Pauling the exception."

"Which became obvious. She might have saved her life by replacing him. Though as Pauling said in his . . . suicide note, she would have died a month later, along with the rest of humanity."

"And suppose Davis does follow her example, and orbits these weapons?"

"I suspect the aliens won't even bother demonstrating with Phobos. They'll just destroy us out of hand."

"A terrible thing to contemplate . . . thank you, Dr. Bell, for being with us on this strange and awful day. This is Marya Washington, reporting from Gainesville, Florida."

"Out," Deeb said.

"Just wrap it and send it on up with no comment," Marya said. "As if."

"You're going to be in real trouble over this," Rory said.

"All of us. Maybe they'll put up a statue someday." She shook a pill out of a vial and took it with the ice water.

She leaned back. "Off the record. It could work, couldn't it?"

"The maser weapon? It's never really been tested."

"I mean in principle. It goes at the speed of light, right? The alien ship wouldn't have any warning."

"Assuming there's only one alien ship, and the beam doesn't miss, and they don't have any defense against twenty-first-century weapons. A lot of assumptions."

"Just trying to look at the bright side."

"Oh, yeah." Rory crossed the room and picked up her buzzing phone. "Buenas."

It was the chancellor. "Rory, what did you do? The governor's been on the phone screaming at me. He wants you fired immediately, yesterday!"

She played dumb. "Because of this morning?"

"He just saw you on the cube. Says you betrayed him and the country and the sacred memory of the president. Divulged top secret information."

"I don't have clearance to *get* top secret information. Was this an interview?"

"Yes, with that black New York woman."

"Well, I did an interview. But it won't be aired until seven o'clock tonight."

"That might be what they told you. But the governor sure as hell saw it."

"So I'm fired? Just like that?"

"No, no. But I have to give you a sabbatical, get you out of the public eye. Out of the line of fire."

"No longer head of the committee?"

"No. In fact, off the committtee altogether. You have other

things to pursue—go do them until mid-January. Full pay. You don't have any classes this semester?"

"No, because—"

"So do some research. Preferably somewhere far away. Turn your phone off and disappear."

"Is that an order, Mal?"

"You know it's not. Just advice, good advice." His voice was tight. "For all of us, Rory. You should've heard the governor. *Our budget's in committee!* He's liable to do anything."

"Okay, I'm out. Won't make a fuss over it. Can I choose my own successor?"

"Sure, of course. Thanks, Rory. I know you could fight it."

"And win. Academic freedom." She took a deep breath. "Pepe Parker would be the logical successor. I'll see whether he wants the job."

"I owe you for this, Rory. I haven't seen the interview my-self. . . ."

"The governor's probably right. I was not respectful of the late president. But then she was a lunatic."

"Rory . . ."

"I'm off-camera. Are you?"

"Sure."

"I'm coming to think that Pauling was a brave man. He didn't see any other option, so he gave his life to save the world. You were *there*, Mal. Am I wrong?"

There was a short silence. "No. I don't think you're wrong. But don't ask me to back you up, not until after the governor signs the budget."

"Understandable. I'll call Pepe." She pushed the "off" button without saying good-bye and stood there looking at the phone. The other three were looking at her.

"You got the axe?" Marya said.

"Yeah. Until the aliens go home or the world ends, or what-ever." She punched two keys.

Pepe

His phone buzzed but he didn't answer it. His boss was on the cube, committing political suicide.

"... nobody on Earth could have done it. The signal started our way long before the conference call—" The cube went blank and Carl Lamb appeared. "That was Professor Aurora Bell, in a transmission—" Pepe stabbed a finger at the phone. "Buenas?"

"Pepe . . ." It was Rory. "The shit has really hit the fan."

"I just saw it."

"The governor wants me tarred and feathered and run out of town on a rail. You want my job?"

"You make it sound so attractive."

"I'm serious. Mal Barrett just put me on sabbatical indefinitely. Nobody else but you can run the thing."

He knew that, of course. "Sure, okay. Where are you now?"

"Up at the office."

"I'll be right up. Buenas?"

"Sí, buenas." He turned off the phone and slipped it back into his pocket.

"What was that?" Lisa Marie said.

"My boss. Ex-boss." He finished off his beer and set the mug down with a thump. "Looks like I've been promoted." He took out a card and slid it through the pay slot. "I've gotta run. Don't know how long this will be. I will be with you tonight, though, as soon as I can get free. Call when I know."

She nodded. "Dinner if you can. I'll get us some steaks or something."

"Deal." He kissed her on the cheek. "Buenas."

"Sí, buenas. Muy buena suerte."

He went a block and a half before he realized he'd left his

umbrella back at the café. It wasn't raining hard, though, and Lisa Marie could use it.

This was how it happened. Rory sacrificed her job, making sure the world knew the truth. So he would be standing down at the Cape with President Davis, to meet the supposed aliens.

He passed a woman who was sitting on a park bench, sobbing, her face in her hands. Her white dress, saturated with rain, revealed her alluring figure. He vaguely recognized her—a student?—and slowed to say something, but then went on. She didn't want company in her grief.

Gabrielle

She heard his steps hesitate—please stop, talk to me, hold me—but he didn't stop, would she? Probably, it didn't happen all that often, you come home and find your cat lying dead, and then the president and all those others, she had poor Happy's body in a shoebox and didn't know what to do with it.

Am I being punished for sin, is my mother's God really up there counting the times I put a camera up my cunt to pay the bills? No, cats die, presidents die, snap out of it, you know better, you know better. Her nose was running and she didn't have anything in her purse; she blew into her wet hand and scraped the mucus onto the bottom of the park bench, then splashed her palm in the puddle at her feet, and rubbed her nose hard against her forearm.

Aliens dropping out of the sky, a science father figure blows up himself and everybody in the room, a perfectly good cat drops over dead, and I'm ten minutes late for an anal-intercourse shoot. Which I'm not going to do. Even if it means my job. Louis is gentle but he's just too big around. It's not the proper use for that opening; things are supposed to come out, not go in.

"Oh, sweetheart. Things can't be that bad."

She wiped her eyes and looked up. It was the old lady with the shopping cart. She sat down next to her. "What is it that's so bad?"

She looked into the old kind face. "My cat died."

"Oh, my." She lifted a corner of the sodden shoebox and looked inside. "What was her name?"

"His name. Happy."

"Never had a boy cat. Lots of girl cats. You want one?"

"Not now, no. Thank you, no."

"You got cat people and dog people, you know? My husband, he was a dog person. One reason I had to get rid of him."

Gabrielle smiled. "He take the dog with him?"

"No, that would be cruel. I kept the dog, even though he smelled bad." She leaned close and whispered. "He had gas. Both of them did."

Gabrielle wiped her eyes. "How long ago was that?"

"Thirty-some years, I guess. Buried him when Hull was president. Hardly anybody had the cube back then."

"You still think about the poor thing."

"Oh, yeah. Buried him under a big piece of plywood out in the swamp. Mall there now."

"You couldn't just bury him in the backyard?"

"No. Gosh and golly. Way too big. Laws, too."

"There are laws about burying dogs?"

She nodded slowly. "Some kinds." She looked over Gabrielle's shoulder. "Afternoon, Officer."

Rabin

He touched the brim of his plastic cap. "Good afternoon, Suzy Q. Are you ladies all right?"

"Nobody's all right, Officer. Nobody's all wrong, nobody's all right. We all of us stuck in the middle."

He smiled a little. "It's a hard day for everybody. Can't I give you a ride to the shelter?"

"We gone through that before, Officer. I don't want nobody preachin' at me."

"You could stand it for a little while. It's a roof over your head."

"Ain't nothin' wrong with my *head*."

He held up a hand. "I just don't want you to get pneumonia again. You remember two years ago?"

"I remember *eighty* years ago. Don't you worry about me."

"She won't catch penumonia from exposure," the beautiful woman said. She touched the old woman's hand. "But he's right. You should get out of this rain."

"You should, too, ma'am. You're not exactly dressed for this."

"No." She startled him by taking off her hair and wringing it out. "What I'm dressed for is getting fucked in the ass."

"What?"

"People do it," Suzy Q. said in her defense. "Where you been all these years?"

Rabin swallowed a couple of times. "Sure. But you're wet. You're cold and wet."

The beautiful woman patted her hair into place and favored him with a brilliant smile. "It's a living. Not the cold and wet. The other."

"You aren't a whore, are you?" Suzy Q. said.

"No. No, I'm an actress. And a medical student." She looked up at Rabin. "No laws broken. I just do cube for the Institute of Sexual Studies here." Still smiling, she started to cry. "Could you do me a favor? Could you do something with my cat?"

"¿Perdón?"

She pushed the shoebox an inch toward him. "My cat died. He just died, with the president. I don't know what to do with him. And I don't want to go to work and I wish it would *stop raining*."

He carefully picked up the sodden box. "Sure, don't worry about it. But will you do something for me?"

"Sure. That's what I do, is do things for men."

"Get yourself and Suzy inside somewhere. I don't want her to die on my shift."

"Okay. Is that a deal, Suzy?"

"Okay. Let's get a cuppa coffee." They headed toward Main Street, the beautiful woman pushing the cart. She wasn't wearing underwear, and her buttocks clung to the translucent fabric, rolling. Rabin's heterosexual fraction watched with interest. What would it be like to do that with a woman? Just different scenery, he supposed.

His civilian phone rang. He wiggled it out of his pocket. "Yeah?"

"Qabil, this is Felicity."

"What?" The dispatcher? Why wasn't she calling on the shoulder unit?

"I'm downstairs, on the pay phone. Look, you're friends with Norman Bell."

"Well, I . . ."

"You're friends. He and his wife have to disappear *right now*. I was just up in the boss's office and he got a call from some FBI guy. The feds are gonna pick them up tonight and take them to Washington for questioning."

"About what?"

"You didn't see the cube? Of course not. Look, they're suspected of being foreign agents. For France or her allies."

"What bullshit!"

"Yeah, and they know it is. He joked about it; they just want to lock her up and throw away the key. It's serious, Qabil. A presidential order. From that senile old Indian."

"Allah. Thanks, Felicity. I'll call him right away."

Norman

Exasperated, Norman hit the "save" button on the Roland and touched the phone screen. It stayed blank.

"Turn off your house," said a voice he didn't recognize. Another blackmailer?

"House, turn yourself off for thirty minutes." It chimed. "Okay. Who are you?"

There was a click, the distorter going off, and a heavy sigh. "Norm, it's Qabil. There's real trouble."

"Yeah? ¿Qué pasa?"

"Is Rory home?"

"No. I expect her any minute."

"You have to pack up and leave as soon as she gets home. The FBI's going to pick you up tonight, take you to Washington and bury you."

"What, that damned interview?"

"I guess; I didn't see it. They claim you're agents, working for France."

"For *France*? We've never even *been* there."

"Well, you can stay at home and talk it over with them, or you can be missing. That's what I'd advise. It's not like the cube; these guys are a law unto themselves."

"So I've heard. How long do we have?"

"Maybe until dark. I'd leave as soon as possible. Do you have cash?"

"A little."

"What I'd do . . . take a cab down to Oaks and max out the ATM, then get on the first train to Archer. From there you can use cash to get anywhere, short trips. Go to Canada or Mexico, someplace you don't need a passport."

"But she didn't break any *law*."

"All I know is that the FBI is after her. I think they can find a law."

"Jesus. When it rains, it pours."

"Don't worry about the rain. Just move as fast as you can."

Norman had to smile. How long did you have to live in a country before you picked up the catchphrases? "Okay. If Rory agrees, we'll be out long before dark."

"If she doesn't agree, you leave by yourself, okay? All this shit in Washington."

"Sure. I'll get packing. Buenas." Qabil said good-bye and Norman turned off the phone. Of course he wouldn't really leave Rory behind. Both or neither of them would go to Washington. To be buried. In shit? He wondered what Qabil meant by that.

He'd pack for both of them, though. He set out two bags, small enough for carry-on, on the bed, and neatly stacked warm-weather clothing in each. He assumed Rory would rather go to Mexico, for the winter, than Canada. Besides, she didn't speak Canadian.

With both of them packed, he carefully lifted out the contents of Rory's bag. Let her check through and make changes.

She should be here by now, he thought. He went to the phone and punched RR, Rory roving.

"Buenas?" No picture, of course.

"Where are you, darling?"

"In a cab. Home in two minutes. Where did you think I'd be?"

"Just making sure."

"How are you taking it?"

"Um . . . not on the phone. Talk to you in two minutes." He pushed the "off" button and rummaged through the drawer under the phone for a joint. It was old and dry. He found a match and lit it. Took one puff and stabbed it out in the sink. Wrong direction. He poured a glass of port and sipped it, waiting, thinking.

This might not have anything to do with the interview. The FBI might have linked him and Rory to whatever that superweapon was, that may or may not have been an invention of Pepe's.

The doorknob rattled and Rory knocked. Of course her thumb-print didn't unlock it unless the house was on. He went down the hall and opened the door.

Aurora

"What, is the house off?"

Norm held the door open and shut it behind her. "Yeah. The shit has hit."

She nodded. "I know. Goddamn governor on top of everything else. But why the house?"

"The governor?"

"Yeah. Why's the house off?"

"The FBI. What did the governor do?"

Rory rubbed her wet hair with both hands. "The governor got me fired, you know that? Did he call the FBI?"

"Fired?"

"You didn't know." Norman opened both hands and made a noise. "The governor leaned on Mal because of an interview I did this morning. So I'm on sabbatical. What does the FBI have to do with it?"

They were in the breakfast nook. "Sit down. Let me get you something to drink."

She sat down. "Just water. What's the FBI? The assassination?"

"Somebody got assassinated?"

She kneaded her forehead. "Of course. Why would you know? The president and all her cabinet, killed in a bomb blast. The vice-president, too."

"My God. Bombed! Was it France?"

"No. Grayson Pauling carried a briefcase full of explosive into a cabinet meeting. Suicide-murder."

"Pauling."

"He was serious about changing the agenda. Lunatic, martyr, I don't have it sorted out. What about the FBI now?"

He got a bottle of water out of the refrigerator. "Qabil called."

"Oh, good. That's all we need."

"No. That's not it. He found out, as a cop, down at the station, he heard the FBI is coming to get you. Take you to Washington."

"Oh, shit." She took the water but didn't drink. "They can't do that. I didn't break any law."

Norm sat across from her with a small glass of wine. "I don't know. Maybe we could talk our way out of it. What Qabil said is they think we're agents for France—"

"We've never *been* to France!"

"Verdad. I think they know that. It's just an excuse."

"Was it before or after the assassination?"

"Just now. I think Qabil assumed I knew about the president dying."

She shook her head. "State of emergency, I guess. But do you really think they can just call us spies and lock us up?"

"I don't know. That's what Qabil thinks. And he's sort of in their line of work."

"Oh, hell. Double hell." She slid the water bottle back and forth in a small arc. "Is that port you're drinking?"

"Get you some?"

"Ah, no." She threw out the water and went to the refrigerator and squeezed herself a tumblerful of the plonk. "So what does your boyfriend recommend that we do?"

"He's not my *boy*friend. He's just looking out for us."

"I'm sorry." She sat down and leaned into her hands; her voice was muffled. "It's been such a day."

"And it's just begun."

She sipped the wine. "Qabil said?"

"He said we should disappear. Before night. Stay on local transport so we can pay cash, and make our way to a country that doesn't need a passport."

"Canada, Mexico, the Caribbean?"

"You'll do it?"

"I'd like about thirty seconds to think about it."

"Go ahead. I'm going to pack some music cubes."

"Packing? You'd leave without me?"

"Of course not. I just want to be ready if you decide to go. I can hear the hounds yapping." He found a cheap plastic box that held a hundred cubes, and started at the beginning, Antonini.

"Oh, hell. Put some jazz in there for me." She stood up. "I'll pack some clothes."

"I already put out a few things. Warm weather?"

"Yeah. Canada doesn't really appeal."

He heard her opening and closing drawers, slamming them. "How about Mexico?"

"Cuba's closer," she said. "Some stuff I wanted to check there, too."

He pulled a couple of handfuls of cubes from her jazz collection, totally random. "Cuba it is." They would have to avoid the

Orlando-Miami monorail, unfortunately; that was ticketed like a plane. Have to zigzag their way down.

He took the cube box and a small player into the bedroom and put them in his bag. Rory was almost packed, rattling around in the bathroom. "You have the sunscreen?" she said.

"Both kinds, yeah. Though I guess we could buy it in Cuba."

Rory came out with a plastic bag of toiletries, put it in the travel bag, and zipped it closed. "So. You ready?"

"Yes." He held out a hand. "I'll take your bag."

"I can—"

"On my bicycle. We can't risk a cab."

"Oh, joy." She handed him the bag. "Mother said if I married you I was in for a rough ride. But bicycling through the rain in December?"

"Fleeing the FBI. Sort of strains your sense of humor, doesn't it."

It wasn't too bad, though. The rain was a cool mist, and they only had to go a mile, to the Oaks substation.

They left the bicycles unlocked, trusting that it wouldn't take long for thieves to remove that particular bit of evidence of their flight, and walked into the venerable, not to say crumbling, mall.

It had seen better days, most of them more than a half century before. A whole block of stores had been demolished, their walls knocked down, to make space for a huge flea market, and that drew more customers than the low-rent purveyors of cheap imported clothing and sexual paraphernalia.

There was a weird youth subculture that had taken over one part—the beatniks, who dressed in century-old fashion and smoked incessantly while listening to century-old music. Rory liked the sound of it as they walked by, but it made Norman cringe. They had to go through there to get to the ATMs.

They thumbed two machines to get the maximum from different accounts, four thousand dollars each. The machines didn't hold any denomination larger than one hundred, though, so they wound up with a conspicuously large wad of bills.

Rory looked around. "Uh-oh." She turned back to the machine. "There's a guy staring at us. From the café."

Norm glanced sideways. "Yeah, I see him in Nick's sometimes. Always writing in that notebook."

"Yeah. Now that you mention it."

‖‖‖‖ The historian

They don't look like the kind of people who come down to the Oaks, he thought, familiar from somewhere. The Greek restaurant. He drank off the rest of his strong sweet coffee while it was still warm. He snapped his fingers twice to get the waitress's attention—a very local custom—and shook a pseudo-Camel out of its package. He lit it with a wooden match and got a sudden rush of THC. Real tobacco must have been something.

He had been staring for a half hour at the image of the *Gainesville Sun* for 24 November 1963, the last time a president had been assassinated. Maybe getting back to work would cut through the feelings of despair and helplessness. He had gotten up to the year before the year he was born.

He tried to ignore the old-fashioned but seductive Dave Brubeck chordings and rhythms, and toggled through the two old newspaper articles that were relevant to this part:

> *Local government found itself in a condition beyond chaos when, in the fall of 2022, the mayor, two city commissioners, and the entire county commission wound up in jail for violating a cluster of real-estate laws, mostly about zoning and eminent domain— but really about bribery on a stunning scale. The result of their machinations, the Alachua/Archer monorail, changed Gainesville irreversibly, in ways that not everybody agreed were bad.*
>
> *City revenues declined as industries moved north to Alachua*

and south to Archer, for cheap real estate and tax relief. But the net result was to give the city back to the university, making it again the college town it had been for most of the twentieth century.

There was a short but intense crime wave in 2023, which led to a five-year suspension of the fraternity system at UF, when it was discovered that four of the fraternities had aligned themselves with individual street gangs. They would pinpoint lucrative robbing sites and then help the boys hide and "fence" the stolen goods. In exchange, they took a percentage of the ill-gotten gains, and bought alcohol for the boys (at the time, the drinking age in Florida was twenty-one), as well as illegal ammunition, which is what led to the discovery. The federal program of "tagging" ammunition had begun secretly, and the so-called Gunfight at the Gainesville Garage was one of the first times it had been used as evidence.

Two policemen and five members of a gang called the Hairballs died in the altercation, and the gang's ammunition was traced to a member of the Kappa Kappa Psi fraternity, who, under interrogation, detailed the depth and breadth of the fraternity's involvement with the gang, and implicated the three other fraternities. . . .

in December

An unprecedented heat wave scorched Australia and New Zealand, thousands of people and millions of cattle and sheep dying in the heat and drought. Canada and Alaska and northern Europe all suffered protracted blizzard conditions, which took hundreds of lives.

The war in Europe entered into an uneasy truce, the peace talks moving from Warsaw to sunny Rome, as troops on various borders scraped ice and snow off their war machines, and then went back to huddle around fires. The peace was partly due to logistics—no one was really prepared to fight in an unrelenting blizzard—and partly due to apocalyptic suspense as the calendar counted down to the Coming.

Preachers and priests and even a cautious pope saw a connection between the hellish weather and the Coming. The aliens had not denied a connection with God and Jesus, and there were appropriate prophecies in the Bible, as well as a lesser authority, Nostradamus. In his prophetic quatrains, the farthest in the future where he had predicted a specific year was 2055, the year the aliens were going to land. Writing in 1555, he said:

For five hundred years more one will take notice of him
Who was the ornament of his time:
Then suddenly a great revelation will be made,
Which will make the people of that century well pleased.

One "ornament of his time" was Nostradamus's contemporary Thomas More ("for five hundred years *more* . . ."), who wrote *Utopia*. To some, this was proof positive that the aliens were going to bring about a heaven on earth. Of course that word "more" doesn't appear in the French—*"De cinq cents ans plus compte l'on tiendre"*—but the people who write for the tabloids probably didn't know about that, and certainly didn't care.

A musical group that had renamed itself 55 Alive went to the top of the charts with a convoluted song, "We're Coming," that used all of the words of the Nostradamos message recombined into a message of hope, which could be interpreted in either secular or religious terms.

The survival stores came back, and merchants who didn't overstock for the two-week wonder made a quick and large profit. It did take a pessimistic kind of optimism, or vice versa, to assume that the aliens would leave humanity alone, but humanity would turn on itself.

The United States launched its killer satellite in a state of total secrecy, which lasted less than a day. An international coalition of scientists and engineers came forth with absolute proof that the deed had been done. They demanded that the weapon be destroyed in place. President Davis called their documents "a bucket of bullshit," saying it was just a weather satellite, and God knows we could use a few.

A gallup showed that 62 percent of French citizens considered the launch an act of war. In America, only 18 percent believed the president was telling the truth, but 32 percent "stood behind his actions."

During the month of December, the leading cause of death in the United States was suicide.

Aurora and Norman felt conspicuous in their flight; almost all of the trains were nearly empty, most of the nation staying home glued to the cube. There were plenty on the Miami-to-Key West "Havana Special," though; people hoping to lose themselves in that island's peculiar attractions.

Of all possible points of exit from the United States, Key West was probably the best one for people who didn't want to be identified. The same fine old Italian families who controlled gambling and prostitution in Havana owned the boats that made the ninety-mile trip, as well as the dock where people stepped aboard the boats, in total anonymity, safe even from overhead orbital surveillance. Some patrons bragged about their "Havana weekends"; others claimed to have had a great time at Disney World.

Aurora and Norman bypassed the fleshpots of the capital city and found a modest apartment in the nearby fishing village Cojímar. Norman rented a keyboard and MIDI recorder and continued to refine his composition. Aurora had her own research project, which took her all over the island. Fortunately, travel was dirt cheap compared to America.

By December 21, orbital telescopes were able to form an image of the approaching spacecraft. It looked like a cross with a gamma-ray star in the center, which made some people rejoice, but their joy was premature. The next day it was obvious that the image was of four tail fins surrounding the exhaust of a very hot engine. The aliens were coming in tail first, braking, the way a human spaceship would.

The gamma-ray beacon disappeared on the twenty-fourth, as the ship abruptly changed course, detouring toward Mars with a profligate waste of fuel. It swung around the red planet, as promised, and cracked Phobos in two. Hubble III gave a tiny image of the ship passing close, and a bright flare. Then the two halves of the small moon tumbled apart.

No word of warning or welcome. They just kept coming, decelerating.

On the morning of the thirty-first, when they were about a half-million miles away—twice the distance to the Moon—four large satellites were disintegrated in the course of one second. One of them was Davis's weapon. The aliens broke silence long enough to apologize, saying they couldn't tell which one it was, hoping none of them were inhabited.

Rory saw the news when she got off the Mafia boat in Key West. She was about to retrace their circuitous route. Norm had obeyed her request that he stay in Cuba for the time being.

There were things she had to know.

January 1

Pepe

He had slept through the early evening, and dropped by Lisa Marie's party long enough to have one glass of champagne and watch the ball drop over Times Square. He had kissed her good-bye and gone to the office.

He snapped on the lights and was going through his top drawer, looking for the stimulants that would keep him sharp for the next couple of days, when there was a light knock on the open door.

He looked up. "Aurora?"

She nodded and sat down in a chair by the door.

"Where have you been? We've—"

"Cabo de Cristobal. Cojímar, Holguín, Havana."

"¿Y?"

"I want to know who you are."

He didn't blink. "I am who I am."

"Who you are, who you work for, and how you managed to wind up in charge of this enterprise, whatever it actually is. You might explain the spaceship part, too."

"Or what? What will you do?"

"What we used to say was 'I'll blow the whistle on you.' Expose you."

"But you say you don't know what I am."

"What you *aren't* is Pepe Parker. There is no such animal. Birth records stolen from Cabo de Cristobal. Grade school burned to the ground. High school records destroyed in the Outage of thirty-nine—"

"Everybody's were."

"Most of them were restored. There's no actual record of your existence until you began graduate work at the University of Havana. After your doctorate, you got a blue card and came here."

Pepe realized he was sweating. He wiped his face with a handkerchief. This couldn't be happening.

"So tell me what's going on. Or I'll blow the whole thing up."

"You can't do that."

"I can indeed. And if something happens to me, Norman—"

"No, no. I wasn't threatening you. What I mean is you *mustn't*."

"I'm willing to be convinced. You could start by telling me who you work for."

"Humanity. I work for all humanity."

"That's no answer."

The phone buzzed and he pushed the button. A dim gray picture of a man in NASA fatigues who spoke over the low thrum of a helicopter. "Dr. Parker? We're closing on Gainesville. Be on your roof in four or five minutes?"

"Gracias. I'll be waiting."

They signed off. "So you're going to the Cape," Rory said.

"As you would have. I'm sorry I can't invite you along."

"I'm still a wanted woman?"

"They call about once a week, the FBI. They've never explained anything." He found the pills and popped one, crunching down on its bitterness. "All-nighter, I'm afraid."

"I guess I could go to the FBI. Tell them what I know, what I don't know."

"No! Please!" He snapped open his attaché case and checked its contents. "Let's make a deal."

"I'm listening."

"Just watch what happens today. Afterward, we can talk forever about it. If you want to blow your whistle then, I won't stop you." He closed the case. "Right now I have to catch that helicopter and go join the festivities." He reached in his pocket and pulled out a key ring. "Here—stay at my place. You know where it is?"

"Still over at Creekside?"

"Yes, 203. Your place might not be safe."

"Okay. You've got a deal. But tell me this . . . do you know who they are? The aliens?"

"I . . . I really can't say."

"But they aren't actually aliens, are they?"

He looked at her silently for a second. "As alien as me."

They both heard the whisper of the helicopter approaching, the pitch of the blades deepening as it landed. He kissed her on the cheek and ran out the door.

Aurora

As the helicopter faded, she crossed the hall to her old office. It was locked, but her old key worked. She said, "Lights."

Nothing had changed. Neater than possible, but she had straightened up for the expected interview. A layer of dust.

Would she ever work here again? She'd know in a few days.

Her shelves of old books seemed untouched. On impulse, she took the latest acquisition, the volume of century-old photographs from *Life* magazine, turned off the lights, and locked the door behind her.

It was about a mile down to Creekside. She was tired, but didn't dare use a cab; most of them weren't set up to take cash, and the ones that did took pictures of their suspicious customers. But at least the sidewalks wouldn't be deserted, not with revelers rolling from party to party.

How many people, though, were sitting at home, terrified, waiting to die? On her way downhill, she passed two churches and a mosque, and they were all doing a brisk business.

A block from Creekside, she stopped at a convenience store and bought an overpriced bottle of domestic champagne.

It came out of a barrel of ice water. The clerk dried it off for her and put it in a bag. "I hope we have something to celebrate tomorrow," he said. "I hope we're *here* tomorrow."

"I wouldn't worry about that," she said. "If they wanted to destroy us, they would have done it by now."

He nodded and took her cash, and clumsily counted out change. "Do I know you from somewhere, ma'am?"

"No. Just passing through."

She crossed the bridge over Hogtown Creek and hurried into the apartment building. There were a lot of people sitting, partying, on the grassy banks of the creek, and she didn't want to be recognized.

She tried four entrances before she found the one with P. PARKER, 203. Whatever his real name was.

She'd expected a spare bachelor flop, appropriate for a man with no history. But it was an eclectic, even baroque, collection of furniture and decorations from all over the world.

Japanese screen, coffee table from Bali or someplace, Mexican bullfight poster, a cuckoo clock from Germany or Switzerland. A pile of cushions in front of the cube, imported from exotic Taiwan. There was something odd about the collection, which suddenly struck her: everything was the same age. As if he'd gone into Pier Three and said, "I'll take this, this, and this."

No champagne flutes in the kitchen, but she did find two wineglasses of Waterford crystal. So it wasn't all Pier Three. She popped the cork on the champagne and poured herself a glass, and put the bottle in the refrigerator.

It was empty, and spotless.

She checked the cupboards and there was no food, not a can of sardines or a box of cereal. Just matching plastic salt and pepper shakers.

Nothing sinister about that. A lot of bachelors ate in restaurants all the time, or brought takeout home.

She took the champagne back to the living room and turned on the cube. It didn't respond to the clicker, but the manual controls were clear enough. She put it on CNN and turned the sound down to a whisper. She set her glass on the Balinese table and curled up on the Taiwanese pillows and opened the musty old book.

That was also a world-changing time, World War II. The stridently upbeat tone of the magazine probably meant people were as worried as the young man who sold her the champagne. But that was protracted—she checked the dates, six years—and the enemies were just people, beatable. Not aliens who could destroy your planet on a whim. Or said they were.

She put her book down, finished off the glass in a couple of gulps, and went to refill it. From the kitchen she could hear a commotion going on outside. She filled the glass and took it out onto Pepe's balcony.

A circle of young people was dancing in the creek, laughing and singing. About half were naked, in spite of the cold water. Crowds on both banks were clapping and shouting. "Take it off, take it off."

Well, they were expecting a message of peace and hope in a few hours. What would they actually get?

She closed her eyes and suddenly opened them, just in time to keep from dropping the expensive crystal over the balcony. Her arms and legs were heavy with fatigue. She went into Pepe's bedroom and manually set the clock to wake her at five forty-five, not trusting the voice controls. Exactly three hours of sleep. She was unconscious before it said two forty-six.

When the clock woke her she staggered downstairs and got breakfast from machines, guaranteed bad coffee and a candy bar. They didn't have any Mars bars, unfortunately, so she picked one at random. Did they still make Mars bars? She hadn't bought a candy bar in twenty-some years. The chocolate was unpleasantly rich and sweet. But it would get her through to the end of the world.

She was mildly surprised not to have been rousted out of bed by FBI agents. Whatever Pepe was, he was evidently not on their side.

She turned on the cube and switched it to Channel 7, hoping to catch Marya. Some male voice-over was describing the procession of notables, showing footage of one helicopter after another alighting on the same landing pad, dropping off this or that president or prime minister or movie star. A large stand of bleachers filled up with people not accustomed to sitting in bleachers. The rising sun was behind them; the sky was salmon deepening to perfect blue.

At precisely six, a U.S. Marine Corps helicopter, number 1, came in and disgorged President Davis and his retinue, including a squad of heavily armed marines. Rory smiled at that. They wouldn't be much help against planet-busting aliens, but they might prevent him from sharing the fate of his predecessor. She had been following his career from Cuba; he was the least popular president since Nixon. A majority of the House and Senate wanted him impeached, if not actually hanged, but they were putting it off for a few days. Maybe the aliens would vaporize him and save them the trouble.

After the old man was safely installed on the dais in front of the bleachers, seated uncomfortably close to the secretary-general of the UN, the cube switched to a telescopic view of the alien ship. It didn't seem fundamentally different from a human spaceship, which could just be form following function. Or perhaps they wanted to reassure us.

Or, most likely, it *was* a human ship, part of the biggest hoax in history. With Pepe somewhere near the center of it.

Her certainty had grown as the evidence accumulated that Pepe had obviously been planted in her department, set up to be her second-in-command. If it was a hoax, it was an enterprise larger than the Manhattan Project. The early data could have been faked, someone hacking the input from GRS-1 and its lunar counterpart. But eventually other telescopes picked it up. It *did* come from outside the solar system, though perhaps not from nearly as far or going as fast as they thought.

And it did apparently crack Phobos in two, though that could conceivably have been set up beforehand. The figure of a hundred thousand megatons—"give or take a factor of a thousand"—came from Leo, but through Pepe. She'd never checked, and Leo died.

Like the president. Like Pauling, and the rest of the cabinet.

She and Norman would have been out of the picture, too, except for the coincidence of Qabil hearing about the FBI.

The four satellites, destroyed by an invisible ray—that was the easiest to explain. Simple sabotage.

In less than an hour, the last piece would fall into place, though it probably would not be conclusive. Hollywood had more than a century of experience in creating aliens.

The president gave a neutral, optimistic speech, blessedly free of spoonerisms and hysteria. The secretary-general of the UN followed, speaking in his native Bantu. Except for glottal clicks and such, it was pretty much the same speech as Davis had given. A great opportunity awaits us; we welcome our friends from space with open arms. Now that they've destroyed our *other* arms.

There were lots of vehicles parked behind the bleachers—white NASA vans, a couple of military trucks, two ambulances, and a fire truck. She wondered whether one of them might conceal a last-resort bomb, and if so, who controlled the trigger.

And how big a bomb? A high helicopter showed the NASA causeway as crowded as a subway station, all the way to the dikes; over a million people waiting to watch the alien craft land. She was glad not to be there.

The cube shifted to a shimmering telescopic view of the alien craft, which had begun to deorbit somewhere over Australia.

It might pass by overhead on its way to the Cape. She went out on the balcony to check the sky, but it was the usual gray blanket.

The partying students were gone, and had not left a mess behind. Kids nowadays. She heard muffled news broadcasts from apartments all around her, and kept the door open so she could listen for Marya or Pepe on the cube.

Not hearing Marya was no surprise. She hadn't had a chance to disappear after the "accidental" broadcast, and even if the FBI didn't take her, the network would probably have fired her or put her on ice for a while.

Overhead, the familiar double crack of a sonic boom; a spaceship on its approach path to Cape Kennedy. She went inside and sat in front of the cube.

There was Pepe, on the dais with nine other notables, behind the president, who slowly got to his feet. They all did the same.

The ship was dimly visible, descending. Rory realized she was holding her breath.

It touched down precisely at the end of the runway, about the size of a regular shuttle. It would have to be, of course, if this were a hoax—they couldn't have secretly built a spaceship from scratch. It was prettier than a regular shuttle—shiny, like chrome, and somehow it didn't use a braking parachute to slow down.

It rolled to a stop a few hundred meters from the dais, and then, with a slight hissing sound, continued on to stop directly in front of the president. A door opened in the side of the craft and a stairway unfolded to the ground.

Two human-looking figures walked down the stairs. They wore shimmering silver skintight suits, obviously male and female. They didn't walk like people who'd been in zero-gee, Rory noticed. Then she noticed they were both beautiful, despite complete hairlessness, not even eyebrows. A nice touch.

When they stepped off the staircase, it folded back into the ship. As they walked toward the dais, the ship started to hiss again, and rolled slowly down the runway.

They walked up the steps in no rush, the woman leading, and when they got to the dais, they ignored the standing notables and went straight to the microphone.

The woman spoke first: "We are not aliens from another planet. We are aliens from earth. We come from five hundred years in your future."

The man continued: "It was the largest engineering enterprise in the history of humanity. The energy we displayed approaching you was only a small fraction of what was required to bend space and time and send us back. That required the total destruction of a small star, the kind you call a brown dwarf."

"We bring a message of hope and caution," the woman said. "The message of hope is that we *are* here, and therefore you do have a future. Knowing that is going to change you. The catastrophic war that seems about to begin will evaporate—and a series of things will happen, starting today, that will make war impossible within the lifetimes of most people now living."

"It's been decided," the man said, "that we cannot—and we know from historical record that we did not—tell you what these things are. You have to find them out for yourselves. Experience them as they happen."

"This has never been done before," the woman said. "We have to assume that so long as the two of us conform to historical record, subsequent events will occur as our history books record them, and there will be peace. But history does not allow us to remain with you, visitors from an impossible time."

The man gestured at the spaceship. "Likewise, we have to dispose of the spacecraft. If one country took possession of the ship's secrets, it would dominate the world."

The ship had reached the end of the runway. It pivoted slowly and then started to roll back toward them, the hiss of exhaust building to a scream. It was already airborne as it passed the reviewing stand, and it arced upward into a vertical climb with such acceleration that within seconds it was a dot, and then it disappeared. Then it exploded, a brilliant perfect sphere of light, in total silence, outside the atmosphere.

"Now there is only one artifact from the future, besides our clothing," the woman said. She held up an ordinary data crystal, and stepped forward to hand it to a technician surrounded by cameras. "Show this a few minutes from now."

"Of course, we are both also artifacts from the future," the man said, "though we're just people." The woman joined hands with him. "You have many ways to extract information from us."

"There was no way," the woman said, "to make us not know things that might be potentially dangerous to your survival."

They looked into each other's eyes and said in unison, "So, good-bye." They both slumped to the floor.

The next few minutes were a fast confusing drama of swarming medics, stretchers, helicopters, but Rory hardly noticed it, lost in thought.

She saw what Pepe had meant. Sure, it was a hoax, audacious and mind-bendingly expensive. But of course she wouldn't blow the whistle. There was a big chance it might work; it might become a self-fulfilling prophecy. So long as the secret was kept.

All she wanted to know was how they managed it; how could they put all the pieces together without somebody spilling the beans? Who was in on it? Certainly not fools like Davis.

She watched the crystal the "dead" woman had handed the technician, and it indeed showed their landing, speech, and "death." At least she *hoped* that was part of the choreography, and they hadn't called upon two people to sacrifice their lives to make the hoax more realistic. The introduction to the scene was convincingly futuristic to her eyes and ears; the voice-over with an unearthly accent, the beginning and ending shots showing a planet of peace and plenty. Cities floating in the air over forests and fields restored to nature. But then the throwaway spaceship showed how big a budget they'd had to play with.

The sun was breaking through the clouds, a rare thing, everybody off the roads. She decided to take a walk. Go up to the astronomy building and see what happens. Maybe reckless, but she had a feeling that the government was going to be a little too busy to pick on her for a while.

The building was deserted. Everyone was probably down at the Cape.

Pepe's office was still unlocked. Feeling a little bit guilty, voyeuristic, she went in to snoop around.

On a worktable under the window there were three neat stacks of paper, the last assignments and finals for Pepe's three classes.

There was a letter to his secretary, detailing the disposition of these papers, thanking her, and saying good-bye. He would be in touch.

Rory had a feeling that he would not be.

Coda

In a quiet corner of Barcelona, the man who was not Pepe Parker relaxed in a situation of modest wealth and perfect privacy. He had a cook, a servant, and a gardener, and walls of books in various languages.

Buried in the basement, there was a weapon that would turn a man into a torch.

With his full white beard and darkened skin, no one would connect him with the youthful Cuban scientist who had run the Coming Committee and mysteriously disappeared.

He spent most of his time reading, in the garden when it was fine, or in front of the fire when it was cool. Sometimes he dined out with beautiful women who thought he was a retired scholar, independently wealthy. Which was true, as far as it went.

In a safe-deposit box at Banco Nacional de Catalunya, there was a single sheet of paper which only he could read. It had a schedule of conservative stock purchases, and the names of the winners of the Kentucky Derby for the next fifty years.